The
Martian Girl

Also by Andrew Martin

FICTION

Soot

The Jim Stringer Novels

The Necropolis Railway
The Blackpool Highflyer
The Lost Luggage Porter
Murder at Deviation Junction
Death on a Branch Line
The Last Train to Scarborough
The Somme Stations
The Baghdad Railway Club
Night Train to Jamalpure

Bilton

The Bobby Dazzlers
The Yellow Diamond

NON-FICTION

Night Trains: The Rise and Fall of the Sleeper
Belles & Whistles: Five Journeys Through Time on Britain's Trains
Underground, Overground: A Passenger's History of the Tube
Flight by Elephant: The Untold Story of World War Two's Most Daring Jungle Rescue
Ghoul Britannia
How to Get Things Really Flat
Funny You Should Say That

The Martian Girl

A London Mystery

Andrew Martin

corsair

CORSAIR

First published in Great Britain in 2018 by Corsair

1 3 5 7 9 10 8 6 4 2

A CIP catalogue record for this book
is available from the British Library.

ISBN: 978-1-4721-5246-6

Typeset in Bembo by M Rules

Printed and bound in Great Britain by Clays Ltd, Elcograf S.p.A.

Papers used by Corsair are from well-managed forests
and other responsible sources.

Corsair
An imprint of
Little, Brown Book Group
Carmelite House
50 Victoria Embankment
London EC4Y 0DZ

An Hachette UK Company
www.hachette.co.uk

www.littlebrown.co.uk

I am indebted to the Author's Foundation for a grant
that helped fund the writing of this book.

A. M.

Prologue

On the mattress on the floorboards, Jean was lying more or less on top of Coates. He was a thin man, but he provided just enough elevation for her to see through the window, where she could make out what appeared to be soft red stars in the darkness. But these were in fact the aeroplane warning lights on the tops of the cranes surrounding the old power station. When it opened for business at around the time of the Martian Girl (1900 or so), the Lots Road Power Station had got through seven hundred tons of coal a day, and had been known as the Chelsea Monster. Now the Monster was on life support, as the cranes – and an amazingly small number of foreign men in fluorescent jackets – converted it to luxury flats.

Not today though, because today was Sunday.

'I want you to sign the contract,' Jean said, looking down at Coates. 'That's why I *wrote* the contract, and you will have noticed that I typed out a dotted line specially for you to sign on.'

'Yes,' he said, 'I did notice that. The whole document was highly impressive, with all those "hereinafters" and "aforesaids".'

He was in magnanimous mood, not minding, for example, about Jean being still on top of him, even though they'd finished having sex a quarter of an hour ago.

'So why won't you sign it?' she said.

He gave one of his twisted smiles – a sort of anti-smile.

'If you don't sign it,' Jean continued, 'you won't be able to sue me if I don't pay the money back, and I actually *want* you to sue me if I don't do that.'

Coates was groping for a cigarette; she'd have to get off him in a minute.

'What you don't appreciate,' he said patronisingly, 'is that your having *written* the contract would support the idea that we had a verbal agreement, by which you intended to be bound.'

Being slightly pissed (Coates always brought wine to their Sunday afternoons), Jean nodded gravely. As a lawyer, Coates would know about these things. Having lit the cigarette, he was kind enough to avert his head slightly as he exhaled smoke. Jean rolled off him, and Coates began fiddling with his phone.

Jean was thinking about the Terms and Conditions of Tobin's Supper Rooms. She had hired Tobin's in order to break out of journalism, which she would accomplish by the triumphant performance of her show, which was technically a *one-woman* show, although she hated that term, since it implied that the woman in question couldn't get anyone to be in the show with her. Also, she was not sure whether the

2

thing she was writing actually *was* a one-woman show. It had certainly started out as one, complete with strangely egocentric stage directions ('I enter from stage left'), but was now starting to look more like her debut *novel*, and furthermore the subject had changed. Her first idea had been to tell the stories of several Victorian music hall artists, but it was now boiling down to the story of just one of them: Kate French, the Martian Girl.

Despite having no apparent interest in music hall in general or the Martian Girl in particular, Coates had forwarded her seven hundred pounds so she could make the down payment on the Rooms. She had accepted his money only after drawing up a contract stipulating that she would repay him in full if the show made a profit.

Having put out his cigarette, Coates seemed to have decided to begin round two, but in spite of what his rather elegant fingers were doing, she was still thinking about Tobin's. It was a small cultural outpost in an incredibly desolate part of London: the Rotherhithe–Deptford borders, where a lot of riverside buildings had been pulled down and nothing very convincing put up in their place. Tobin's had appealed to Jean because the Martian Girl had made her name in another theatre in the area: the beautiful (and long gone) Rotherhithe Hippodrome. If Jean cancelled her show, she would lose the seven hundred pounds – or Coates would. In four weeks' time, another seven hundred pounds would become due, which Jean herself would be paying – and losing if she then cancelled. The final eight hundred would come from the ticket revenue accrued during the week-long run of the show.

Coates now performed a skilful if rather violent manoeu-vre, after which *he* was on top of *her*. So Jean forgot about the show for five minutes.

Afterwards, she walked over to the table to collect her laptop. Being with Coates was like having mild flu: you spent most of your time sweating slightly in bed, and when you got out of the bed, you felt shivery and keen to get back into it.

'Can I show you something?' she said, returning to the mattress on the floor. She was always petitioning Coates.

'Hard-core pornography, presumably?'

Jean logged on to YouTube and found the clip of Ada Reeve. Ada belonged to the 1890s, so she was plump, wore a big hat and had crooked teeth. She was one of the half dozen or so music hall artistes Jean had intended to cover in her show, until she had discovered Kate French. When Jean pressed 'play', Ada began to perform a song called 'Foolish Questions'. Jean tilted the screen towards Coates, and she watched him as Ada sang . . .

Did you ever give a girl a box of chocolates after tea and notice how she grabs it, and then says 'Is this for me?'

Rather than smiling, Coates gave a slight nod. His mind was clearly elsewhere, and he seemed to drift away entirely in the next verse, during which Ada sang of telling someone that she'd been to the funeral of a certain Fred, and this person had replied, 'Why? Is he dead?'

'A foolish question, you see?' said Jean.

Sometimes, when abstracted like this, Coates would move

4

his lips in a worrying way. Before this could happen, she said, 'It's funny, don't you think?'

Coates nodded, and reached for another of his American Spirit cigarettes. When they had first met, it had interested Jean that they both smoked this fairly obscure brand: Jean the roll-ups, Coates the ready-mades. It hadn't interested Coates very much.

'Is this one of the women you're going to be taking off?' he said, lighting the cigarette.

Jean reached out to the laptop and banished Ada.

'No. I was going to do Ada Reeve, but I've changed the subject of the show. Do you want me to tell you what it's about now? I believe I've told you six or seven times already, but I'm happy to go over it again.'

'What's more important,' he said rudely, 'is whether you've told the theatre.'

'Tobin's? They're fine about it. Didn't even want to see a draft.'

'I suppose they're more interested in getting their two grand than worrying about art,' he said. He stood up, naked, and looked down on Jean, who was very far below him. He smiled at the discrepancy, then set off towards the bathroom. On the way there, he put out his cigarette in the ashtray on Jean's table. He only smoked them about a third of the way down, which was probably something to do with his being extremely vain, and forty-eight years old. Most likely he had smoked cigarettes all the way down when he was a younger man, and death a more distant prospect. He entered the bathroom and closed the door, but the door was badly fitted, and after a few minutes, steam came rolling from under it, Coates having embarked on one of his long, thunderous showers. For such a dirty-minded man, he was extremely clean. In their first weeks together, Jean had sometimes joined him in the shower, but he hadn't seemed to like that, and just carried on sluicing himself down while saying things like, 'Could you pass the shampoo, please?'

Jean addressed him from the bed, knowing he couldn't hear:

'Kate French was a mind reader, Mr Coates, and a jolly good one. She performed with a man called Joseph Draper. I've seen a few reviews, but not much is known about her. She seems to have just disappeared in 1898, which is pretty odd, wouldn't you say?

'According to the census of 1891,' she continued, rolling a cigarette, 'an Esmeralda Kate French, aged fifteen, had been living at number three Stanley Buildings, Pancras Road. She was the daughter of Frederick Mathias French, and those two were the only "household members", so the mother was presumably dead. They kept no servant, Mr Coates. Pancras Road you'll know, although you probably don't *know* you know it. It's right in-between King's Cross and St Pancras stations, and it used to be a proper road with shops and pubs, now it's a sort of taxi drop-off area. One block of Stanley Buildings survives, but not as flats. It's converted into a "business centre" – all part of the general tarting up of King's Cross. Flat number three was on the ground floor.'

Jean watched the steam rolling over the floorboards, which were very good floorboards, the kind that didn't need to be covered by rugs, which was just as well, since the cost of them had ruled out the purchase of rugs.

'Now . . . ' she said to the steam, 'Fred French was a policeman with the Metropolitan Police, which I found out because Kate was registered as a pupil – later a pupil *teacher* – at Collier Street School, King's Cross, and the document of registration gives the occupation of the "parent or guardian". He'd joined in 1882, then left in 1891, with the rank of sergeant. He'd been in the police band, or one of them. He then *re*-joined the police in 1897, but he retired after less than a year because of chronic bronchitis. He would have qualified for a pension, but only a small one because he didn't do enough years. How to account for the gap between his two stints on the force, you must be wondering, Mr Coates? Well, between 1892 and 1897 he and Kate seem to have gone north in an attempt to "make it" in show business – Kate as a singer, dancer and comedienne on the Halls, her father as a violinist. She only became a mind reader later on, you see?'

Jean got out of bed and put the laptop on her table, which was what she called her desk, so as not to be intimidated by the idea of writing at it. She picked up a piece of paper and returned to the bed.

'On one occasion they performed at the Royal Albert Music Hall in Manchester. I think it must have had delusions of grandeur, Mr Coates – the Royal Albert I mean – because it combined music hall with classical concerts. I found the bill on the internet, and I printed it out.'

She fell silent as she read over the document:

7

CHAMBER CONCERTS
Season 1895–6
CONCERT to be held at the Royal Albert
Music Hall, November 9th 1895.

ARTISTES:
Violin – Mr Frederick French
Violin and Viola – Miss Leila Backhouse
Violincello – Miss Dorothy Peters
Vocalist – Miss Kate French
Piano – Mr Reginald Duckworth

Such lovely northern names, Jean thought (apart from 'French', of course). The programme included the Sonata in E Major by Handel. Kate had sung 'Four Leaf Clover' by somebody called Lambert, and 'O! Sweet Content' by somebody called Noble.

Jean resumed her shouting towards the shower. 'So far, Mr Coates, I have been unable to find any registration of death for Kate or Joseph Draper. Or, come to that, for a man called Hugh Brooks, who had performed with Draper before he recruited Kate. But it might just be that there are too many similar names . . .'

The shower fell silent. Coates emerged and began dressing – good quality white shirt; nice, battered tweed jacket; then the blue Crombie with velvet collar. He wasn't called Coates for nothing, but were those garments starting to look a little threadbare? How would he feel about losing his seven hundred quid? Even though he lived in a flat in Chelsea with a magazine-editing wife called Camilla, Coates gave alarming signs of being broke. When they first met – back in February – he'd presented himself as a successful barrister, but it turned out he'd quit the chambers to which he'd belonged shortly before they met. This was not, technically, one of his many lies – once a barrister, always a barrister; the qualification was for life – but Coates's success in the job was all in the past, which was disturbing because Coates *looked* like a barrister and obviously *belonged* in a barrister's chambers. It was very easy to picture him reading a brief with his feet on the desk and some female barrister looking on with a mixture of disapproval and lust. Jean wondered whether it was absolutely necessary that her lover be successful. Yes, probably, because Coates was ten years older than her. He'd had more time to be successful, so he *ought* to be successful; also that success would justify his somewhat arrogant personality.

'What about Wednesday?' said Jean. Sunday and Wednesday afternoons were their possible 'windows', but they could have longer on Sundays if Coates's wife and daughter went to 'the country' and he didn't go with them.

No reply from Mr Coates, because he was checking his mobile phone again.

Jean said, '*I* have a tendency to ask rather foolish questions, don't you think?'

'Frankly yes,' said Coates, pocketing the phone. 'But I assume you do it for your own amusement.'

He smiled, and the trouble was that it was a very good sort of smile: vulpine. He walked over, bent down and kissed Jean.

'I'll call you,' he said, which meant: 'You call me.'

PART ONE

A month later

When Coates saw that Jean was calling him, he pressed 'decline', before turning off his phone altogether. Having failed to speak to him, she would always text, just as though there were no such thing as 'missed call'. It was irritating.

Jean was the second to last person Coates wanted to hear from just then, the *very* last one being his wife. On this dark Sunday afternoon, he was on his way to Number Four, to obtain something he couldn't get from either. He had walked from his flat in Chelsea, shadowing the river, as dictated by his Number Four ritual. As he passed the Albert Bridge its lights came on, making it resemble a kind of golden harp in the misty rain. When Coates reached Pimlico, the darkening of the day was more or less complete.

He turned north from the river, walking along Vauxhall Bridge Road before making two further turns. On the face of it, Pimlico was blandly respectable but Coates detected a special enigmatic quality here, making it the ideal place to harbour Number Four. In Pimlico you might easily see a milk float at three in the afternoon; there were Indian restaurants with endorsements in their windows dating from the seventies. If you walked past a barber's shop, one of the barbers might be cutting the other's hair, to keep his hand in, there being no customers. Yes, Pimlico had the river, but the river didn't seem very interested in Pimlico; it was just passing through.

Coates always called into a certain riverside pub on his way to Number Four. It was a sedate pub, with a sedate name: the Duke of Hamilton. The interior was not as old as it pretended to be, and the supposedly real fire was gas. A party of four sat in the corner, two women and two men: the kind of middle-aged, middle-class Londoners becoming as rare in the centre of town as red phone boxes. They were talking of golf – a mixed foursome, you might say. Coates approached the bar. He always hoped to be served by the manageress, with whom he conducted a silent flirtation, but it was the manager who stood before him.

'Evening,' said the manager. He didn't attempt any further small talk: the stare Coates was giving him had seen to that.

He took the wine out into the pub's front yard, sat down under a sunshade left over from summer, and lit an American Spirit. A wind was getting up on the river, and the cigarette burned down quickly. The ritual dictated he should smoke two, but with the second one, he simply watched the smoke flying in all the wrong directions, hardly putting it to his lips. The woman – the manageress – was watching him from the pub door. This was annoying, even though she was quite attractive in the unimaginative, Pimlico way. Blonde, with a backside nearly – but not quite – too big. She looked at him and smiled, and he smiled evenly back, giving as good as he got. Coates wondered what she saw: a handsome forty-eight-year-old running to seed, but slowly – almost certainly more slowly than whoever had the mixed blessing of being the man in her life. The woman stepped out from the doorway and made an adjustment to the chairs at the next table. She obviously wanted him to speak.

'Blustery day,' he said.

'Just a bit,' she said.

He finished his wine, and she pointed at the empty glass, asking, 'That dead?' She seemed to specialise in unnecessary remarks. Coates nodded, blowing smoke. The whole scenario was ridiculous, like the start of a bad porn film. She picked up the glass and walked away. Coates was perfectly confident that she had emerged from the pub purely in order to show him her arse.

He put out his cigarette; it was time to go to Number Four.

———

Jean looked through the window at the sleeping Monster, which stood amid the particular type of rainy darkness she associated with Sunday. It was five thirty, and Coates had not replied to her call or her text. Obviously, he hadn't been able to leave his wife's side for long enough. Or, of course, he was just ignoring her. Coates would be 'in the country' today, so he'd said. In Jean's mind, this 'country' of his was full of married couples who were forever walking hand-in-hand through pretty woods, clinking glasses in oak-beamed inns, or drinking hot chocolate next to log fires, always using two hands to hold the cup.

In practice, it was unlikely that Coates's wife conducted herself so meekly. She was called Camilla, and her journalistic by-line was Camilla Rowe, not that she did much writing any more, being the editor of one of the bigger women's magazines. Jean had once pitched an idea to her by email, eliciting a brisk rejection, and Jean did wonder whether she was capable of having started an affair with a man just because his wife had turned down her feature idea. She liked to think not.

On the mattress lay the forty pages of her monologue, a word almost as distasteful to her as 'one-woman show'. It was far too reminiscent of 'monotonous' – and she had no idea how it was going to *end*. Jean took the script over to the sofa with her green tea and her rolled-up cigarette. She smoked the cigarette rapidly down, crushed it into the tea dregs and began to speak, in her 'Kate' voice, which was more ingenuous and charming – she hoped – than her own:

'Raining, is it . . . ?' she began, addressing the stove.

This definitely wasn't going to work. Jean took the chair from her table by the window, put it in the middle of the room, sat on it. Then she stood up again. She checked her phone, because maybe a text had come in when that gull had been screeching on the window sill: one of those stupid ones that mistook the river for the sea. (Was there such a thing as a seagull that had never seen the sea?) But there was nothing, so she put the phone under the sofa cushion. A call was practically *guaranteed* when she did that, because the phone didn't like to be rebuffed. She stared at the cushion for a while, then returned to the central chair. On the actual stage, for the actual show, she would have one chair for Kate and another for Joseph Draper, although Draper would never appear. His voice might be heard occasionally, if Jean could get the sound design together for that.

'Tell the story,' Jean muttered to herself, 'tell the story.' (She had heard proper actors say this to each other before going on stage.) She cleared her throat quite unnecessarily. She must become Kate: the young, sweet-natured Kate French, summoned to a meeting on the empty stage of the long-gone Rotherhithe Hippodrome. It was 1898, a different world. Queen Victoria was seventy-nine; the Rotherhithe Hippodrome was brand new. A perfectly normal supper was bread, cheese and cocoa; all men smoked; you could buy a revolver for ten-and-six (which to the best of Jean's understanding was about fifty pounds) and it was perfectly legal to own it, but if you shot and killed somebody with it and were caught, then you were hung (or was it 'hanged'?).

But the weather was the same – and so Jean had decreed that it would be raining on that dark Sunday afternoon too, and Kate would be sitting with wet feet, owing to leaking boots, and toying with a skimpy umbrella as Mr Joseph Draper, mind reader, perused her letter of application, as forwarded by *The Era* newspaper. Kate would have been thinking of her sick father – 'The Dad' – and how it was essential for both of them that she land this job.

The music halls were 'dark' on Sundays – in other words there were no performances – and Kate and Draper would be the only people in the theatre; their voices would be echoing.

She began ...

'Raining, is it?' said Draper, as I sat down on the chair he had somewhat grudgingly indicated.

He was scrutinising my letter of application, so it did not seem that any answer was required to this 'greeting'. As to his surmise about the weather, no great feat of clairvoyance had been required from the eminent mind reader, since I had become soaked to the skin during my walk from the station. But since it might seem rude to leave the question unanswered, I said, 'It is somewhat, yes.' That didn't seem quite enough, however, so I added: 'Fortunately my boots are so full of holes that the water drains off pretty quickly.'

This amusing sally earned no response from the mind reader, who merely continued to examine my letter of application with every appearance of scepticism. Eventually, he said, 'Now, you describe yourself as "a pathetic singer".'

'Sad, you know,' I explained. 'I can make the whole house feel sad.'

'I daresay you can,' Draper muttered, reading on.

I looked down at my umbrella, which had not kept the rain off my head to any significant degree as I had walked along the very appropriately named Lower Road in Rotherhithe, and yet now had the nerve to be discharging a great deal of accumulated water across the boards of the stage. It didn't *stop* rain, this benighted object, but merely perpetuated it indoors. I sentenced it, there and then, to the dustbin; and no doubt Mr Draper was doing the same to me, his perusal of my letter being merely for form's sake. He was now looking up from that wretched document with an expression of incredulity: 'You say you were repeatedly engaged at the Royal Albert Hall?'

'The Royal Albert *Music Hall*,' I corrected him. 'It's in Manchester, where I lived for a few years with The . . . with my father, he being a musician at the time, a violinist, connected occasionally to the famous Hallé Orchestra.'

'But this Royal Albert Music Hall . . . I don't believe I've heard of it?'

'Oh, it's quite new – and small. It is, by its own admission, the Handsomest and Most Comfortable Music Hall in the North West. Do you really not know it, Mr Draper? It is illuminated throughout by *electricity*!'

It goes without saying that I was not as cheerful as I was attempting to appear. When I thought of those Northern days, I always pictured myself and The Dad on a certain platform at a benighted railway station in Manchester (a town full of benighted railway stations) which lacked a roof, in spite of being located in Britain's rainiest place. We stood in the middle of swirling rain, The Dad clutching his violin case, and me holding the carpet bag that contained the majority of our possessions. I dated the onset of The Dad's emphysema from that moment. Emphysema was the staging post between bronchitis and bronchopneumonia which all the medical dictionaries in all the reference libraries in Manchester and north London insisted was 'invariably fatal in children and adults'.

On the very day I had written my letter of application to Draper, Dr Theodore Mortimer of Pentonville Road had taken me aside after examining The Dad. He said, 'As your father has aged, his lungs have become smaller, lighter and the elastic tissue has degenerated.'

'And what might be done about it?' I had asked – and rather crossly, since I had thought him rather too fond of saying all those words.

'Nothing,' he had said. 'Except to make your father as comfortable as possible for the year or so that remains.

You must ensure he is well-rested, not over-exerted; that he has a good supply of milk, fresh eggs, green vegetables and cod liver oil. You must buy a steam-making machine—'

'You mean a kettle?' I cut in. 'We have one of those.'

He did not mean a kettle. He meant something that cost two pounds from Bell & Croydon, pharmacists of Marylebone. In other words, the means of alleviation lay in the accumulation of cash. It was imperative, therefore, that my application to Draper should succeed.

He had returned to my letter. He was no doubt concluding that I had never had an established 'turn', and therefore could not be called a true turner. All my engagements had been small, and more often in singing rooms and free-and-easies than actual halls; I had been a half-timer in the business, and never a real 'pro' in that I had always of necessity combined performing with assisting in various crowded classrooms, which was why nobody had seen fit to do me the honour of taking a tenth of my income; hence the reason my letters must bear the address of the flat I shared with The Dad in Pancras Road, rather than some smart agency in the West End. I contemplated telling Draper about the little bit of stage work I'd done since coming back from the north. At Collins's Hall in Islington, I had done a week with two friends of The Dad: Tom Anderton and Al Firth, who had a comedy police skit in which they took the part of two detectives. Tom Anderton was a neighbour of ours in King's Cross, and the turn was particularly amusing to The Dad, who had found the men of the real Detective Branch to be overly pleased with themselves during his time on the force.

Yes, Anderton and Firth jolly well *had* been funny, and I would tell Draper about them.

'They performed as Holmfirth & Watford, you see. Tom Anderton, as Holmfirth, wore a deerstalker hat and smoked a sort of bent pipe. He was taking off—'

'I *know* who he was taking off, Miss French,' said Draper.

'In the skit,' I said, 'they were investigating a murder.' At this, Draper folded his arms and fixed me with a look of such outright hostility that he stopped me in my tracks. 'Ought I to cease speaking?' I said, and Draper nodded, but then shook his head, hostility having apparently given way to confusion.

'I played the corpse,' I continued, 'but I wasn't really dead, merely stunned. Anderton asks Watford to inspect my coat pockets. "Nothing in the left pocket," Watford informs him, whereupon he tries the other one, reporting, "Nothing in the right pocket either." "Ha!" says Holmfirth. "Ambidextrous!"'

Draper was nodding slowly, still apparently dazed. Perhaps I should ask *him* a question about his *own* past? The Dad had discovered that Draper had performed mind reading with a man called Hugh Brooks, but they had separated for some reason about five years ago, and Brooks had emigrated to Australia. The Dad had relayed the news in a rather frowning way, and it was surely the case that the partnership of Brooks and Draper would not have broken up for any very *good* reason. So I decided not to ask about it.

Turning to my right, I saw the backcloth, which reminded me of the rain, in that it showed Tower Bridge on a *sunny* day, with the drawbridge (I know it's not called that) open, and a pretty white ship sailing through, and several pretty white clouds sailing over. Turning to the left, I contemplated the auditorium, as much as I could see of it, for only one of the glims was lit, and the carbide hissed as it burned in its box, so that I seemed to have been 'getting the bird', as the turners say, ever since I'd sat down. The flickering illumination went as far as about the fifth row of the stalls, and disclosed the shadowy outline of the front of the circle. From the absolute blackness beyond, a great coldness seemed to come, mixed with a smell of past tobacco and orange peel.

'Now,' Draper said, after yet more ponderosity (a word I made up while waiting), 'you toured the provincial houses for a while with a strongman?'

'Indeed,' I said, 'the world-famous Mr Jim Barratt!'

If Joseph Draper had ever heard of Jim Barratt, the name caused no great access of enthusiasm. He simply sat opposite me on that empty stage, now not even reading my letter, but merely eyeing me balefully and simply *breathing* on his chair, which was appropriately throne-like, being left over from some Shakespearean skit. He wore thin wire spectacles. If you can see the innermost secrets of people's minds, I reasoned, you shouldn't need glasses to perceive more everyday objects, such as your hand in front of your face. As to that face, it was pudding-like: a suet pudding – wide – and his shoulders were broad, contradicting the message of the flimsy glasses. He said, 'Barratt billed himself as The World's Strongest Man, did he not?'

'Barratt?' I replied, effortlessly continuing my impersonation of an imbecile. 'By no means. That was Harry

22

Wheeler. Far from being The World's Strongest Man, Jim Barratt was The Strongest Man *in the World*, thereby avoiding a law suit. But the main difference was that Barratt was a comedy weightlifter.'

'How can weightlifting be funny?' asked Draper.

'With difficulty, Mr Draper. At the climax, Barratt would pick me up and revolve me above his head.'

Draper was good enough to nod, which might be taken as some slight sign of encouragement. Either way, I pounced with a witticism: 'I may not have been around the world, Mr Draper, but I have been *whirled around*!'

Jean walked over to the sofa and retrieved the phone, which remained comatose. *I must go back and put the stage directions in*, she thought, looking at the manuscript splayed on the floor. She picked up her rolling tobacco and returned to the window.

The power station cranes were rocking slightly in the wind, and the rain was flying all over the place. Bloody Coates. Since this particular Sunday afternoon was on the brink of being Sunday evening, she'd been trying to find out from him about Wednesday. She hoped he *was* in the country rather than at the flat in Chelsea, because he'd *said* he was going to be in the country. She began trying to imagine the interior of the Chelsea flat, but then her mental camera wandered into a room in which a little girl sat, innocently doing her homework. Coates's daughter was about ten, and every time Jean remembered her, she resolved to break it off with Coates. She ought not to be having an affair with a married man in the first place, for God's sake, but at least she minded about it. Coates didn't seem to mind about it, or anything. But then you never knew, what with the long silences that interspersed his cynical conversation: he was obviously brooding about something. Clearly, the man was trouble. Some women subconsciously wanted trouble, but Jean did not believe that she herself was in that category.

She contemplated the mass of papers on her table. She would distract herself by doing some journalistic work. Or should she lie down and go to sleep?

———

The top bell of Number Four was marked 'Le Business'. Coates rang, and was admitted without a word being uttered through the entryphone. He climbed the stairs, passing a flat in which a radio was playing the news; somehow this implied the occupant was respectable. Light showers in the south would give way to heavier rain as the evening progressed.

The girl called Eve admitted him to the flat, and to the room he thought of as the reception. It bothered him that the TV showed Sky Sports, albeit with the sound turned down, but not quite all the way. 'He's just a box player,' he heard a football moron say, 'scores goals in the box.' The TV had always been switched off in the past, and Sky Sports suggested the presence of a man behind the scenes. Coates had never seen a man in Number Four, and he didn't want to either. None of the girls was paying attention to the TV: they were all looking at their phones.

Besides Eve, there were four other girls in the reception all sitting on armchairs, and all showing a lot of leg while otherwise fully dressed. The legs were the calling cards, in effect.

Eve introduced them with an outstretched arm, like a charmingly shy hostess, but Coates was a regular, so she began, 'I think you know ... Maxine, Helen, Sarah, Monica.' He did. Everyone smiled foolishly. None of the girls were drug users as far as he knew, but he chose not to look too closely for the signs. They all seemed to be English, which was also good – meant they were less likely to be enslaved to some East European gangster.

Maxine gave him the biggest smile, then returned to her browsing. Of course, she knew she was in for it. But Maxine was a game girl: he had known that on his first visit, just by the look of her; but he hadn't gone with her that time. He'd gone with Eve who, having asked his preference, had attempted to accommodate him with a pair of stockings. She demonstrated how they might be loosely knotted, saying, 'It's only a fantasy, after all,' clearly failing to grasp that there was no 'only' about Coates's fantasy. He had gone along with Eve's tame scenario, but they had had a proper talk afterwards – a kind of professional consultation, both sitting cross-legged and half-dressed on the bed – and Eve had said she knew two girls who might be better suited to him, if he could ever come in on weekends. Saturdays were difficult for Coates. He always spent Saturdays with Camilla and Lucy. But on Sundays, Camilla took Lucy to her mother's place in Oxfordshire, which left Coates free to visit either Jean or – on about one Sunday every two months – Number Four.

He was looking at the girls now, as Eve handed him a glass of white wine. Every punter, he believed, was entitled to a complimentary glass of wine. All in all, it was a very nice situation. It was rare enough for Coates to be sitting in a Tube carriage with four such attractive women in front of him, let alone any four from whom he might take his pick, but although he looked politely at each girl in turn, it was Maxine who rose to her feet, picking up from beside her chair a black leather bag.

Maxine led Coates to another room. She was perhaps the oldest of the girls, and perhaps the least pretty. She was very pale and a bit too thin, with eyes of electric blue. Her quite frizzy dark hair was tied into a sort of vertical ponytail, as though someone had recently tried to hang her from her hair – and what Coates liked about Maxine was the suspicion that she might have gone along with that sort of notion. She looked appealingly like a tragic Victorian doll you might find at the back of an antique shop.

The room into which she had led him contained an iron bedstead with a cupboard by it. There were flowers on the window sill, and what with the slight smell of disinfectant, it was reminiscent of an old-fashioned hospital. Maxine undressed to her knickers. She looked a question at him, and when he nodded, she removed these as well. Then she took some thin white ropes out of the black bag. You'd have thought she was a mountaineer; but Maxine was not a mountaineer, and Coates tied her up in the way he – and, he genuinely hoped, she – enjoyed, with her wrists attached to her ankles behind her. But the main thing was that he enjoyed it.

'Well, here we are again,' she said.

Coates sat on the bed and moved his hand through her hair. She seemed perfectly relaxed, and a girl who was relaxed in

26

that situation was (unfortunately) one in a million. He stood, and looked out of the window as he took off his trousers and unbuttoned his shirt. The rain was landing on the window glass in a curious way, making numerous glittering X's against the dark. Over the road were some of the usual Pimlico houses. The moon had turned up early and was loitering not far above the chimney pots; a red bus rolled along the street. Its conductor, a trim black man, struck a dandyish attitude on the rear platform. The Moon over Pimlico. It ought to be a novel, written by some frustrated female in the 1930s. Perhaps Jean would one day write a novel like that, instead of just talking about writing a novel . . . or it might be a still-life. Coates wanted the moment to last.

He looked down at Maxine, whose name, he assumed, was a sort of stage name. 'Are they too tight?' he said.

'What?' she said foolishly. Evidently the ropes were not too tight. 'I was nearly asleep just then,' she said.

He could think of no response to that, but he was pleased. Coates continued to count his Pimlico blessings. This room was warm and quiet; he had the girl on the bed, and the clock on the bedside table was proceeding slowly towards half past six; he had the full moon, and still a nearly full glass of fairly decent white wine. His phone was switched off: so no wife, no Jean. Ideally, he would sit in the corner of the room, sipping the wine and smoking a cigarette while occasionally asking Maxine questions about anything at all.

Coates looked at his packet of American Spirit on the bedside table. He felt he couldn't smoke one, because then Maxine would be subjected to passive smoking in a too-literal way. It would be crass. He removed his shirt, and she

27

was watching him. Still trim, in spite of all the wine; he had the bike to thank for that. Wearing only his boxer shorts – now necessarily somewhat askew – Coates sat down next to Maxine, who rolled rather awkwardly onto her side, and he ran his hand over her breast.

He had three hundred in his wallet, and his visit would account for all of it, but that was fine. It was money well spent, even though he couldn't afford it. Maxine said, 'Don't you want to see about down below?' Coates was moving his hand in the direction indicated when a dark-haired man in a football shirt entered the room. He was holding a small exotic tea glass. 'For Christ sake,' he said (very definitely 'Christ' not 'Christ's'); then he turned and departed, but he had broken the spell. Coates stood up, ran his hands through his hair.

'Who the hell was that?'

'Just some fellah,' said Maxine.

She knew but wasn't saying. Coates began to undo the ropes, making clear the encounter was over.

'If you know who he is,' he said, 'please do tell me.'

'He's the owner,' Maxine said, eventually.

'The owner of what?'

She sat up and began neatly folding the ropes, which were her personal property, after all. 'The business and the flat.'

A criminal, then: the East European gangster Coates had identified as the last person he wanted to see on the premises. 'What nationality is he?' he asked.

Maxine shrugged. 'Foreign.' She walked forward and they shook hands, which was how they usually finished. 'I'm sorry he interrupted,' she said. 'It was nice ... we can knock something off, if you like.'

Coates smiled at this preposterous expression. Approaching the reception again, he could hear the sound of Sky Sports – it had been turned up. The Yob sat in the armchair, inflicting football talk on Eve, who was sitting on another of the chairs with a magazine on her bare knees, looking very prettily 1960s somehow. What a great time Coates would have had were it not for this Yob. Eve rose as Coates approached.

'Everything all right?' she said.

'We were interrupted,' he said, eyeing the Yob.

'I'm sorry about that,' said Eve.

'By *him*,' said Coates, indicating the Yob.

The Yob still did not look at Coates, and Eve seemed torn between the two men. Coates paid in full, with a fifty-pound tip for Maxine, and it irritated him that this might look like cowardice. Again, he indicated the Yob to Eve.

'Try to make sure he doesn't get his hands on it,' he said, and now the Yob turned in his chair.

'You,' he said, 'you get the fuck out, and you no come back . . . Disrespecting the girls.'

'I do not disrespect the girls,' said Coates, turning squarely towards the Yob. 'You, I disrespect.'

'You fucking pervert man.'

'There's a lot of perversions,' said Coates. 'One of them's called voyeurism.'

This was lost on the Yob, who had gone back to watching the TV. Coates waited but the Yob did not turn towards him again. So Coates began to descend the stairs.

On the street, he headed back towards the river, passing a sign that slowly flashed its modest offer: MINI CAB . . . MINI

CAB. Coates walked past that sign every time, always switching on his phone as he did so. He was quite relieved (but also quite irritated) to see that there was no message from Jean. There was a text from his wife, though. He clicked it open, resigned to seeing: *I am leaving you because you go with whores.* In fact, it said *Remember Dan and Diana's thing tonight. It's til late, so you can BE late. Love, C.*

Coates was now passing a typical Pimlico scene: behind net curtains two old people were inspecting a bulky desktop computer, but the sight did not give him the satisfaction it ought to have done. He realised he was shaking, and he knew he had gone white. The Yob had effectively stolen three hundred pounds off him, and he had done nothing about it. Coates was short of money. He could not afford to spend three hundred pounds for no return, yet he had just walked away. Too many people were taking advantage of him.

Ahead lay Millbank, and the river. He could see the water over the wall, a black shine moving along it, the bad weather in preparation. Something made Coates stop in the road and look back.

The Yob was approaching.

'Good,' said a voice in Coates's head.

———

Jean, sitting at her table, watched the moon floating over the chimneys of the Chelsea Monster. Some stars played a supporting role. Before her was a pile of the Sunday papers, whose pages she prowled for slots the freelancer might fill: up-for-grabs columns with lonely-sounding names like In My Opinion, Speaking for Myself. The Sunday papers presented a swaggering front, but they were all dying, just as all the dailies and all the magazines were dying. Jean's regular slot on the 'edgy' (the editor's word) men's fashion and lifestyle magazine, *Beau*, paid less now than it had done three years ago. Her column was in the 'outrageously named' (that was the editor again) Women's Bits section, where a few women had their say. Other than this, it was a matter of the odd book or music review, the occasional radio broadcast, some DJing. To put it bluntly, Jean was being subsidised by her parents, and this could not go on, partly because *they* could not go on. Hence the Martian Girl play, to which most of the mess on the table related.

As well as numerous works of late Victorian social history, Jean had a *Gazetteer and Railway Plan of London (Eastern District)* dating from 1896, which was near enough to her target date of 1898, and plenty of books about – and maps of – the river Thames, south-east London and King's Cross. She had a high pile of books on music hall. Only a couple of these mentioned Kate French, and one of the mentions had been the germ of the whole MG idea: 'Little is known of Kate French's later years, if indeed there were any.' It had come as the culmination of something equally elusive ...

In 1898, some five years after the break with Hugh Brooks, Joseph Draper teamed up with Kate French (aka The Martian Girl, but their billing varied). They became favourites for a while in east London, with a turn that – thanks to the input of the charming yet wayward French – seems to have been something more interesting than stage mesmerism done 'by the book'.

31

The 1891 census had provided Jean with an address for Joseph Draper: 2 Providence Road, Rotherhithe, where he lived (presumably not in the conjugal sense) with Mary White, 'a servant'. There was nothing left of Providence Road, but the old maps showed that it had run at right angles to the river. On Jean's table was a downloaded and printed-out photograph of Draper and his previous mind-reading partner, Hugh Brooks. Draper looked like a minor official: an impatient, cross man in a boring suit and round, wire-rimmed glasses. Brooks was more flamboyant, with a goatee beard, longish hair and a better cut of suit: a sort of restrained, English version of Buffalo Bill; and he carried an expensive-looking cane with what was possibly a silver top. In the photograph, Brooks had turned slightly away from Draper, as though they'd just had a falling out, which they might well have (Draper looked like a man easy to fall out with), but the pose was probably meant to convey that they did not need to look at each other, or indeed to speak, in order to communicate.

Jean had found the picture on a website devoted to music hall arcana, and she had downloaded a picture of Kate from the same place. This was an illustration rather than a photograph, and it showed Kate on her own, wearing a blindfold, head upraised, like a noble person about to be executed. Running along the bottom were the words *Kate French, the amazing Martian Girl. See her at the Silvertown Empire, in mesmeric communication with Mr Joseph Draper.*

Jean had exhausted the internet by now (surprising how shallow it was when you really knew a subject), but two weeks ago she had found a treasure trove in the archive of the British Theatre Memorial Fund, located in a mixed-use office block on Marylebone Road. The archive had been established in the 1950s by some rich actors who intended to open a museum, but the plan foundered, leaving behind a haphazardly indexed mountain of documents overseen today by some retired actresses, if the extravagance of their attire was anything to go by.

Through sheer incompetence, Jean had arrived towards closing time on her first and so far only visit; then half an hour had been taken up by registration, and trying to appear patient as one of the retired actresses explained, with much rattling of bangles, that on the very next day, refurbishment of the lift leading to the archive would put it temporarily out of bounds. Jean would be informed of the reopening date by email ... which was highly frustrating, because in the fifteen remaining minutes she had discovered a very promising file: the correspondence of a man called Arthur Wakelam.

At first, Jean had thought Art Wakelam (as he signed himself) must be a theatrical agent; then she saw that he was frequently writing *to* agents, so he must have been a kind of talent scout, working for both agents and theatre managers. So far, Jean had been able to photograph only two documents from this cache, the first of which had slithered out of the cardboard envelope when she was handed the file, seemingly demanding to be noticed. It was a letter written by Wakelam, rather casually addressed from 'Bayswater Road', and sent to Bill Wise, of the Selwyn & Wise theatrical agency, Piccadilly Circus, London, on Tuesday, November 4th 1898:

My Dear Bill,

You asked for a brief description of the Koenigs' act. There are six people on the stage. Two are dressed as servants, and there are two dwarfs who are dressed as children and nobody knows they are dwarfs. They do the most marvellous tricks, starting with club juggling; then they juggle with hoops, but the tricks and series they do are different from all others, and they put some of their head balancing tricks into this and catch the hoops upside down & c. Then they do their equilibristic stuff, and this ought to be even more sensational for the public than before, as the boy who balances the other boy is much smaller than the boy he balances.

The finish consists of the boy balancing the other boy head-to-head while the top boy balances a long pole on his feet, and spins same with his feet (while still balancing head to head) and at each end of the pole two midgets hang on – wait for it – by their teeth. There is no trick connected with this; it is absolutely genuine, and I'm sure every manager would do well with this act, provided it is advertised properly, that is to say booming it, because of course the Koenigs are quite unknown over here.

. . . all of which was completely irrelevant. It was the post-script that had interested Jean.

PS: I see, as perhaps you will have done, that Draper the mesmerist has found a new partner following the departure of Brooks, apparently for Australia. It's a girl this time, a Miss French. I saw her singing in

Manchester, and she was very pretty and fascinating. In light of our discussion, I am minded to have a word with her. She is at the Hippodrome, Rotherhithe, on Friday, and I had been meaning to go there anyway, having been invited (forgive this lamentable boasting) to backstage champagne with Miss Marie Lloyd herself. I will say nothing more in cold print, but on Wednesday (one o'clock at The Criterion, I take it?) you can advise me on discretion and valour and which is the better part of which in this affair.

Jean had then flicked quickly through the Wakelam archive looking for any further mentions of Kate French, Joseph Draper or Hugh Brooks. She had found a short note, again from Art Wakelam in Bayswater Road, this time addressed to Mr Saul Green, under-manager of the Hippodrome Theatre, Leicester Square, and this was of earlier date: March 1896.

My Dear Saul,

Draper and Brooks are competent thought readers. Rather too competent perhaps, so the turn lacks excitement. I do not see them as bill-toppers, and yet they are expensive. You must negotiate with Draper, the senior partner, who will certainly take the lion's share of whatever is agreed. In fact, you can learn a good deal about these two from the fact that B comes before D in the alphabet, but not in their billing.

Yours ever,
Art.

In the final fraught minutes of her archive visit, Jean had found a confusing letter about three ventriloquists, and this was not written by Wakelam, but by Theodore Selwyn of Selwyn & Wise, who mentioned Wakelam in passing to his correspondent as 'our dynamic young Mr Wakelam – he of the semi-American pedigree, and thoroughly American dress'. At which point, Jean had been required to return the file, since the archive was closing.

————

The Yob was approaching through the rain. He now wore a grey hoodie reading HARVARD.

'Look at this fucking clown,' said the voice in Coates's head, which was the voice *of* the Head – the Head of Chambers.

'Come here man,' the Yob was shouting, 'we going have a fucking talk.' For a Yob, he was very high-pitched. He might have been East European or further east. Turkey?

Coates had just reached Millbank, the north side of it. As the Yob approached, he crossed to the south side – not because he wanted to get away from the Yob but because he wanted to be *on* the south side, near the river. The Yob was now shouting from a few feet behind, 'You disrespect me, you disrespect my fucking girls. Who the fuck you think you are, man?'

Hadn't he said all that before? The black river was slapping against the wall, like a confined serpent.

'Three hundreds for what you do back there, man?' the Yob was shouting as they walked along. 'You fucking *joking* me, man.'

Coates hadn't intended to address the Yob again, but it was necessary to ask a question: 'Did the girl complain?'

'Yes man, she complain – big time.'

No, couldn't be true. He'd had evidence before that she'd quite enjoyed it.

Looming out of the rain ahead of them was a little oasis for the pedestrian: bottle bank, litter bin, lifebelt on a wooden frame, and a bench on a raised stone platform. The platform would enable anyone on the bench to look over the wall and see the river, perhaps while necking a bottle of wine, which they could then responsibly recycle in the bottle bank – which resembled a sort of diving bell. The thing was evidently full: empty bottles sprouted from the holes, and there were others around the base. There was only one small downside: an overhanging street lamp, but nobody would be looking to see what it illuminated. Directly over the road was a dark, deserted office block.

'Here you go, boy,' said the Head.

This was obviously going to be Parrish all over again, and there was nothing Coates could do to stop it.

'You fucking sick, man,' said the Yob, 'so you pay special price. It going to be six . . . six hundreds. You and me, friend – we walk; we find cash till and you pay. You pay you *fucking* bill, man.'

'No,' said the Head. '*He* pays the fucking bill.'

Coates picked up a bottle and swung it into the side of the Yob's face. The bottle broke, but the Yob remained obstinately upright, so Coates jammed the broken end into the Yob's neck, then ducked to avoid the spray of blood that flew up as the Yob went down. It had been automatic, meant-to-be. There was no need for Coates to stand there waiting for all the blood to come out of the Yob, but he did wait, with his hands in his coat pockets, keeping his back to the road. 'Watch out for your shoes, boy one,' said the Head, who would sometimes add 'one' to his usual 'boy' in more affectionate moments. It was a good point the Head had made. He was wearing his black suedes from Church's, which would be expensive to replace. By the time he'd retreated about five yards, the Yob was dead.

There was very little difference – in the dark – between the blood and the rainwater on the pavement. He looked up slowly as a bus came roaring along: the 87, originating from Battersea, heading for Trafalgar Square, then Aldwych. There were only about four people on it. None had looked his way, as far as he could tell.

Coates was still shaking slightly. The Head said, 'You'd kill him again if you could, boy. Am I right? Give him a fucking boot.' So Coates kicked the Yob in the stomach, and that did seem to do some good. He reached into the pocket of the hoodie and took out a wallet and a phone. The wallet held some money and some cards, but he threw the whole lot over the wall into the river. As for the phone, it was smashed. He'd probably smashed it with the kick. Coates lit a cigarette and activated the phone. He saw an image of the Yob, arm in arm with another yob. They both wore the same football shirt, and seemed to be in a football stadium. But it wasn't possible to go any further with the phone. 'It's locked,' said Coates.

'Into the river with it, you daft sod,' said the Head. For a Head of Chambers, the Head was remarkably foul-mouthed, and not very well educated. Of course, he bore no relationship to any actual senior barrister Coates had worked under. If he'd been a real person he'd have been a small, hard, angry man, possibly ex-military. His accent was a bit cockney, slightly reminiscent of Coates's own father's.

Coates threw the phone: a spinning light going into the water. Then another spinning light was hurtling towards him.

'Cop car,' said the Head of Chambers.

But the occupants were going too fast to stop nearby. As if to underline their incompetence, they put on their siren only when they'd gone past, but the flashing light had unsettled Coates. He began to walk east, heading rapidly away from the Yob. He threw down his cigarette and crossed the road.

He was approaching Parliament, which would be surrounded by police, even on a Sunday. Signs on railings read things like No Cycles – Police Will Remove and The Parliamentary Estate is Monitored by Security Cameras. Sheer bravado in most cases. About half the CCTV in London was malfunctioning at any given time. But Coates knew he'd made a mistake in leaving the Yob behind. He should have put him in the water, and he *would* do, but first he needed a drink.

Approaching Trafalgar Square, he turned into a pub. As he entered, a woman frowned at him. 'What's her problem?' he said, possibly out loud. Coates was not accustomed to being frowned at by women, and he was indignant until he realised his face might be covered with blood; that he was a murderer. But he had *nearly* been a murderer for a long time, and he did not regret killing the Yob. The woman was now giving him a half smile while raising a glass to her lips. That was more like it, but he needed to get a good look at himself in a mirror. He saw a sign and read it: GENTS.

As he stepped into the bright light of the gents', he was

confronted by a man coming out, so that if he did have blood on him, it would be too late to do anything about it. Coates approached the mirror above the sink with eyes downcast. Slowly, he looked up. He seemed to look much as he had done before going to Number Four, albeit wetter and paler. Coates took out his comb and began combing his hair, which he always found a soothing activity, and as he did it, the Head was calling him many names – 'ponce', mainly, but other worse ones as well. Then he saw a small mark on his shirt collar – a thin spray of blood. Should he go home and change his shirt before the party? 'No! You fucking idiot!' said the Head quite loudly, because there was still a job to be done with the body of the Yob, and because of Lucy and the babysitter. Also, ridiculous Dan and Diana lived near King's Cross, so a diversion to Chelsea would put him well beyond ordinary lateness. He would have to embellish an already over-complicated story. What *was* the story? Come on now. Here it was: he'd been swimming at the RAC Club in Pall Mall (where trunks and towels could be hired) before having a drink with a semi-fictional old friend, Dawson, who was a member there, and who wanted some advice about . . . what? A buy-to-let mortgage. Coates produced these lies with ease, but he never knew whether Camilla believed them. It didn't matter so much whether Jean believed them.

Coates tried to clean the spot with a damp paper towel. He then went back upstairs, bought a large white wine and took it to a stool by the window. On Whitehall, the rain was increasing. 'This is good, boy,' said the Head, because it would deflect people from walking along Millbank. He watched the silver spray thrown up by the cars and illuminated by their tail lights – so many moving fountains. A beautiful sight, it struck him, of the kind you'd never see from prison. It occurred to him that, having started killing people, he might well be destined to continue, and that he would eventually be arrested and go to jail just as he would eventually get cancer and die. But he wasn't ready for any of that just yet. Therefore, he must not leave the Yob lying around.

So Coates drank off the wine and quit the pub.

―――――――

Having concluded that, since she obviously wasn't going to be doing any work, she might as well go to sleep for a while, Jean had lain down on her mattress … where she had dreamed one of her regular dreams of Kate French, the Martian Girl. This time, Kate was walking along by the river in east London, passing giant, blank-faced warehouses with forbidding words painted in white: DRY DOCK, EMPIRE WORKS, BULLIVANT'S WHARF, SHIPS' PROPELLERS. Every so often there'd be a crane, a ship's mast, or an ordinary house amid the warehouses, and sometimes Kate would disappear behind a building, but she would always doggedly re-emerge, exposed on the wharves or docks of the riverbank as she strode on, heading east towards her unknown future. It can't have been a very deep dream, Jean thought when she woke up. It had been more like a dream of an old black and white film than of an actual event. The backdrop of the wharves and warehouses had seemed to move, rather than Kate herself, as if she were walking on the spot against a back projection.

As usual when she dreamed of Kate, Jean had been unable

to see her face properly – a perpetuation of the blindfold in the poster. But there'd been one intriguing detail: Kate's coat had very definitely had a fur-trimmed collar, much like a Max Mara coat Jean herself had once owned – bought before Max Mara prices went through the roof.

Jean looked at her phone: 18:57. Would she call Coates? A Foolish Question. But no; his phone would be switched off, and she would leave an inept voicemail, such as, 'Just calling to see what you're up to.'

Jean put down the phone, and was proud of herself for doing so. She began outlining the programme of an evening that would not involve moping over Coates. She would go to Battersea – to the theatre called The Space. There were no performances on Sundays at The Space, but the bar and café were open until some peculiar time: nine fifteen, possibly. She could walk it – if she could find her umbrella – and she would go over Albert Bridge, which was so much prettier than Battersea Bridge.

At The Space, Jean would have another conference with Donald, the stage manager. Donald was an elderly Rastafarian, and he knew exactly what could and could not be done in a one-woman show. The Space, being 'in the round', was of no use for Jean's purposes (and too expensive, as Donald had gently pointed out), but he would be happy to advise on the projections and lighting she might use at Tobin's. The projections would be any archive footage of music halls that was available free: East End scenes and river scenes; sailing ships and steam ships drifting through the mist right next to the houses; Tower Bridge being raised up as Kate French headed east to begin her collaboration with Draper, the Union Jack flying from the Tower of London and pointing in that direction.

The main use of projections would come in the mind-reading scenes: an image of a number being written on a blackboard while Jean, as Kate, sat blindfolded. A flat cap, a meerschaum pipe or a handkerchief might be projected: any object presented by an auditor – an audience member – that Draper would convey mentally to Kate. Draper's voice would accompany these shots. An actor would need to be found for those, and Donald thought he had the right man for the job: a person with the preposterously actorly name of Grenville, or possibly Granville, who would do it for 'about a hundred pounds in cash' – in other words exactly a hundred pounds in cash – and who had been in the Royal Shakespeare Company, and so would be difficult to deflect. But Jean worried that anybody of that sort would not have the droning voice she imagined to have been Draper's. For the rest of the soundtrack, Jean wanted semi-abstract noises suggestive of the river at night, also music hall cheering and applause slightly muffled.

Having found her umbrella, she was now looking for her elastic-sided DM boots. It was amazing how much she managed to lose in such a small flat. After a while she found, instead of her boots, an unopened packet of American Spirit rolling tobacco which she had completely forgotten about. It was in the pocket of her cape, which she'd forgotten *had* a pocket – so that was the explanation. She picked up her phone. 19:17. She'd better get on with it.

Ten minutes later, Jean was talking to herself as she hurried over Albert Bridge, on which she was more or less alone, what with the wind and the rain, and it being Sunday. As she walked, she was *being* Kate French, on that shadowy music hall stage.

Mr Draper then enquired point blank whether I had ever heard of Professor and Mrs Baldwin, and for a moment I thought we had strayed into the groves (is it?) of academe, until I recalled that the mesmerists tended to go in for these high-falutin' sorts of names, suggestive of great hidden powers. But I could only shake my head at the question.

'Then surely the White Mahatma?' Draper said.

'The White *what*?' I replied. Things were undoubtedly not going well. He then asked whether I had the faculty of sight, which, since I did not properly take his meaning, seemed a very strange question indeed. 'Well, I can *see*,' I said. 'I am not *blind*.'

'I mean second sight,' he elaborated. 'Many turners in this line claim to have second sight.'

'What an idea!' I said, and it appeared I had at last hit a right note, for Draper said: 'Good, because I don't want a loony. You do realise that any stage mesmerist is constantly pestered with letters from the asylums?'

'Oh, how sad. I assume one replies saying it's only a trick.'

'One doesn't reply at all, Miss French. Now, following your tremendous success as a *characteristic comedienne*,' Draper continued, seeming positively to underline the words with his sarcastic contempt, 'you are presently ... unemployed?'

'I am at liberty,' I corrected him.

Draper eyed me. His eyes, behind the glasses, were

extraordinarily small and perfunctory. They were pale blue, but only because they had to have *some* colour or other. Perhaps the smallness was an illusion created by the glasses, and I pictured a diagram of the sort seen in science books, showing a lens of Draper's spectacles ('Fig. 1') and the much smaller lens of his eye ('Fig. 2') with complicated lines going between them marked *a*, *b* and *c*.

'You are plainly lacking in experience, Miss French. Can you give me one good reason, plainly stated, why I should take you on?'

I am inoculated against smallpox, I nearly said. *I always came top in the spelling bees; I could read Shakespeare at the age of eight; I once made my own small museum of interesting objects. At school, I had the medallion for 'Never Absent, Never Late' three years in a row.* What I did say, indicating the letter, was, 'I can't remember if I put in about the dancing.'

'Dancing is irrelevant to mind reading,' Draper pointed out.

'Up North,' I stupidly persisted, 'I was briefly in a troupe called the Fancies, with Solly Fisher. Sol was a very good, if rather curious, comedy dancer, Mr Draper, veteran of not only the Fancies, also the Bouncing Bucks, the Terpsi Corps, and all those names that will live as long as theatre itself. As a solo artiste, he was always billed as The Man With Somebody Else's Legs, but he didn't push himself properly, and was somewhat scatter-brained. At the Bradford Alhambra, I heard him ask, "Which side is stage left in this theatre?" What Sol Fisher could have done with, Mr Draper, was somebody else's *brain* ... And as you have probably realised, sir, the same could be said for me. Evidently, I have been wasting your time. Please don't trouble to deny it. I see now that I was very rash in thinking I might take to mesmerism. It was just a thought that came into my head. A lot of things come into my head, Mr Draper.'

'And go straight out again,' he said. 'Would that be right?'

'Mr Draper,' I said, rising to my feet, 'I was crediting you with having avoided outright rudeness. I see that I have finally provoked you to it. Good afternoon to you, sir ... or good evening, as the case may be.'

... For it might have been any sort of time in the unnatural light of that lonely music hall, as I commenced to exit stage left, my footsteps echoing about the vast auditorium, as though several other people were leaving at the same time. I had just stepped into the wings when I heard Draper's upraised voice.

'Miss French,' he called, 'will you kindly come back here?'

Jean came to a dead stop, as Kate French would have stopped on hearing Draper's voice. Jean had not heard any voice; she had merely recalled that there would be no point in continuing her walk to The Space. It would not be open after all. There had been a catastrophic leak – reasonable enough in view of the incessant rain – and the place was closed for repairs that were expected to take ten days. She had been told of this, now she came to think of it, two days beforehand by an email, but the price of being involved in any way with The Space was that you received half a dozen emails a day

46

from them, and so the news had been somewhat submerged. She had resolved on having a Coates-free Sunday and would stick with the plan. Therefore, she would take that bus, the number of which she couldn't remember, but which ran from Battersea to the West End, crossing Vauxhall Bridge and running along Millbank, and she would go and see – since there were no plays on Sunday – a film.

Feeling only slightly foolish, Jean turned through one hundred and eighty degrees and began walking back in the direction she'd come from, while looking up suitable films on her phone. It was 19:41.

————

It was nearly eight o'clock as Coates approached the bottle bank once again. A pedestrian, approaching either very slowly or not at all, was a long way off to the west on the river side. 'Wino,' said the Head. That was probably right, and they could generally be discounted as unreliable witnesses. There was another new element a hundred yards away on the water: a bus-like boat with seats under a glass canopy, blue light within. Seemed to be empty, but the light indicated there might be crew on board somewhere.

Down in his stone trench, the Yob was getting on with being dead. The distant figure remained distant. As far as Coates could tell, he was looking at the river. Coates heard the roar of an approaching bus: another 87 taking . . . nobody at all, as far as he could see, towards the West End.

Then came an additional roaring from the direction of the river: the boat was moving away, and the overspill of light allowed Coates to read its name on the hull: *The Midnight*

Bell. He was glad the boat was moving away, although it was taking its time about it, seeming to grind its way along the water. The wall of the Embankment was too high and wide for the Yob to be lifted over with ease. But then Coates knew how he was going to accomplish this: the Head might have told him, since he was muttering something about 'Thirty yards west; all laid on for you.' There was a small garden, like a layby, partly screened from the road by some sickly trees and a small sort of white stone temple. This muddy little plot hardly deserved a name, but it had one, announced by a sign: Victoria Tower Gardens.

There was another bench in this garden. It was on a platform like the one by the bottle bank, because the river wall continued at the same height. But in this garden were stone steps leading to the top of the wall, which at that point was surmounted by a stretch of railings and a small gate.

Coates entered Victoria Tower Gardens. He stopped for a moment to note the dark green of the trees. Colour was good: when he was very down, the colours would leak out of the world in a way that made him furious. The gate on the wall was locked, and there were spikes on top of it, but both gate and spikes were low. There was a laughable, antique sign on the gate: GREATER LONDON COUNCIL WARNING: CHILDREN MUST NOT PLAY ON THESE STEPS. On the other side were more steps, wandering down into the black water. The pomposity and pointlessness of the arrangement . . . it was quite incredible. Coates returned to the Yob. Another bonus: the annoying river gazer seemed to have gone. Coates waited until there were no cars, then he dragged the Yob by his hooded top onto the pavement proper, and from there into Victoria Tower Gardens. At the foot of the steps, Coates had to stop and wait. A bus was coming: another 87, but going the other way from the previous two – back towards Battersea.

Coates was about to start pulling the Yob up towards the gate when he was horrified by the chime of a mighty bell. And there was Parliament, suddenly very near – and Big Ben going about his official duty of striking the hour. The hour was eight, and by the time of the fourth strike, Coates had got the Yob halfway up the steps; by the time of the eighth, both the Yob and Coates were on the top step. Coates was thinking of those descriptions of the 'Missing' on the Marine Police website, which he had often looked at while making his plans for Parrish: *Adult male, found in the Thames at Gravesend. Age unknown.* Unknown, because the fishes had eaten half of him, or he'd been liquefied by a boat propeller. Or just rotted in the water. But then Coates heard himself saying, 'The Marine Police always say the majority of bodies are recovered and identified.'

'You fucking mug,' said the Head. 'Of course they're going to say that. They're not going to go around recommending the river as the perfect waste disposal. But that's what it is, boy, that's what it is.'

Yes, he must have a point. Coates would have saved himself a lot of trouble if Parrish had gone into the river. But that was ancient history.

The legs were taking too long. The spikes had either penetrated the Yob's hooded top or the skin of his stomach – it didn't matter which. Coates had been trying to drag him over, when a series of lifts was required. But now another bus was

49

coming, this one heading into town. Coates was getting a bit sick of these 87s. It was an unnecessarily good service. He had an impression of passive profiles in the brightly lit windows: about four of them.

Within another half minute, he'd got the Yob over. It hadn't been a case of 'one more heave', more like about six quick ones, which had left Coates bathed in sweat as well as rainwater. A less fit man could never have done it. Even now the Yob was not in the river, but only on the steps leading into it. Coates climbed over the gate and began kicking the Yob, more or less at his leisure, into the black water, where he watched him roll. 'Looks like he's trying to swim the fucking crawl,' said the Head. But soon enough he was going under and away – pretty fast, too – heading for Lambeth Bridge from where he would probably make his lonely voyage to the open sea without troubling any missing persons list. That would depend on whether anybody missed him. 'Doubt it,' said the Head. 'Anybody that knew the cunt will probably be overjoyed to see the back of him.' And that was always possible, of course.

———

'You're soaking wet,' said Camilla when Coates arrived at the party. She was looking him up and down, assessing him. But that was quite normal, and Coates didn't mind, on the assumption that she liked what she saw, aesthetically if not morally.

'How's Lucy?' he asked, as he always did.

'Fine.'

'She went riding, did she?'

Camilla nodded.

There was a stable near her mother's house, with ponies for children as young even as ten-year-old Lucy to ride. Coates couldn't bear to watch Lucy ride in case she fell off, which she had done twice. Coates had had an argument with some negligent moron of a stable lad on the last occasion. There'd been no shouting, at least not from Coates. He'd wanted the stable lad to admit that he'd not been paying proper attention. If he didn't admit it Coates intended to hit him, but Camilla had called him off. So now horse riding was one of the Lucy activities he was not allowed to supervise. Apparently, he was over-protective. Reading was in danger of becoming another, but his fault there was that he pushed her too hard. He would spend hours reading with Lucy, especially since he'd quit chambers. He knew that he tired her out, and sometimes she'd cry, at which point he would always back off. He would never consciously upset Lucy. She was the one person for whom he had complete respect. Camilla came close. Jean? She was a little further down the scale, because Jean was whimsical, but that was fine; a nice contrast. It was good to have the two of them.

'The white wine's over there,' Camilla said. 'It's perfectly okay.'

And so he was being dispatched. Here was his wife's cynicism in microcosm: she wanted him to know she suspected him of behaving badly, but hadn't pressed the point. They would usually operate separately at parties. They'd have a debrief in bed afterwards, unless something had come up that caused her to go to the spare room.

Heading for the wine, Coates passed himself in a mirror.

51

Not too bad. He'd opened the window in the taxi so as to partially dry his hair. He'd got out at King's Cross station, then walked into next-door St Pancras International, where the T.M. Lewin shop had been unexpectedly open, so he'd bought a new shirt of more or less the same blue as the stained one, which he'd then put into a bin in the gents'. He'd had a glass of champagne on the concourse bar. Twelve pounds. He couldn't afford to spend that kind of money on booze, especially given the amount he would sometimes spend on sex. By drinking champagne he'd been trying to draw a line under the killing of the Yob, but it hadn't worked. He knew he was in for months of agitation, just as the agitation caused by Parrish had started to fade. They'd have a good chance of making an identification if they did find the body. The Yob had probably been fingerprinted at some point. If not, the dental records would do it. He must have been to an NHS dentist. Probably why he came here in the first place. Health tourism. Coates also couldn't help thinking he might have left a bit of his innards on that railing in Victoria Gardens.

Dan and Diana had an ill-advised Pop Art theme in their flat: framed, stylised posters of Bowie, the Stones etc. They thought these suggested youth whereas in fact they suggested age. Coates drifted off into vacancy, exhausted by bad thoughts. The Head had departed for the night. He only liked to be around for the exciting times. Coates found, after an unknown period, that he was watching Camilla talking to some man whose face was dominated by his thick black glasses. He had in effect exchanged his face for his glasses. He was probably in media. By and large, Coates hated people in media, as he often explained to Camilla, who edited a magazine; but he believed she had married him precisely because he was the opposite of the feline males she was surrounded by at work. She was now frowning towards Coates over the man's shoulder, as if to say: 'For God's sake talk to somebody.'

Coates had already rebuffed a couple of opening gambits, both from women. 'Can I help you to some food?' one of them had asked. 'No,' he'd replied, following up with a tardy and grudging, 'Thanks.' The other had been bolder: 'How do you know Dan and Diana?' Resenting the idea that he should know any two people so ridiculously conjoined by alliteration, he'd said, 'I don't. They're friends of my wife.' It was par for the course that women should come up to him. He calculated that he was about the best-looking man at the party: certainly the best for his age, just as Camilla was the best looking in her age bracket, and Lucy was in her own category (year five), from what he had seen of her classmates. But for how much longer would he hold onto the two of them without a job?

Clearly, he had wanted a greater revenge on the Yob than could be gained by killing him. But look on the bright side: he might be out past the Isle of Dogs by now. When a body reached the open sea, the Marine Police said it had 'gone out', like a jail break. They wouldn't have the expression if it never happened. Coates drank another glass of wine, mood improving somewhat. He saw his hostess across the room, looking at him. She nodded and gave him a slow, reluctant smile – more of a smirk. He liked to elicit reluctant smiles, or better still a reluctant laugh, because then the woman was doing it despite herself. It meant he had got at her in some way. Coates was well aware that most women were on their guard in his presence. His reputation preceded him.

Diana came up to him. He liked her hair; didn't like her party dress. She had a very good nose, he realised.

'What are you up to these days?' she said, and without waiting for an answer (just as well, since there was no answer), she asked him why he'd left the law.

'You have to be a toady,' he said. 'You have to suck up to these people – solicitors – who are your inferiors.'

'How so?'

He frowned; didn't like that phrase. 'Almost invariably physically,' he said, 'academically . . . morally.' She was forcing him to think about Parrish again, therefore also the Yob.

'*Morally?*' Diana asked.

He nodded. 'They're not called "solicitors" for nothing. They would have been barristers themselves if they'd had the courage to be freelance.'

'It's the solicitors who give the barristers the work, isn't it?'

'Yes.' He was coming over as pompous, uptight, and there was no need. He pictured those yellow signs that dot the river walls: DANGER STRONG CURRENTS. He said to Diana: 'I kept being asked to drinks parties with solicitors. My clerk would bring me the invitations, and he'd encourage me to go, to network. My line was: if they like my advocacy or drafting, fine; but I'm not interested in them as people.'

'Which they must have found very charming. What *was* your work? What sort of law, I mean?'

'Mixed,' he said. 'Mainly landlord and tenant and trust work.'

'I hope you weren't evicting people.'

'I did a lot of evictions,' he said. 'You are now seeing horns growing out of my head.'

'Oh, I saw them long ago.'

She was like everyone in the room bar Coates himself: from a privileged background – and the privilege had somehow made her sanctimonious.

'They were mainly commercial tenants who'd calculated that the landlord wouldn't go to law,' he said. 'So I wouldn't lose much sleep over them.'

'Trusts ...' she said. 'Sounds sort of Dickensian. It was a trust in *Bleak House*, wasn't it?'

'In the sense that all executors of a will are trustees, yes.' Coates now smiled at Diana. 'You know my favourite sort of trusts?'

'No.'

He leant towards her, whispering: '*Secret* trusts.'

She smiled back – smiled *in spite of herself*. So ten minutes of flirtation ensued, which Diana ended by asking the wrong question:

'But weren't you about to become a QC?'

'That didn't interest me,' he said. 'As a Silk, you have to charge so much more that the work falls off. You might be five years trying to get back to the level you were at before.'

He walked away. Later, dancing started. Camilla danced with the man in glasses, but that was all right. Coates liked watching her dance, and he couldn't believe she was interested in the man. You couldn't fall for a pair of glasses.

———

On the way home in the car, Camilla, who was driving, said, 'You've got a new shirt.'

'Correct.'

'It's nice. It's like the other one, but slightly different.'

'Right again. Well put.'

'What happened to the other one?'

Coates brushed his hand through his hair. 'Threw it away.'

'That's extravagant. Why?'

'It was dead.' She couldn't object to this. It was Camilla who'd introduced into their marriage the concept of dead – lifeless, washed-out – clothes, and she would weed them out of his wardrobe.

'It just suddenly . . . died?' she said.

'I looked at myself in the mirror after squash, and thought: I need a new shirt.'

Coates realised his mistake immediately. There was one chance in a million that Camilla wouldn't have spotted the mistake. The only real question was whether she'd choose to pick him up on it. She did.

'But I thought you were going swimming?'

'We played squash afterwards.'

That would just about do. Coates *had* been to the RAC Club, albeit not today, and there *were* squash courts there, and all the gear could be hired.

The silence that followed was magnified by the fact that the Prius is a silent car.

'I'm out tomorrow night,' said Camilla. 'Yoga. What about you?'

Coates nodded. Offered the chance to be out, he'd take it. He needed time alone to get his head around what he'd done on Millbank. What the Yob had made him do. He'd say he was off to a Haldane Society event. He was a member of the Haldane Society, a club for left-wing lawyers, which he'd joined as a student, when he *was* left wing. It had come in very useful ever since.

As they closed in on their street, which was off the King's Road, she asked, 'How *is* Dawson?'

'Having a mid-life crisis,' said Coates.

'Oh yes?'

'The details are pretty sordid,' he said, but now they were into the whole business of looking for a parking space.

When they were in the flat, it was Coates's job to pay the babysitter. He paid for less and less these days, but it was ritualistic that he paid the babysitter, while Camilla went to make sure Lucy was asleep. If Lucy was *not* asleep, there was a good chance Coates would never see this particular babysitter again, because Camilla would have deemed her incompetent ... which would be a shame because she was very pretty and petite. She seemed to have made a charming cocoon for herself amid the old cashmere blankets they kept on the sofa, like a dormouse. Seven hours after killing the Yob, Coates was finally beginning to feel himself again. He had half enjoyed fencing in the car with Camilla, and it was quite amusing to be handing over cash to an attractive female once again, but this time more innocently.

'How was Lucy?' he asked.

'She's a lovely girl,' said the babysitter, who was possibly called Amanda, 'and so bright!'

There was an empty glass by the sofa. Lucy had probably said to her something like, 'They won't mind if you have some wine, you know.' She was precocious; it was a miracle Lucy wasn't helping *herself* to wine. All too soon, she would be, if heredity had anything to do with it. Camilla now returned to the living room. Apparently Lucy was not asleep, but Camilla did not seem to be holding it against Amanda, since she began asking if she might be free tomorrow. She broke off from this to say to Coates, 'Lucy wants to see you. Don't start reading her a story.'

Coates walked along the corridor to Lucy's room, collecting a last glass of white wine from the small kitchen on the way. Lucy had the best room in the flat, the only one with a fireplace, and she kept all her dolls on the mantelpiece, which she could only just reach. She was sitting up in bed.

'It's way past my bedtime,' she said. (There would often be these charming *mea culpas*.)

'Well, you said it, kid,' said Coates, sitting on the bed next to her.

'Where've you been?' she said.

'What do you mean? I've been to the same place as your mother. To the party.'

'Mummy said you were late.'

'Well you know, it's rude to be *early* to a party.'

Lucy frowned, then leant against his chest, listening, like a small primitive doctor who couldn't afford a stethoscope. She often did this. Last year, Coates's father had died of a heart attack; Coates was pleased about this, because his father was a mad oik, which Lucy hadn't quite been old enough to realise. After debating various lies by which to explain the sudden disappearance of her grandfather, Coates and Camilla had told her the truth. It had been Lucy's first intimation of mortality, and having somehow – being very bright – divined that a son might go the same way as a father, she had been regularly checking Coates's heartbeat ever since.

'Still going?' he asked.

'Obviously,' Lucy said, but she continued to listen.

Coates took a sip of wine.

'I heard that going down,' she said.

'Shall I do it again?'

'No,' Lucy said, lifting her head from his chest. 'You drink too much.'

No doubt a direct quote from her mother, but she might easily have worked it out for herself. Coates kissed his clever girl on her forehead and turned out the bedside light.

———

Jean was walking through the ticket hall of Embankment Tube station. She was about to head left – up Villiers Street and towards Charing Cross – when something made her look right, towards the Embankment itself. Two police cars were present, and a small crowd. The focus of attention was a big concrete pier, permanently moored a hundred yards east of Hungerford Bridge. It was for pleasure cruisers, which seemed a silly term now, on this gloomy late afternoon with rain falling, and there was no such boat to be seen at the moment. Instead, there were two floating counterparts of the police cars, resembling tugboats, only with blue and yellow checks. Another boat was black, with a winch on the rear – the stern. There was at least one frogman in the water and he kept coming up, like a seal. Some of the action was concealed behind a dirty, flapping banner advertising RIVER CRUISES, but this was obviously something serious.

'They've found a body,' a man turned around to tell her. It was a sufficiently sensational piece of news to justify addressing a stranger. Jean thanked him, which was ever so slightly ridiculous of her. It would not be seemly to hang about waiting for a glimpse of the body, even though the man who'd addressed her was one of about fifty people doing just that. She began climbing the slope of Villiers Street.

Jean was on her way to see her new friend, Vincent. Because he couldn't make a living from his number one passion – which was ventriloquism – Vincent worked in a magic shop: that is, a shop retailing magic tricks and theatrical memorabilia down an alleyway off Charing Cross Road. Jean did not know who owned the shop, but it wasn't Vincent.

Vincent was steeped in show business, all the unprofitable parts of it. As a boy, he had apparently won prizes in children's ballroom dancing classes. He was unfortunately now quite fat, and pale with thinning curly hair and a goatee beard. He always wore a dark suit and a black, ribbon-like tie, so that he looked like an opera singer, or the maître d' of an Italian restaurant. Vincent was about twenty-five, and had clearly been born at least a hundred years too late, but he did have a website, which Jean had discovered in her music hall investigations. It promoted his ventriloquism – which he conducted with a three-foot-high replica of himself called Little Vince – and offered snippets of music hall history. Jean had emailed Vincent, and he'd invited her to drop by the shop at any time, which she'd done twice in the last fortnight, when they'd talked about Kate French, the Martian Girl. Vincent had heard of Kate, and had undertaken to find out more about her on his own account. Jean was carrying her laptop in her handbag, in anticipation of some joint internet searching with Vincent.

The alleyway was barely wide enough to accommodate Jean's umbrella. A kind of sluice ran down the centre, off-loading rainwater into Charing Cross Road. As she opened the shop door, a bell rang loudly – and futilely. The shop was deserted apart from Jean, and it remained so after the ringing had subsided.

The shop was under-lit. It was as if the lights had been dimmed for the start of a show, but the show had never begun. Forty years ago there would have been many more items on the shelves; in five years' time there would presumably be no shop at all. Jean began inspecting a set of 'champagne bottles', some of which fitted inside others. There was a bundle of suspiciously truncated ropes, a fez, a rather tattered rabbit for pulling out of a hat. On the counter was a display of suspect playing cards. These might or might not be used in mind-reading acts. Jean picked up one of the packs.

'Open it up, if you like,' said Vincent. He'd stepped through the curtain behind the counter. She smiled at him and fanned the cards: they were all the jack of diamonds.

'You could have a jolly good game of snap with these!' she said.

Vincent nodded, smiling. He was a really lovely man. 'How's the writing coming?' he asked, kindly absolving her of the necessity of buying anything.

'I've got up to where Draper is just about to take her on,' said Jean, replacing the cards. 'But I can't quite see why he *would* have taken her on. I mean, she was very inexperienced at that point, and he was a real top-liner.' Jean always tried to use correct music hall terminology in the presence of Vincent. For example, she was always careful to call ventriloquists 'vents'.

'Well,' said Vincent, 'Draper was no longer with Brooks.'

'Yes, why?'

'Brooks died.'

'But I thought he went to Australia.'

'Yes, well; one or the other. Nobody really knows.'

'I'm hoping to find out from the archive of the British Theatre Memorial Fund,' Jean said grandly. 'Have you been there?'

'Not for a long time.'

It occurred to Jean that Vincent had something up his sleeve.

'Perhaps,' she said at length, 'Draper saw that Kate was desperate. I mean, she was living on Poverty Corner . . .' (She gave herself a tick for that Edwardianism.) 'Perhaps he took pity on her?'

Vincent looked at her, smiling.

'I would say that's rather unlikely,' he said. 'Friend Draper was pretty hard-headed, by all accounts. I've got to close up now; then I'd like to show you something, if that's okay?'

Jean nodded, slightly nervous. Vincent was being unprecedentedly confident.

She took a step back as he emerged from behind the counter. It was as if a seaside automaton had emerged from its glass case. He flipped the sign on the door so that it read CLOSED on the outside and OPEN on the inside, but that was fine: it was six o'clock, closing time (or very nearly). And Vincent was now *locking* the door, which was presumably also par for the course. All shop doors were locked when shops were closed, but Jean did wonder whether Vincent might be dangerous, as well as weird. Certainly, he *was* weird, but perhaps not more so than any ventriloquist. If you met a ventriloquist who wasn't weird, you'd feel short-changed. 'Just have to sort a few things,' he said. 'Have a seat.'

He indicated a stool next to the counter, and Jean sat on it as Vincent bustled about, performing the closing ritual. After some business with the till and a big, battered ledger, Vincent went into the back room. He returned carrying a smaller version of himself: Little Vince. Big Vince laid him rather roughly on the counter, then went into the back room again, leaving Little Vince on his back staring fixedly at the ceiling. It was extremely hard to believe he was not about to tilt his head towards Jean and wink. Jean had watched Vincent's act on YouTube, where it appeared in two versions. The first had lacked sound, and there'd been some interludes where Big and Little Vince had seemed to stare, completely motionless, at the audience. (Jean hoped very much that there *had* been an audience, and that they were laughing or applauding in those moments.) The second clip did have sound, and the dialogue perhaps embodied Vincent's lack of self-confidence. He had opened by asking Little Vince, 'Are we going to give these people a really good laugh?' 'I doubt it,' Little Vince had gloomily replied. The theme was that Little Vince wanted to break away and go solo, and not as Little Vince, but just as Vince, 'like Sting'. Big Vince had warned that he might have difficulty as a solo artist, because he was, after all, 'made of wood'.

'Always have to make it personal, don't you?' said Little Vince.

Big Vince now returned from the back room, carrying a customised black suitcase with red velvet lining, and he placed Little Vince inside it, much to Jean's relief. She had feared he would place the figure on his knee and start doing his act for her. Vincent was shutting the suitcase, with some difficulty.

'You have a gig tonight, do you?' Jean asked.

'Nope,' said Vincent. 'Actually, I was wondering if you'd fancy a quick drink?'

This was bad, Jean thought. Was Vincent getting the wrong idea about her visits to the shop? But she said, 'Yes, sure. Would that be after or before you show me whatever you were going to show me?' Because she was getting a bit impatient on that front.

'After,' he said, and he swung the suitcase down onto the floor and fished in his top pocket, producing a memory stick with a flourish. 'Kate,' he said, 'found her on the web.'

'*What?*' said Jean. If this was actual footage, it was more than she'd ever hoped for.

Vincent put the memory stick into the laptop on the counter, and the footage started to play, flickering like a black and white fire, and it was immediately exciting because the film was clearly going to show an external location, not just a fixed shot of a music hall stage. The first thing Jean saw clearly was a glass roof, and what appeared to be steam, which gradually became *actual* steam – this was a railway station – and the camera moved shakily down past a dangling notice that read PLATFORM 1 to show a crowd of happy people, standing beside a locomotive. In spite of the glass roof, it appeared to be raining heavily inside this railway station, but that was just scratches on the film.

'When is this?' asked Jean.

'December 1898,' said Vincent.

'And where is it?' Jean asked. 'I mean, it's a railway station, obviously.'

'Charing Cross. They're all turners.'

'So it's a tour?'

'Yes.'

They were all waving bits of paper – their tickets.

'What was special about the tickets?' Jean asked, because surely it wasn't such a big deal to be in possession of a railway ticket, even in 1898.

'Hold on,' said Vincent, and a few seconds later a caption – fancy white letters on black, taking up the entire screen – explained: *Free Travel Today!* Then it was back to the turners, still waving their tickets.

'Turners were generally on the move on a Sunday,' said Vincent. 'The Music Hall Railway Rates Association fought for them to get discount tickets.'

'But the caption said *free* tickets,' said Jean, wondering why she didn't just shut up and listen.

'Ah, yes,' he said, 'but here's the thing. The usual discount was three-quarters of the fare. But sometimes, a railway would give them *completely* free travel on a Sunday, as a sort of promotion.' He was pointing at the screen. 'There's Kate French.'

Vincent was indicating a very gorgeous woman on the end of the row: the Martian Girl. She wore a coat with a fur collar: the same coat, surely, she had worn in Jean's dream of her. Well, a coincidence ... Either that or a message had flashed through a hundred and twenty years. Kate French did not look late Victorian; did not look like Ada Reeve, in other words. She was the opposite of plump, blousy and gap-toothed, and she did not wear a hat with a bowl of fruit on it, or any hat at all. Kate French was dark and slight, with a very modern beauty.

The camera was threatening to wander away from her, so Jean asked Vincent to freeze the frame. Her hair was mid-length, with ringlets at the sides. But it was the eyes that you noticed: there was a deep glitter, but also a reserve as – when Jean asked Vince to restart the film – she smiled and waved her ticket. The cameraman had noticed it too, because having moved away from Kate French at the end of the line, he quickly moved back to her.

'She's very pretty,' said Jean, who found that she was almost in tears.

'And there's Joseph Draper,' said Vincent.

Draper was *not* pretty. He stood next to Kate, wearing a homburg hat and wire glasses; he was waving his ticket, but he was the only one not smiling. He was making it pretty clear that he was waving his ticket because he'd been told to do so.

'He doesn't look very nice,' said Jean, cursing herself for a second insipid word choice ('pretty' having been the first).

'Do you know what I think?' said Vincent, looking up from the screen.

'That he killed her?'

Vincent looked directly at Jean for once; he began to nod as the screen went black.

Jean's phone rang. She ought not to take it, given the point her conversation with Vincent had reached, but she knew she would do if it was Coates. It was Coates. She'd held off from calling him for an entire twenty-four hours, and she'd got her reward: *he* had called *her*.

'Vincent,' said Jean, 'will you excuse me? I'm going to have to take this.' But with his natural magnanimity, Vincent had already retreated into the back room.

After the preliminaries, Coates said, 'By the way, sorry about yesterday. I was in the country.'

'You said. What was it like?'

'Wet.'

'You could have called,' Jean failed to prevent herself from saying. 'Well anyway,' she said, 'nothing to be done ... I'm trying not to say that word, by the way ... '

'What word?'

'"Anyway."'

'Why?'

'It doesn't mean any*thing*. Anyway ... I was busy yesterday. I went to The Space.'

'The Space?'

'*Time Out* called it the liveliest and most diverse arts centre south of the river.'

'I bet it is.'

'It's in Battersea.' Jean decided to elide over the fact that she'd aborted the mission. 'Afterwards, I went into the West End.'

'How?'

'*How*? Well, Battersea's not on the Tube, so –'

'You went by bus?'

'Yes.'

Silence down the line. Of course, he went in for silences,

but there seemed something different about this one: it arose, Jean instinctively felt, from not knowing what to say, as opposed to just refusing to say anything. Jean ought to ride it out, testing its possibilities, but after about four seconds she lost her nerve. 'I could've walked, but that would have taken half an hour, and the weather was terrible.'

'An eighty-seven?' he said, after some time.

'What?'

'You took the number eighty-seven.'

'Probably – they all look the same to me. It went along Millbank to Trafalgar Square.'

'You got off there?'

'Yes.'

'Why?'

'Because that's where I *wanted* to get off. And that's where it terminated.'

'The eighty-seven terminates in Aldwych.'

What was this? The Transport for London helpline? 'I went to see a film.'

'What time was the film?'

'Most people,' Jean said, 'would ask what the film *was*. It started at about nine. But I don't quite see why this is relevant.' Jean was proud of that third sentence. It took gumption.

'We came back early from the country,' he said. 'I was thinking of biking round to see you, and I was wondering whether you would have been in.'

'You were thinking of coming round?' she said, amazed. However early he'd returned from the country, he would still not be at her place until the evening, and the two of them didn't do evenings. 'Well, it's a purely academic matter now, isn't it?' she said, giving one of her nervous laughs, which she was also trying to eliminate.

Then the longest pause – followed by the oddest remark of all:

'I could come round to you now if you like.'

Was it really possible that evenings were now on the agenda? Mondays as well, since this *was* Monday.

'I'm not at home,' she said, at once annoyed and pleased about the fact.

'Where are you?'

Something different was definitely going on. What did it matter where she was? They only ever met in her flat, and she was not in her flat. It occurred to her that it would sound ridiculous to say where she actually was, but she could see no alternative, with Vincent almost certainly listening from the back room, although probably doing his best not to.

'I'm in a magic shop,' she said.

'Researching for the show.'

'Yes.'

'Is the show about magic?'

'Sort of. You know what it's about – I've very often told you.'

'Where is the shop?'

'West End.'

'I could come and meet you.'

He's unilaterally changing the rules of engagement, thought Jean. Was their relationship about to go public? The thought scared her. She'd assumed it was primarily about the need for sex – Coates's need for it in particular – which was both very bad and quite good. Sex was so important for

Coates that to be his sex object was quite a compliment. That was one way of looking at it, anyway. And if their relationship was a sex-only thing, that would impose natural limits; including a temporal limit, because they would get bored of each other eventually.

'We could go for a drink,' he said.

'I couldn't see you until eight,' she said, amazed at her own ruthlessness. 'I have to see someone else before then.' How traumatic this must be for poor old Coates: not only did she leave her home occasionally, she also knew other people.

'All right, where?'

Jean named a pub called the Punch Bowl. Like the magic shop, it was down an alleyway (this one off Wardour Street), which was probably why she'd thought of it.

'Eight o'clock then,' Coates said quietly.

Vincent reappeared from the back room. 'Everything all right?' he said, ejecting the memory stick from the laptop and handing it to Jean.

'For me?' she said, taking the memory stick. She'd asked a classic 'foolish question', but she was disorientated. Vincent nodded. She said, 'I'll make a copy and give it straight back.'

'Keep it,' he said, and Jean thanked him while wondering if this was her reward for having put Coates off until eight o'clock, because Vincent probably *had* heard her doing that. She said, 'Do you know the Punch Bowl off Wardour Street? Do you mind if we go there? Someone else will be coming along, but not 'til eight.'

'Sounds a good plan,' said Vincent.

He began doing something with the till. Jean did hope he would be leaving the Punch Bowl at – or before – eight. The idea of trying to bridge the gap between Vincent and Coates; between an alpha male and a sort of beta minus . . . That was unfair, but the idea of saying to Coates, 'Meet Vincent, he's a ventriloquist . . . '

She and Vincent stepped out of the shop and into the alley. Vincent put down his suitcase. As he was locking the shop door with several keys, a man was approaching along the alley. He wore a camel coat, had a ponytail of grey, dead hair.

'Oh hello there, Mr Worsley,' said Vincent – or it might have been Horsley or Wolsey. Vincent didn't seem to like saying the name anyway. 'Do you want to go in?'

'Obviously. How was today?'

'Oh, pretty slow. We did about a hundred and fifty. Mainly books.'

Worsley (that was the name, Jean decided) scowled at Jean as Vincent unlocked the door, holding it open for Worsley as a servant would. 'We had two telephone queries about the Beginner's Course, Mr Worsley. Both worth a follow-up, I think, if we don't hear anything.'

They wouldn't be hearing anything, Jean thought, and they both knew it.

'That was Mr Worsley,' said Vincent, when they were walking down the alley. 'He owns the shop. He can be a bit . . . '

Charing Cross Road had become extremely dark, rainy and crowded since Jean had last been on it. Vincent – too shy to share her umbrella – maintained a position just beyond its range as they walked in silence. The rudeness of Worsley had obviously demoralised the poor boy. After a while, Jean said, 'You really think Draper killed Kate?'

'Well, *you* said that,' said Vincent.

'But you agreed, didn't you?'

'Possibly. It's possible.'

'Because of something she found out? Something to do with Brooks? But I think someone might have saved her. She had a white knight, maybe. He was called Art Wakelam. Have you ever heard of him, Vincent?'

He frowned. 'Maybe ... An impresario of some sort ... And of course you can do anything you want with your story.'

'But I would like it to be based on fact, because that's a guarantee of truth. It's a terrible thing for a creative writer to say ... but why lie if you don't have to?'

'Yes,' said Vincent, 'absolutely.'

They continued in silence, Jean thinking about the 87 bus and Coates's bizarre obsession with it. Since everything with him came back to sex, he probably suspected her of having another man, and somehow the 87 bus was tangled up in his mind with this thought. There *had* been a slight erotic element to her top-deck activity: she had been checking the Facebook of Paul Dean, an old university friend who'd been in love with her ever since, in spite of presumably having lots of other opportunities, since he was quite successful in some City job, and not bad looking. Jean considered him a sort of lover-in-reserve, and it was unfortunately the case that she toyed with him much as Coates toyed with her.

They had now reached the alley that led to the pub. Jean turned into it first. There was a kink in this alley, and Jean knew that when she got beyond it she would see an enormous period lantern, hanging over the pub door. Jean turned the corner, and she did see the lantern, but not the door, because

Coates was standing directly in front of it. He was an hour and a half early.

———

'This is Vincent,' said Jean, feeling quite badly shaken, 'he's a ventriloquist.'

'Sorry I'm early,' Coates said, kissing her – his usual light, moreish kiss, this time with the added feature of his hand on her shoulder: a slightly fraternal touch, to show the wholesomeness of their arrangement. Turning to shake Vincent's hand, he continued, 'Something fell through. But I know you two want to discuss the show, so I'll let you get on with it. Shall we go in?' he said, indicating the pub as though he had lately acquired it.

The pub was crowded, and made to seem even more so by the fact that everyone was kaleidoscopically reflected in the Victorian glasswork for which it was famous. The glass was neutral in tone, but the colours were supplied by the people, especially the many red-faced males. Of course, Coates immediately found a table, which was in a kind of mirrored booth, so they would be seeing each other from all angles. 'Can I buy you a drink?' Coates asked Vincent.

'Oh,' said Vincent. He was trying to fit his suitcase under the table, and appeared flustered.

'Gottle o' geer?' suggested Coates, which was nearly rude.

'Pint of bitter, please,' said Vincent, 'I'll just see what they've got.'

So he must be one of those real-ale people. As Vincent pushed past on his way to the bar, Coates did not do the obvious thing: raise his eyebrows at Jean, as if to say, 'Where did you find this loony?' Instead, he pushed back the side of her hair. 'What about you, kid?'

'Red wine, please,' she said, with contemptible meekness.

'I mean it,' he said. 'I won't bother you for an hour.' And when he returned with the drinks he began being as good as his word, averting himself slightly from Jean and Vincent and beginning a deep engagement with his iPad.

'Do you think,' Jean said to Vincent, 'that Draper thought Kate could really read his mind, and that unnerved him? I'm thinking of developing it that way.'

Vincent nodded for a while. 'It's also possible he became jealous of Kate,' he said.

'Professionally jealous?'

'Yes. Or it might have been an argument about money.'

'But why *jealous*?'

'She had a sort of mystery about her that people liked,' said Vincent. 'But he had no mystery. You can tell a lot about him from the bill matter he wrote. His first act he just called "Draper & Brooks: Two Minds as One".'

'Boring,' said Jean, 'uninspired.'

'It is when you think of The White Mahatma and so on. Then he changed it to Draper & Brooks: Mental Telegraphy.'

'They might as well have been called Draper & Brooks: Mental Postage,' Jean said, '. . . thoughts delivered same day! But when he teamed up with Kate, he billed her as The Martian Girl, which is pretty flamboyant.'

'Ah,' said Vincent, who was beginning to get over the baleful Worsley effect. 'I think it was Kate who came up with that. There was quite an obsession with space travel at the time, and the technology of communications, hence Martian

Girl. And they were sometimes Draper & French, Transmitter and Receiver.'

'Not bad,' said Jean. 'By the way, he was always the transmitter and she was always the receiver?'

'Absolutely right. Draper was always what was called the agent. His partners were always the percipients.'

'Which was the senior role?'

'Good question. Put it like this: Draper always paid himself more than the other person, because it was basically his act.'

'But they both had to know the codes.'

'Yes, but Draper liked to take on inexperienced people who he'd then *teach* the codes. That way, he always had something over them.'

'But he didn't make up the codes. He didn't own them.'

'No, that's true. He was just good at teaching them.'

By now – Jean noticed – Coates had put his iPad aside. He was sitting silently, looking down at the table.

'A lot of it's done by simple phrases,' said Vincent. 'Say the object a transmitter has to convey is an engagement ring. He might say, "What do we have here?" and that particular phrase refers to a set of objects to do with jewellery. There might be ten items in the jewellery set: bracelet, brooch, signet ring and so on, all in numbered order. Let's assume an engagement ring is number five on the list. Number five in the jewellery set, and object number five in *any* of the sets – and there'd be a lot of them – would be indicated by a certain word. "Tell", for example. So the transmitter says, "What do we have here? Tell me." But for finer detail, like the colour of the stone in the ring, you're into a more complicated code, and it depends which one.

I used to know the Rochelle Code, dreamed up by a guy called Rochelle.'

'It's the one I'm trying to learn,' said Jean.

Vincent nodded. 'Draper and Kate might have used it. In Rochelle, A is H, B is T, C is S, D is G . . . Can't remember the rest.'

Coates was looking at the ceiling in a bizarre way, but Jean was pretty sure he was paying attention.

'Now,' Vincent continued, 'say Draper wants to convey the initials on a signet ring, which are A.C. Remember, it's the first letter of a word that counts, so he says, "Hurry. Since we're losing time." A being H and C being S . . . It's my round, I think?'

Vincent went to the bar; Jean also stood up, and Coates raised a questioning eyebrow.

'I'm off to the ladies',' she said.

He nodded, as though giving her the go-ahead. When she returned, Vincent was still floundering at the bar, trying to catch the barman's eye, so Coates was alone at the table. Approaching him, Jean saw that he was studying his iPad again, but she couldn't see the screen because he was holding it up, like a book. Behind him the wall of mirrors, etched with laurels and flowers. In some facets, the back of Coates's head appeared, showing the incipient bald spot, which must absolutely never be mentioned: but the mirrors gave no sight of the iPad screen.

'I don't know if you came in on the Tube?' Jean said, sitting down. 'At Embankment they were taking a body out of the river.'

Coates closed down the iPad and laid it carefully on the table.

'Did you not come in by Tube?' she said.

He shook his head. The District Line to Embankment would be a logical way for him to travel to the West End from Chelsea. He wouldn't have walked or cycled in the rain, and she didn't believe he took taxis very often, being strapped for cash. But it must remain a secret how he had come. In view of the continuing silence of her supposed lover, Jean thought she'd better try another tack, so she took her laptop out of her bag and inserted the memory stick Vincent had given her. She swivelled the screen towards Coates as the footage began. When the camera closed in on Kate, she said, 'That's her.'

'Who?' Coates said, inevitably. He was slowly returning from about a hundred miles away.

'Kate French, the Martian Girl. The subject of my show.'

'The mind reader?'

'Yes. What do you think?'

'Interesting,' he said, nodding.

'What do you mean by "interesting"?'

'She's very good looking.'

'Oh. I thought you had something more profound in mind.'

'Afraid not,' he said, and he smiled for about half a second.

Vincent now returned, and with him the subject of Edwardian music hall, specifically Tobin's Supper Rooms, where Jean would be performing. Coates sat completely still, not even drinking, as Vincent explained that Tobin's had originally been one of the 'Little Empires', which meant that, although it was small, it had pretensions, hence Moorish decorations on the exterior, a gilded proscenium, plaster statues in alcoves ... But Vincent was losing heart, seeing Coates unmoved by all this plush magnificence. Jean wondered if

Coates had been given pause by what he'd just been reading on the iPad . . .

But wait. Coates was raising his head and smiling at Vincent.

'There would have been an orchestra, of course?' he said.

'Definitely,' said Vincent.

'With the timpani and cymbals just that little bit too loud? And all the men in the audience smoking?'

'Absolutely!' said Vincent. 'Or with a cigar behind the ear for later on.'

Finally, the evening hit its stride. It turned out Coates had a pretty good working knowledge of music hall, not that he'd ever given any hint of this to Jean when she'd talked about the show, possibly because he hadn't been listening. But Coates was clever. He was well read and he had, as he quite often mentioned, 'taken' (that was the verb) a first in history from Oxford before qualifying as a lawyer.

'Ah, now you see we're getting into a fascinating area,' Vincent was saying, two drinks later. The area was the connection between mind reading and the supernatural, and Vincent and Coates now went into a good twenty minutes of back-and-forth about psychic research, spiritualist mediums and communication with the dead or dying. It appeared they were both familiar with a highly obscure book called *Phantasms of the Living*, which they both referred to familiarly as '*Phantasms*'. Eventually, Jean was forced to ask what this flipping book was all about.

'Go ahead, Vincent,' said Coates, deferring to his new best friend, but Vincent insisted Coates take the floor.

'All right,' he said. 'Typical scenario. A retired colonel is sitting in his club in Pall Mall. It's midnight. He's in the club library, reading the paper and drinking a brandy. He looks through the window, and there's his wife's face. He throws down the paper and moves towards the window; but the face has disappeared. He sits back down and orders another brandy. Of course, he's in shock, because it can't have been his wife's face.'

'Why not?' asked Jean, resigned to the fact that he'd have a devastating answer.

'Because the library's on the third floor. And his wife's in Brighton.'

'Exactly,' said Vincent, '*exactly*, and not only that . . . '

'Not only that,' said Coates, 'but his wife turns out . . . '

' . . . She turns out,' said Vincent, 'to have died in Brighton from a sudden illness at exactly midnight.'

Jean had something to contribute here, but Coates was speaking, and rather loudly. 'These were called death wraiths,' he said, pompously, to everyone. 'The Victorians had given up on being able to bring back the dead, but there was this idea that the dead might communicate to the living at the moment of death. It was a sort of compromise position.'

'I'll tell you another compromise position,' said Jean, determined to break in. 'The idea of the collective unconscious. It was related to the meeting of minds that was supposed to occur in telepathy, but in the collective unconscious, the *dead* could communicate their thoughts to the *living*.' Jean sat back. It had probably been quite a silly intervention. But she often thought about the collective unconscious. She pictured it as being like the estuary of the Thames and the beginning of the sea – an escape from a narrow channel into universality. But neither Coates nor Vincent appeared even to have heard her.

'Another drink?' said Coates.

'I was just about to suggest that,' said Vincent.

Talk about two minds as one, Jean thought; talk about transmitter and receiver.

'Impressive guy,' Coates said to Jean as they came out of Charing Cross station. 'I mean, he knows all that, *and* he can speak without moving his lips. At least, I assume he can.'

'Yes, he can.'

'He could lose a little weight.'

They had seen Vincent – and Little Vince – onto a train. He lived somewhere like Bromley, and it had seemed strange that he proved to be equipped with so modern a thing as an Oyster card, albeit kept in a rather mouldering wallet. Jean had half expected that he, like Kate French, would travel on a free pass for 'Theatricals' as supplied by the London, Greenwich & Blackheath Railway Co., or some such antiquated concern.

They had all waved as the train pulled away – as if she and Coates were parents seeing off their child. Whether parents seeing children off would then retreat behind a station pillar for a long snog she doubted, but that's what she and Coates had done. Neither one had initiated the move; they had both initiated it, and this was why she was stuck with Mr Coates. As they broke off, Jean looked about the station, which contained no trains at all now that Vincent's had left – and very few people. She was trying to work out

80

where Kate had been standing in the archive footage. Coates was watching her.

She took his arm as they headed back to the ticket gate. It had been quite a good evening, she thought. On Villiers Street, Coates was sharing her umbrella. It was a novelty to be walking alongside him, and every approaching man provided a reminder of why she *was* alongside him: the shambling, the fat, the bald, the obviously boring: one by one they approached and diverged, shamed by the imperious gaze of Coates. (Actually that wasn't quite right, because he only looked at the women.) He'd gone back to the subject of ventriloquism, which he seemed to approve of. There'd been a vent act he'd seen as a boy in Brighton or somewhere. 'T.P. Collins . . . and the dummy was called Davey.'

'Funny, was it?'

'*I* thought so, when I was ten. I remember the beginning. Collins asks Davey, "Now where were you born?" "London," says Davey. "What part?" asks Collins. "All of me," says Davey.'

Jean laughed. 'Any more?'

'Collins says to Davey, "Now tell me a true story." Davey begins, "Once upon a time . . ." but Collins interrupts: "I've heard it before!"'

Jean liked him telling her this.

As they entered the ticket hall at Embankment, it occurred to her that, however Coates had come to town, he must now intend returning to Chelsea by Tube. She indicated the other entrance, on the side of the river, the stone pier and the River Cruises banner. The flotilla was gone, and there was no sign of official activity. 'That's where they took the body out,' she said, turning towards the ticket machines – she needed to top up her Oyster, but Coates was not following. He remained in the centre of the booking hall, frowning slightly. She knew immediately that she would not be going back to west London on the Tube with him. He walked over and kissed her quickly, saying, 'I think I'll walk it.'

'You're going to *walk* to Chelsea?' she said.

'I'll call you,' he said.

Jean watched as he exited the station on the river side. She waited ten seconds, then walked a little way out of the booking hall to see where he went. He was heading along the Embankment, in the opposite direction to Chelsea, naturally enough. The black water bucked about in the wind and rain – a frustrated sea – as Jean headed back into the booking office. She really was going to have to wean herself off that man.

———

Coates walked fast away from Embankment station. The Yob had progressed no more than a quarter of a mile from where he'd been put in: a completely abject performance. Coates had learnt about if from the tweeting of some Marine Police Unit officer: *Body recovery this PM. Sad business for all concerned.* But who *was* concerned? That's what Coates wanted to know. The Yob had not yet shown up on the missing persons list, which could mean he'd already been identified and claimed by next of kin. He was probably in a 'relationship' with one of the girls at Number Four, and Coates was beginning to think he had made a big mistake; but any alternative to the termination of the Yob had been inconceivable.

He crossed the road, away from the river. The river had let him down, and he wanted nothing to do with it.

Coates did hope he wasn't going to have a problem with Jean, but something was going on there. Why the delay in calling him? *Had* she been on one of those buses: those relentless 87s? She'd travelled along the right route at the right time. Assume she'd seen him, then. How would she react? Would she call the police? No, because that would have been to throw away an opportunity. Would she contact him immediately? No, she would delay, needing time to think. She must have worked out that he was considering moving on from her, but now the power was in *her* hands. So how would she proceed when he called her? Just as she had done: obliquely, by insinuation; couldn't afford to show her hand quite yet. She would mention the bus – an apparent irrelevance – forcing him to wonder why. Further hints would be dropped. She had mentioned that she had seen the body recovered from the river, which she presented as coincidence: she happened to have come out of the Tube station at the right time. But if she had seen him putting the Yob *into* the river, she would be on the alert for news of its re-emergence. She'd be watching the online postings of the Marine Police as intently as he was.

No. Couldn't be. These were all weak thoughts; paranoia, and possibly psychosis.

He suddenly realised he was standing next to another tube station. Temple. This wasn't where he wanted to be. He walked on.

She must have seen him looking at the Marine Police website on his iPad. How? In a reflection: that pub was a hall of mirrors. She wouldn't say what she'd seen because she wanted him to believe she could read his thoughts ... or vice versa. She would not need to say anything directly, because she had the means to present things in a metaphorical way: the farcical notion of mind reading, which her play, all of a sudden, was about. Previously, it had been about a variety of oddballs from the Edwardian halls. Now – as of last night, he suspected – she had focused on just one oddball: the woman Kate, the so-called Martian Girl, a mind reader who had discovered the secrets of some man: this Draper character.

But he must be wrong. He wanted to be wrong, but that wasn't the same thing.

He stopped and lit a cigarette, which the wind from the river tried to stop him doing. This Vincent character ... seemingly pleasant enough, probably gay but you never knew. There'd been a few yearning looks towards Jean, but Coates had also detected similar looks towards himself, which he often did with men of that kind. The guy had no self-confidence, and you couldn't blame him for that, but you could blame him for the lack of discipline that caused him to be so fat, which in turn caused the lack of self-confidence. Result? He was a ventriloquist – played with dolls. Maybe Jean was going the same way, losing confidence, looking at the fading prospect of luring her man away from his wife and daughter. Jean was putting a bit of weight on herself, he'd noticed. A certain heft had always been part of her attraction, together with an undoubtedly very attractive – if perhaps too wide – face, but it was a fine line. Another one of Camilla's friends seemed to cross that line every month: one minute he fancied them; next minute not even worth a flirtation.

Coates thought back to the time he'd first set eyes on Jean. She'd been playing records in the pub at the end of her road. She was filling in for some other DJ, which – he would learn – was typical of the way she earned money: on the edge of some artistic pursuit already marginal. (Jean was thirty-eight or so, late thirties anyway. She was no genius but had a good brain and she ought to be doing more with her life.) She'd looked the part though, and he liked the way she'd cue up the records while listening through just one of the two earpieces of the headphones, with the other dangling down – like a radio operator in a war film. He'd been with Camilla and another couple, the female half of which had crossed the line long since, although she didn't seem to know it. The man was some kind of consultant, safely in work even if his job was indefinable. Coates, newly unemployed, had resented that.

. . . So he'd been watching Jean, who was obviously looking for a man. She'd gone off twice to the ladies', and come back each time with fresh lipstick. She'd probably been sending out come-on messages with the records she played. It was all pretty slow and sultry stuff. She'd been wearing a short blue dress and mad, stripy tights with those DMs of hers. But her legs were good enough to be downplayed, so it was showing off, in a roundabout way. Her dress had been made even shorter – hoisted up – by the wide leather belt she'd been wearing. Whilst the other man at the table had been talking about how he'd assembled and maintained what he called his 'team' (his fellow parasites), Coates had set himself a challenge: he would get this DJing girl into bed, and she'd be naked all except for that belt.

He'd gone up to her and, speaking quietly, so that she had to lean towards him over the noise of the music, asked, 'Do you take requests?'

She did take requests, as it turned out. But he'd never managed that final part, now that he thought about it: the business with the belt. It had been clear from the start that Jean's tastes did not run along the same lines as his own. Hers went little beyond – to use the vernacular term he hated – the vanilla. But when he took a shower, she was likely to come in and join him, which irritated him, because there wasn't room. She would seem quite aggrieved if he took a shower alone, as if he'd snubbed her. Well, she was possessive; he didn't like this word either, but . . . *clingy*. Even so, this was obviously not the time to move on from her. He must find out what she knew, and what she intended to do with the information.

He had come to Milford Lane: back entrance to the Middle Temple. It had often been his means of approach to chambers, because he would cycle along the river from Chelsea. Coates stood beside the vintage red phone box which guarded the Lane like a sentry: the lawyers got to keep the nice phone boxes and the Victorian street lamps, to demonstrate the timelessness of their patch, and its exclusivity. Coates thought of the shop where he'd bought his first gown, in his Bar School days: Ede & Ravenscroft. What did it say above the door? *Est. 1689.* It had seemed to promise a long career.

Only a few lights still burned in the high windows of the Temple. Two lawyers were coming towards him. They wore the regulation gear: blue coats and suits, polished Oxfords on their feet. One carried a brief bag, his night's reading inside. His monogram was embroidered on the side, so he was clearly a ponce. A lot of barristers were too keen on the trappings of the job, had a stationery fetish: pink ribbons, yellow writing pads and fountain pens. Coates vaguely recognised the other one – the one without the bag – and he nodded at Coates as he went past. Coates met his gaze squarely. Why should he skulk? He was still a member of the Temple, even if not currently practising. He watched the two as they went by, reaching the end of the Lane, heading left for Blackfriars. Coates himself ought to leave the Lane. But he remained, becoming motionless, thinking back.

When he reached the top of the stairs that led to his flat, Vincent was soaked with sweat. He had known since he was about sixteen that a heart attack was inevitable. It would either come when he was climbing those stairs, or when he was dancing. The only question was whether it would be fatal, and if it was not, he would change his lifestyle. This was the deal he'd brokered with himself. He opened his front door and saw Teddy Cooper, sitting on top of the bookshelf.

That was nearly the heart attack, there and then. He'd forgotten he'd left him there. Teddy Cooper was a mid-sized boy, and there was something wrong with his eyes. The sinister thing was that Vincent didn't know quite what, and he'd been messing about with the movements while watching TV.

He put down the case, and the polystyrene box in which he'd been carrying the kebab he'd bought from the place next to the station. The box was empty, since he'd eaten the kebab under the bus shelter around the corner. He seldom took his takeaways much further than the bus shelter: he would be just too hungry. The bus shelter offered protection from the rain, a seat and a light ... but no bin, which was why he brought the boxes home. The hot living room was reeling slightly: the effect of the walk up the stairs, and of course he'd drunk too much. He ought now to down several pints of water, but there were more urgent priorities. His laptop was on the couch, and he tapped in the password to unlock it: BVMPF, all the difficult letters for a vent, followed by his date of birth ... which he got wrong first time around. He was agitated because he knew some bad thing was lying in wait, and indeed the first thing he saw was himself, looking fat, damp and practically bald. He had accidentally left the camera on, a hazard of practising routines in front of it.

One of the old lines came back to him: *Cheeky Boy to balding Vent: 'You've parted your hair differently ... Parted with it altogether.'* If he lost any more hair – and there was no 'if' about it – he'd have to modify Little Vince, because Little Vince was supposed to be his mini-me. (Not his son, as some people thought.)

Vincent switched off the camera. The email counter showed six new ones. He opened his inbox, braced and ready. Five were spam, one was from Tim Scully. Scully was a teacher from somewhere up north like Rotherham; he was also a part-time vent. He occasionally – well, in fact quite often – asked Vincent for advice, and here were two more questions ... which was fine: Vincent was happy to help, and he would get to them in a minute. The main thing was: nothing from Worsley. Vincent pressed Mark All Messages as Read and the email counter disappeared. But danger remained, since Worsley was a Facebook 'friend'. He began scrolling the notifications, and these too seemed Worsley-free. There was one new Like for the picture of the great Len Insull

(1883–1974) that he'd put up. You often saw pictures of the figures Insull made, but you seldom saw the man himself. In this one, he was putting the finishing touches to a freckled girl figure, like a doctor attending to a patient.

Nothing from Worsley! Vincent stood up and did a little buck and wing dance, until he saw the eyes of Teddy Cooper on him, which in turn reminded him of Mrs Bellamy in the flat below, and her migraines. He sat down and read Scully's email. The gist of it was that he was thinking of doing a little vent show at the school where he taught. He wanted to do a pupil–teacher dialogue with his figure, Young Henry, and did Vincent know of any jokes in that line?

Vincent went to the kitchen. He drank a glass of water and made a cup of tea. He took the tea, and a cold sausage, back to the computer with him. *Hi Tim*, he typed. *Good to hear from you. Sounds a great idea for a show. You might have heard of an act called Barrowclough & Boy* . . . Tim Scully wouldn't have heard of it but he pressed on. *Barrowclough was rigged out as a teacher – mortar board and gown, etc – and the Boy was a schoolboy. There's YouTube clips of them on radio in the Forties.* After a moment's hesitation, Vincent looked for, and supplied the links. Well, he was in a good mood, having got the all-clear on the Worsley front. *These might give you some ideas, and I don't think copyright's going to be an issue.*

Ought he to be saying that? Wasn't he suggesting that Scully would be nicking the material, and incapable of writing his own? But he *was* incapable of writing his own, unfortunately.

Vincent signed off with best wishes, and *PS: Good luck with the show!* He went back to the kitchen and drank another glass of water, and ate another cold sausage. The trouble with Tim Scully was that there were a number of things you couldn't say to him. The fact was that he had terrible lip control, which needn't be fatal as long as the vent can bring the figure alive. If people are laughing, they're not looking at your lips. But Scully couldn't bring Young Henry alive.

Vincent returned to the laptop. If he wasn't careful, he'd find himself sending an email to Jean. He could always write a draft and see how it looked. *Hi Jean*, he began. No, wait: that was 'Hygiene', so *Dear Jean*. But did he dare write that? And what would follow? *It was great to see you and Mr Coates*, possibly? But only the first part of that was true: he had been rather scared of Coates. Suddenly, he had a good idea for Tim Scully. He opened another Compose box.

Hi again Tim. Just recalled a line from God knows where – some act from way back. Vent says to boy, 'Define a kiss for me, mathematically' to which the Boy answers (funnier if it's after long thought) 'It's a lip tickle.' Get it?! All best, Vince.

He pressed Send, and then – as so often – he wanted to recall the email. The joke wouldn't work in a school. The kids wouldn't understand; it was slightly indecent, and why on earth had he written 'Get it?!' Tim Scully might be a poor vent, but he wasn't an idiot.

Vincent looked down at the screen. The email counter had gone up to 1.

This would be Scully, thanking him.

But it was from Worsley. Vincent read:

I suppose that was the woman you've been talking to about the Martian Girl. Your conversations on that subject with any third party stop NOW. Last warning. And you'd better let me know this is received and understood.

———

Under the Victorian lamp in Milford Lane, Coates was thinking of a less quaint spot: Pret à Manger on the Strand, brightly lit one rainy morning about eight months ago.

Coates would sometimes go there for breakfast, looking over pleadings, and drinking a cup of tea while eating a smoked salmon sandwich. He'd been sitting on a high stool at a high table when a good-looking woman carrying a bowl of porridge came up and sat on the seat opposite.

He noted the graceless way she parked herself on the stool, almost with a grunt, and the nice glow that came off her – a gust of something real in that ersatz place. She was quite big, in the way that was beginning to interest him, and which had eventually drawn him to Jean. The woman began to eat her porridge, and since she was blonde, she put him in mind of a chunkier Goldilocks. She would be able to handle at least two of the three bears. He watched her eat. When she'd finished, she pushed the remains away and blew upwards, so that her fringe fluttered. 'I feel much better for that,' she said. Then she smiled at him, demonstrating a very promising gap between her front teeth. She wore no wedding ring.

'I could honestly eat another,' she said. 'What do you think?'

'Only you can say whether you can eat another,' he said.

'No, but do you think I *should* do?'

'I think you should, yes.'

'Why?'

'Because it's organic.'

If she thought that amusing she didn't exactly laugh, but they were now in a conversation.

'I'm guessing you're a lawyer,' she said. 'I can always spot lawyers.'

'If we weren't right outside the Temple, and if I wasn't reading a brief, I'd say that was brilliant.'

'I'd say you were a *criminal* lawyer,' she said, with the emphasis on 'criminal'.

'You're going by the frayed shirt cuffs I suppose?'

'My boyfriend's a lawyer,' she said. 'Shall I tell you his name? He's called Owen.'

'How lovely.'

'Owen Parrish. He's just moved up to London from Bristol.'

'And brought you with him?'

'I was here already. We've only been together a few weeks.'

Coates was thinking that this relationship she was describing must have at the outside about five minutes left to run, when it occurred to him that the words 'Parrish' and 'Bristol' were persisting in his mind. But he couldn't say why.

'I'm Helen, by the way,' she said. 'I knew you were going to ask, so I thought I'd tell you.'

Coates told her his own name, while writing his mobile number on a serviette. He passed it over to her. 'I have to go in a minute. This is just in case you ever fancy another breakfast meeting.' She picked up the serviette, smirking despite herself. Then she put on a pair of thick glasses to read it, which was also great. She raised it to her lips. Was she

92

going to kiss his phone number? That was too much even for a sexually confident man like Coates to hope for. Or was she going to use the serviette *as* a serviette before contemptuously crumpling it into the table waste? In the event, her action was closer to the first than the second. She brushed the serviette against the side of her mouth, where perhaps there *had* been a genuine flake of food. Then she put it in her bag, took off her glasses and smiled with downcast eyes; Helen was at rest.

Meanwhile, Coates had been recollecting. There was a new man at the firm of Blakemore & Miller, solicitors of New Fetter Lane, and he had come from out of town, but was straight in at partner level. He might well have come from Bristol, and he might well have been called Parrish. Coates had remembered disliking the name when his clerk, Freddie Lowndes, had mentioned the new man. A big part of the chambers' family and landlord-and-tenant work came from Blakemore's, and Freddie Lowndes always kept up with developments there, which was partly why Coates didn't. The other reasons were that he couldn't be bothered, and he thought it undignified.

Helen, he now noticed, was glancing towards the door. She seemed to have become a bit distracted; there appeared to be some sort of malfunction. 'Here comes Owen,' she said.

A squat man was approaching from the doorway. He had a revolting, scuttling walk, with his arms down by his sides as if they were false arms, his real ones concealed somewhere inside his coat. But he now raised one of those arms and – while staring with hostility at Coates – let the hand on the arm fall onto Helen's shoulder, as if to say, 'This belongs to me.' Helen introduced Coates to Owen Parrish and vice versa;

it didn't go particularly well, and she and Parrish then left. He wasn't fit to be anyone's boyfriend, let alone such a nice piece as Helen; but he must be rich.

*

On Milford Lane, Coates looked towards the gate: a dog stepped through it and began to approach him, breaking off a couple of times to sniff parts of the wall. Coates waited for some affected, countrified lawyer to emerge in its wake. People would bring dogs to work, in the backs of Range Rovers crammed with green wellington boots; thought they were country squires. There was something wrong with the dog. It had only three legs. The dog stopped and tilted its head in a questioning way. It had a superior look, despite being scrawny, not particularly clean, and a leg short. Its head was half black and half white, as if it stood in permanent shadow. Coates made a clicking noise, to see whether the dog would come towards him, but it turned around and walked back into the Temple, just as though it knew what he'd done in that Lane. It was quite a hammy performance on the part of the dog, he thought, and it failed to prick his conscience. Very few things did prick his conscience. Coates did not regard himself as immoral, but as a man who would only put up with a certain amount of provocation.

———

When she got home, Jean – knowing she wouldn't sleep – took refuge from the strangeness of Coates, in a late night, slightly drunken writing session.

*

It had been settled that Draper would teach me the art of clairvoyance for ten pounds, which I need not pay in advance (which was just as well, since I did not *have* ten pounds) but would be gradually extracted from my wages in the first month of our starting work. He envisaged a series of 'fill-ins' which he seemed to know how to secure: performances for one or two nights only rather than bookings for a week, which was the usual way. These 'fill-ins' were to be local affairs (local, that is, for *him*, meaning east London) and would last a month, during which I was on trial. If my performances proved satisfactory Draper would seek longer engagements further afield. If I proved *un*satisfactory, and he was obliged to ditch me (he had some other term for this), the money would still be owing, and I would still be obliged to re-pay him. If I should seek to dissolve our partnership prior to the completion of one hundred performances, I would be obliged to refund the ten pounds.

My new employer lived at Providence Road in Rotherhithe which, like all of Rotherhithe, was near the river. Providence Road *smelt* of the river – mud, rain, dead fish – and as I approached number 2 on the first morning of my instruction, the mast and spar of a ship loomed from the misty rain at the end of it in a rather salutary way, like a giant crucifix. Perhaps the captains of sailing ships had lived on this street, because the houses were quite grand, or at least very tall (if rather thin) and some had stone medallions on the front, in which appeared a little carving of a ship; and two of the houses had flagpoles coming out at an angle from the front, but neither had a flag, and most of the houses had been sub-divided into lodgements.

It was eight o'clock in the morning and men would keep spilling out of the houses. They were clerks, judging by their black suits and umbrellas, who would have nothing more to do with the river than to take the train running through the tunnel beneath it to reach the City. (I had just alighted from that train myself.)

Draper's house appeared, from the outside, to have remained whole, but it had neither medallion nor flagpole. What it did have was a little brass sign reading 'No Hawkers'. The bell of the nearby church was actually chiming the hour of eight as I rapped the knocker, so perhaps Draper would compliment me on my punctuality. That would get us off on the right foot, I thought, and – as the door was slowly opened – the chimes of the hour were released from inside the house as well. But it was a maid or skivvy who answered my knock, and she said very little, but admitted me to a cold hallway with rather depressing linoleum on the floor, and a grandfather clock resembling an upright coffin.

The depressing linoleum continued in the front parlour, to which I was now shown by the silent maid. Mr Draper was dressed as though for the City, but of course he wasn't going there. He stood by the fire, but I don't know why he bothered, since there were only about six coals upon it, and only two of them alight. A large, circular table was covered with a black cloth, like a shroud. There were some papers on it, and – most surprisingly – a typewriter. (I believed those machines cost a small fortune, and I'd never seen one outside an office before.) This was not the kind of diggings you'd expect a turner to live in: there were no old bills on the

96

walls, no framed photograph of the householder on stage. After our preliminaries, and the rather grudging offer of a cup of tea, I mentioned this to Mr Draper. 'There are plenty of bills in fact,' he said, indicating some of the papers on the table, 'and I endeavour to pay them promptly.'

So that was the small talk out of the way, and we got down to work. After inviting me to sit at the table (he himself did not sit), he began by asking whether I had any notion of how stage mesmerism worked.

'By the use of linguistic codes,' I said, and he seemed disappointed that I had immediately hit the nail on the head. He asked if I had even the remotest notion of how these codes might work. 'No,' I said, and he nodded, preparatory to embarking on the explanation. 'But I have a pretty shrewd idea,' I cut in. 'Let's say you wish to convey to me a piece of fruit. Say for instance a pineapple. You address me as follows. "Is it a cherry I am thinking of, Miss French?" I answer, "No." "Is it a lemon I am thinking of, Miss French?" "No again," I say, after a little thought, designed to convey that a lemon might very well have been a possibility. "Was it," you ask, "*by any chance*, a pineapple?" "Yes!" I say, "a pineapple it certainly was!"'

I smiled at Mr Draper, who did not smile back. The tea came; it was cold, like the room. I did not care to think of all the equally depressing rooms stacked on the top of this one. There was a bookshelf near the fireplace – not a big one, and not many books on it. In fact, four. I tried to make out the titles. One was called *Curious Things*, which struck me as rather unexpectedly whimsical. It had a subtitle I couldn't make out. The second was called *A Tour of the American*

States. The third was *Physical Training for Men*, which might account for the tightness of Draper's suit coat; the fourth, *How to Play Golf*.

'What you have just described, Miss French,' said Draper, who was scowling at me for having inspected his books, 'would be suitable for the sort of drawing-room entertainment indulged in by silly, inebriated people after supper.'

'Thanks,' I said.

'The professional, however, uses a more sophisticated code.' He pushed towards me a pen, a bottle of ink and some blank paper. 'You will wish to take notes as I speak.'

———

Coates had walked back to Embankment Tube station, but he hadn't been able to face the flat, and Camilla, so he was in the wine bar opposite the station, which was a kind of dank basement, candlelit and full of young females, more of them than usual unaccompanied. In the absence of a man to praise them they were tending to look at themselves on the screens of their phones, using them like little compacts. In quite a number of cases, the gaze strayed from the phone towards Coates, who stood at the bar with his bottle of white, which had cost seventeen pounds. To think that he was financially dependent on his wife. He wished she would be a bit less magnanimous about it, and all his other lapses from domestic perfection. It might almost be a strategy to humiliate him. And then there was the strategy of Jean: her mind-reading conceit. It was revoltingly elliptical. Why couldn't she just say what she thought, or what she knew? A woman in her position was bound to turn hostile eventually, and you never knew what weird form the hostility would take. Perhaps he should count himself lucky that she had remained benign for as long as she had done?

No; he was not lucky, because the odds against a man being as vindictive as Parrish had proved after the Pret encounter were enormous. Coates sipped wine, remembering . . .

*

There'd been a case from Blakemore's on which – the day before Helen – he'd attended a conference. That had gone satisfactorily, but when the papers were sent through – on the day after Helen – it was the name of a junior colleague on the back sheet. When another brief was diverted away from him a week later, Freddie Lowndes offered to call Blakemore's 'to see if everything's all right'. But Coates wouldn't play the supplicant in that way, even via a third party.

Then, one misty workless morning, he had been approaching the Temple fountain on his way from chambers to Fleet Street. Parrish had been approaching from the opposite direction. Seeing that Parrish was aiming to go left of the fountain, he had intended to go right, but he realised that was cowardice, so he diverted left, forcing Parrish to sidestep him, possibly being hit by some of the spray from the fountain as he did so. After they'd crossed, Parrish had called back to him: 'Just to let you know, you'll be getting no more work from my firm.'

'On what grounds?'

'On the grounds that you do not meet the ethical standards we require.'

'In other words, Helen fancied me. By the way, I suppose she's left you?' Coates was trying to get him to say, 'How dare you?' because he seemed the type, but Parrish continued with the false mildness: 'Well, now you're living up to your reputation for arrogance.'

'Arrogance is not in itself unethical.'

'No, but sexual harassment is!' So there was his little rhetorical coup, and there was something laughable about the way the fountain splashed blithely on. 'You are damn lucky,' Parrish began shouting over the noise of it, '*damn* lucky not to have been reported to Bar Standards!' No colleague's wife was safe from Coates, it appeared, and as Parrish continued with what was turning out to be quite a lengthy bill of indictment, Coates was looking at him. The look, surely, could only be interpreted as meaning 'Stop now or I'll kill you', and Parrish did stop eventually. But by then it was too late.

Towards the end of that day, the Lane had been full of grey fog. Coates waited by the phone box, watching the gateway by which people came out of the Temple. He was smoking, and praying for Parrish to come along. The Head was present – one of the first times he had 'come in' – and he was talking rapidly, giving a sort of briefing inside Coates' skull: 'This Parrish bastard lives south of the river, and when he leaves his office on New Fetter Lane, he cuts through the Temple to catch a cab on the Embankment. He does it every night, boy, but the time varies.' An hour or so went past, with Coates so intent on the gate that he hardly noticed the time; but looking back, he worked out that it had been about eleven fifteen when Parrish had appeared. He was stopping under the first lamp in order to belch, and to check his messages. 'Pissed,' the Head had pointed out. Parrish's stupidity in turning up proved he deserved what he had coming; but it wasn't coming yet, even though the Head was shouting, 'Take him out, boy! Take him out!'

Coates retreated onto the Embankment before Parrish saw him. If Coates had done him that night, he would have been in the frame, and nicked soon after, because their row at the fountain would have been observed from the windows of the chambers roundabout. But Coates had established that Parrish was a Milford Lane man.

He had decided to wait a month.

He was pretty monstrous in that time, he had to admit; on a high. Runs along the King's Road at 5 a.m., evening sessions in the Coal Hole – a long, narrow pub on the Strand where everybody drank too much in a kind of raucous bus queue at the bar. He'd picked up a certain Barbara there, an elegant woman of perhaps fifty who'd been a ballet dancer. The point was that Barbara's choice of shoes – black high heels with leather ankle straps – had not been arbitrary, as he discovered when they'd gone back to her flat near Borough Market. Mrs Coates had also received a lot of attention in bed, which she had taken in her enigmatic stride.

The Head of Chambers came and went, but when a foggy and moonless evening arrived in the third week, he insisted.

In the Lane, the redness had apparently been seeping from the phone box and making a halo around the Victorian lamps. He watched from the Embankment, smoking. He'd made sure to wear gloves. 'Here's the mark,' said the Head, as Parrish came scuttling through the gate at about eleven – he'd been on his phone. Coates advanced, making it quick. He took hold of Parrish's head and drove it into the wall. There had been a kind of sad, soggy breakage, and when Parrish went down, his eyes rolled upwards in the correct manner for a dying person. The Head was saying, 'Now give the fucker a kick, boy.' But Coates had said, 'No, I think I'm done,' and after taking the wallet and phone to make it look like a mugging, he'd just walked away.

The next morning, Coates had cycled in, anticipating a Witness Appeal notice at the top of Milford Lane, because it was the City police, and they were hot on witness appeals. Yes, the yellow sign was there – he saw it as soon as he got off his bike – but it was headlined with the wrong word: not MURDER but SERIOUS ASSAULT. So that was the start of a horrible morning for Coates. He'd had to take the Tube to Snaresbrook for a mitigation at the Crown Court, and as he closed in on that Gothic courthouse, which resembled a miniature Tower of London, with its own ravens (some of which were looking contemptuously down at Coates from the roof turrets), he could think only of prison.

Freddie Lowndes had intercepted Coates on his return to chambers. Lowndes probably knew Coates had done it, but he was on Coates's side. They were old allies, and Coates had given Lowndes's boy, Mike, five grand when he was trying to go professional as a racing cyclist. They had taken a walk together around the frosty gardens: a crisis meeting masquerading as a little constitutional. A beautiful sunset was developing over the City skyscrapers, making a cinematic catastrophe: the fire of London. (Coates had decided he would pay for a girl that evening. As a condemned man, he had every right to do so.)

According to Freddie Lowndes, Parrish had been unconscious the whole night, so there were going to be consequences from this injury.

'Yes?' Coates had said, eager for the worst.

Parrish had sustained post-traumatic amnesia. Over the next few days, Freddie came back with further bulletins: the condition had settled down as retrograde amnesia, not post-retrograde. In other words the right sort: Parrish could not remember anything of the run-up to the accident. But, being a cunt, he was working with a memory specialist. Time seemed to move very slowly for Coates over the next few days, and the Temple fountain iced over, even though it was supposed to be spring. What would the memory man unearth? Coates had little or no work in that time.

A week after the event, Lowndes had come up to Coates and told him that Ivor Jenkins QC, real-life head of chambers, had wanted to see him. Coates had looked towards the closed door of Jenkins' office. But Freddie Lowndes said, 'He's in El Vino's. He wants to see you there right now.' That couldn't be right. El Vino's was a wine bar, and Jenkins didn't drink.

'I don't think it's that sort of meeting,' Freddie had said.

Jenkins had been sitting at a table with a glass of water in front of him; a solicitor called Ian Hadley was on the opposite side. Coates knew Hadley was a partner at Blakemore's, therefore a colleague, if not a friend, of Parrish. Hadley nursed a small glass of red, but there was no welcoming bottle on the table, and no smile from either of the two as he approached. It was all over in five minutes.

'Sit down,' said Jenkins. 'Ian has something to tell you.'

'We know you attacked Owen Parrish,' said Hadley. 'We think we can build a case but we're minded not to try, on one condition.'

He nodded to Jenkins, who said, 'I want you out of chambers, and out of the Temple.'

'Shouldn't there be a chambers meeting about this?'

'We've had a meeting. We can have another one, and you can come if you want. But I don't think you'd enjoy it very much. I have the full backing of my colleagues. There's been concern about your behaviour for some time.'

'Don't I get an official warning?' Coates had asked, which caused the Head of Chambers in Coates' skull to pipe up with: 'Stop whining, you cunt.'

'You nearly killed the man, for Christ's sake.' This was Hadley speaking; you'd almost think Parrish had been his friend.

'Are the Bar Standards Board involved?'

'They can be.'

'You appear determined to make this a full-blown scandal,' said Jenkins. 'We're doing you a favour; you don't seem to appreciate that.'

In other words, they would push for a prosecution (and disbarment) if he resisted. He must hand in his chambers key fob; he would be blocked from the IT, and at that news, the other Head of Chambers came on again: 'Why not take these two queers out right here and now? Steak knife on the table to the left, boy one! Or are *you* queer as well?'

'No,' Coates had been aware of saying out loud. Jenkins and Hadley hadn't quite known why he'd said 'No', so they were checked for a moment. But then Jenkins resumed. He and Hadley had employed a private detective and he'd come up with some things that might or might not amount to admissible evidence. The matter of Coates's work from Blakemore's drying up – that supposedly went to motivation;

and then Coates might be on Embankment CCTV. There was probably enough to bring a charge, if not to convict, and the charge alone would end Coates's career. In the old days, Jenkins would have given him a pistol and shown him into a quiet room . . .

*

And in this other wine bar, Coates found himself thinking of the old days, as represented by a framed, mildewed music hall poster on the wall opposite. He was looking at a list of blocky names in red, some relatively tall and thin, some relatively short and fat, and Coates wondered if the shape of the letters had reflected the shape of the people. Sometimes the names were preceded by smaller words, which were hard to read from this distance in the candlelit gloom, but LEO PICARDO was probably 'The Great'. HARRY LIMBRICK was followed by a procession of three words in smaller type, possibly BY ROYAL APPOINTMENT, or some such nonsense. A person called DUFAY was perhaps preceded by their own first name – and now Coates's phone was ringing. It had possibly been ringing for some time. It was Camilla.

'Hello,' he said.

'It's eleven thirty.'

'Yes,' he said, 'it is.'

'I was expecting you back by now.' This was unusual. More like a Jean line.

'Yes, sorry. I got a bit . . . distracted.'

'You sound drunk.'

'Well, I haven't had anything to eat, really.'

'That would not in itself make you drunk.'

'I ... *We*'ve got through a couple of bottles of this ... I don't know what it's called. It's ideal partnered with any roasted white meats and fresh salads.'

'How do you know, if you haven't eaten anything?'

'I'm reading the label,' said Coates, and this at least happened to be true.

'Who's "we", anyway?'

This was too Jean-like: wheedling. Looking at the music hall poster, he nearly said *Leo Picardo*. 'It's that publisher I told you about. Leo Sutton.' He had never told her about any publisher, as she probably knew.

'I don't think I've met him,' Camilla said. That was more like it: old style, telling him she knew he was lying.

'You haven't missed much,' said Coates, putting his feet up on the empty chair opposite. 'He's currently doing a wee – in the gents', I hasten to add. He wants a book for undergraduates: *So You're Thinking of Being a Barrister?* Something like that.'

'But you've decided to stop being a barrister.'

'Yeah. He wants both sides of the argument. How's Lucy?'

'She's asleep.'

'What sort of day did she have?'

'If you'd been here, you'd know, wouldn't you?'

He treated her to a longer silence this time, but when he realised he was creating an opportunity for her to say, 'I'm leaving you,' he panicked. If only the Yob hadn't turned up in the river. 'I'm beginning to think I might go back into practice,' he heard himself saying. 'What do you think? Well, I know what you think.' *Was* there a way back? Parrish had

106

not even died, after all. He was still in practice, for God's sake, albeit in more easy-going Bristol. He was epileptic now, according to Freddie Lowndes; and he had a stutter, which put advocacy beyond him. Coates said, 'Lucy had a maths test today, didn't she?'

'She came top. Your coaching paid off.'

'I just told her not to be scared of it. Where did Verity come?'

Verity was Lucy's best friend and greatest enemy.

'It's enough that Lucy came top, wouldn't you say?'

'But I bet you asked as well.'

'Verity came well down the rankings.'

'That's excellent,' said Coates, and he laughed, and poured himself another glass. Camilla might well have been laughing too: she often appreciated his malice. 'I'll be home in an hour,' he said. 'Don't wait up. We'll go out to dinner tomorrow.'

'Yes. Maybe.'

He would finish the bottle and have another glass for the road. He was looking again at the poster. Two words at the bottom. He moved towards the poster, moved towards the words. THE MARTIAN GIRL. So this poster – or this person on it – was part of the conspiracy. But you couldn't kill someone who was already dead; and Coates would never do a woman. Turning back towards the table, he saw he'd knocked his chair over when standing up.

———

Jean looked down at her manuscript, which she had printed out again. In the absence of any paying work, she had made good progress. Regarding Mr Coates, the possible Wednesday had come and gone with no message. On Monday, when she had seen him walking away from Embankment station, she had thought *good, let him go,* and she had maintained the thought in the four days since. That he had been walking *in the wrong direction* – in relation both to Jean and his poor wife – had seemed to underline his unknowability in a preposterous way. Perhaps he was developing a transport phobia, which might explain his close questioning about the 87 bus. He ought to know there was a fine line between being mysterious and being exhausting to think about. She might make the same point to Vincent while she was about it. She'd emailed him on Tuesday morning, thanking him for footage of Kate French. She'd heard nothing back, in spite of the email having contained some polite questions.

There'd been nothing for it but to escape into her manuscript, which was rapidly becoming a novel. She was going to have to go in person to Tobin's Supper Rooms and explain that she was pulling out of her contract. She'd also have to apologise to Rasta Donald for wasting his time on questions of staging.

There were just too many words for it to be a play, and this was a new sort of writing for her: it carried her away, and she didn't need to play music to draw it out. Her Technics 1210 turntable – her most valuable possession – was accumulating dust, and her vinyl stacks had not been disrupted for a week. She was leaving music behind, or vice versa. She hadn't DJed since that fateful night of her meeting with Coates, partly because Coates himself winced whenever she tried for a seductive musical mood. It was very difficult to believe that she had ever peddled 'easy vibes and old school R 'n' B', or that the excruciatingly punning 'Four beats to the bar with Jean Beckett' had ever appeared on pub flyers and Facebook. As an auditory phenomenon, four beats to the bar were guaranteed to banish any thoughts of late Victorian England. The only record in her collection that conjured the right imagery was from her small classical sub-section: *Chopin Nocturnes* brought Victorian scenes to mind with their slow, smoky sparkle.

Jean made a cup of green tea and brought it back to her table, where she began rolling herself an American Spirit. She was wondering why she bothered to drink green tea, with all its healthy antioxidants, if she was only going to accompany it every time with a cigarette. At least drinking wine while smoking showed some consistency, since both gave you cancer. But it wasn't yet time for wine. It was 4 p.m. In terms of light, the day had barely seemed to begin, as if Mother Nature had said to herself, let's get this one over with quickly.

Then again, something was happening with the Monster for once. In the past two days, an unusually high number of lorries had come and gone; the cranes were in a different position, and there was a temporary indentation in its side, which gave Jean a glimpse of the Thames: rolling, shiny black like an oil slick. If he really was 'Father Thames', he was the kind of father who beat his children.

She lit her cigarette, began to read.

'The basic letter code,' said Draper, 'is as follows. 'A is H, B is T, C is S, D is G, E is F, F is E, G is A, H is I, I is B,

J is L. Now there is a special arrangement for K, it being hard to begin a sentence with that letter. If the object to be conveyed began with K, I would begin a sentence with the word, "Pray", as in "Pray tell this article?"'

There were also special arrangements for U, X and Z, and I made rapid notes accordingly. But still, I would glance about the room. It seemed that Draper also taught by correspondence because on the table beside the bills was a document headed: *Are you interested in mind reading? Would you like to break the bonds of material existence? Then please send a postal order for three and six to P.O. Box 215, Rotherhithe, London E.* Draper saw me reading this, and he did not like it, but he kept silence.

We spent the first two hours on the letter code. Afterwards, more cold tea was brought in, and we had a short break. 'I was thinking about the bill matter,' I said. 'What are we to call ourselves?'

Draper said, 'We won't be calling ourselves anything unless you learn those codes, Miss French. However, I have been revolving the idea of Draper & French – the Two Mentalists.'

'Mmm ... good. But also remarkably dull, don't you think? How about Completely Mental!'

'Another possibility,' said Draper, ignoring my suggestion, 'would be Draper & French – Two Minds but a Single Thought.'

'That makes us sound rather stupid, wouldn't you say? How about Draper & French – It Comes in Flashes.'

'What does, for heaven's sake?'

'THE ASTRAL LIGHT! Or might I be The Martian

Girl? I read a story about the Martians, and they could read each other's thoughts, or anyone's. They had blue skin as well.'

'We come,' said Draper, laying down his teacup, 'to the basic number code.'

In this, numbers were denoted by words.

Number 1 was 'Say' or 'Speak'.

2 was Be, Look or Let.

3 was Can or Can't.

4 was Do or Don't.

5 was Will or Won't.

6 was What.

7 was Please or Pray.

8 was Are or Ain't.

9 was Now.

10 was Tell.

0 was Hurry or Come.

'Well' meant repeat the last figure.

'You must pay attention,' Draper had said, while pacing before the perpetually dying fire, 'only to the first word of a sentence. Say the number 1234 is required. You would hear the following from me: "Say the number. Look at it. Can you see it? Do you know?"'

'And would you say it as quickly as that?'

'I was about to add, Miss French, that I would not say it as *slowly* as that. By the way, I will frequently allude to your "seeing" but you will be blindfolded. I will be speaking metaphorically.'

That was all I needed: metaphors on top of number and letter codes.

'Incidentally,' he said, 'do you know the principal objects that give rise to the number codes?' He stopped pacing and eyed me. From somewhere beyond the end of the street, a ship blew its horn rather foggily.

'Bank notes, possibly?' I said.

'Wrong,' Draper replied, in his amiable way, adding for good measure, 'I wonder that you were ever on the Halls at all. The numbers occur most commonly in connection with railway tickets. Well over half the auditors in any hall will have a railway, tram or bus ticket about their person. All these tickets carry serial numbers.'

'Yes,' I said slowly, 'I suppose they do.'

'Fortunately for you,' he said, 'there are only, including zero, ten numbers.'

But we were very far from being done with them yet. In conveying a number to me, Draper might also be conveying the colour of an article, for these corresponded to the numbers, as follows:

1 was White.

2 was Black.

3 was Blue.

4 was Brown.

5 was Red.

6 was Green.

7 was Yellow.

8 was Grey.

'Suppose,' he said, now standing fixedly before the fire, and so absorbing into the back of his trousers such little heat as it gave out, 'the article presented is green in colour. The question will be "What is the colour?", the word

"What" being six and green being sixth on the colour list. Is everything quite clear up to now?'

'Quite clear,' I said, heartily wishing I had stuck with comedy dancing.

Draper said, 'We now come to something much more difficult.'

'Oh,' I said, 'good.'

But it seemed we would be coming to it on the next day, since Draper had a luncheon appointment. As I rose to my feet, I stepped a little way towards the bookshelf, where I made out the subtitle to *Curious Things*. It was *Some Psychical Phenomena*. So the subtitle was even more unexpected than the title. Draper ushered me into the hallway, where he called out 'Mary!', which must be the name of the maid. We waited in the cold hall while the clock struck twelve, an incredibly laborious process that must have left the poor thing exhausted. The maid had not appeared, so Draper discovered my coat and gloves for himself.

'I will see you tomorrow at eight o'clock sharp, Miss French,' he said.

I must admit that I lingered outside the front door when he had closed it on me, in expectation of Draper's shout of rage at the poor maid. For she must appear, and it must come. It did so as I was walking away.

———

The offices of the magazine were east of London Bridge, in one of those new glass buildings jostling for a view of the river. Not that the river put on much of a show. It was just a sullen mass of black water on a forced march to the sea. The features meetings were conducted in the boardroom on the top floor, so that Camilla and her colleagues were up in the cold, dark blue sky. In these offices, Camilla felt as though she were exiled from somewhere: from Fleet Street, perhaps, where her father had been managing editor of two national newspapers in succession, and where the buildings were of stone, therefore permanent and rooted to the spot, unlike these conditional glass boxes.

The meetings happened every Friday afternoon. They were formulaic because the magazine – like all magazines – was formulaic. At the long glass table, Camilla presided over a dozen writers and editors. Her key lieutenant was Jane Harvey, her deputy, who secured a beautiful actress or pop singer every week, like a joint of meat, for the lead story and the cover. It was increasingly the case that Camilla had never heard of these people. Then there was Gigi Forbes, the fashion editor. Gigi had taken to bringing a lapdog to work, and it was wheezing away on her knee right now. You had to be a genius to bring a dog into work, and Gigi Forbes was nothing more than a reasonable stylist with an unobjectionable prose style. But Camilla quite liked Gigi – and therefore tolerated the dog – because Gigi was always very complimentary about Camilla's appearance. She seemed to approve of the pencil skirts and Miu Miu stilettoes Camilla favoured on dressy occasions – and which had been bought for her by Coates. (They reflected his pervy taste, which Camilla shared sartorially, if not erotically.)

Those shoes, costing six hundred pounds, had been purchased in the days when Coates had a job and therefore money: a perfect time, in retrospect, when Camilla had just got the editorship, and Coates was safely quartered at the

Temple on the opposite bank of the river. There was a balance about it: he worked with the men, she with the women, and they would converge in the evenings on Blackfriars Bridge, each thrilled at the handsomeness of the other.

The writers were contracted freelancers. They had their own regular columns, and also pitched longer features, in which they provided more of the same. There was Diana Vickers, agony aunt; Simon Kendall, of the motoring column, who Camilla had gone to bed with, even though he couldn't write. There was Dr Peter Lewin, who wrote a psychology column, with the 'Dr' incorporated into not only his by-line but also his email address. There was Patrick Williams, an Old Etonian foodie, who irritated Camilla with his inverted snobbery. (A very characteristic line of his would be, 'Don't diss the humble fishfinger.') There was Polly Mitchell, who was about twenty-two and wrote about clubs in a way that made Camilla feel exceptionally old, which was fine: that's what a young journalist was supposed to do, and a forty-three-year-old editor must take it on the chin. For a while, Polly's favourite adjective for describing a club was 'banging', but this had recently given away to 'pumping'. When you watched Polly typing a text with her thumbs – which she did incessantly, including right now – it was like watching a film of a person typing a text that had then been speeded up. Once, Camilla had spent the whole night awake, having sent Polly a very silly email. It had been bothering Camilla for a while that the word 'night' had fallen off the front of 'nightclub', and she had asked Polly, *These clubs you write about – they are NIGHTclubs, aren't they?* The question – she realised, as soon as she'd pressed Send – opened up numerous possibilities for devastatingly sarcastic replies, e.g. *Well, they're not GOLF clubs!* In the event, of course, Polly had not replied at all. No doubt she would have a novel out soon, and it would be turned into a film, or she'd just go right ahead and write the film; but Polly Mitchell had fat legs, and her face wasn't quite as pretty as it should have been.

Next to Polly was Lee Christian, who was not actually a regular, but provided occasional pieces – which always had to be rewritten by Mark, the chief sub – about London crime. He'd been the crime correspondent on a paper, in the days when papers had crime correspondents, and he was forever ghosting the autobiographies of people who'd taken part in the Great Train Robbery. His role was to terrify the readers: tell them how easy it was for their children to buy drugs or get stabbed (if they were boys) or raped or molested (if girls). He was dark and quite distinguished; looked a bit like Count Dracula, and he kept sending in new by-line photographs. Lee Christian was personally acquainted with a lot of criminals and you'd think he would have been killed by now, because he was an idiot. Objectively, he ought never to be commissioned as a writer: a TV presenter, maybe, but not a writer. Therefore, it had been occurring to Camilla recently that Lee was in her debt . . .

He was talking now about people trafficking. The word 'gang-master' kept coming up, and it seemed Lee Christian was personally acquainted with one of those charmers. The gang-master was Chinese and he lived in Wapping – in an opium den, no doubt. 'Sounds absolutely fascinating, Lee,' Camilla said, when he had begun to repeat himself. 'Lifting the lid on the white slavers. Fifteen hundred words?'

'I think it's a bigger story than that, love,' said sexist Lee. 'It could easily stretch to three ... three and a half thousand.'

'Let's say two thousand five hundred,' she said, but Lee Christian would write three and a half anyway, and Mark looked up from doodling to flash her an accusatory look. Big cutting and rewriting job in store for the poor boy. But it was just too bad: she wanted to keep Lee Christian on side.

Sally Wilkinson was speaking now. Sally was small, quiet, and plain-but-with-potential – a dark horse. Insofar as ordinary people featured in the magazine, this was because Sally had tracked them down. Ordinary people could be in the magazine if they'd had a sufficiently appalling experience – serious spinal injury, sole survivor of a house fire – or if they just *were* appalling. Young women who were prostitutes, say. Those pieces followed a very strict formula. They always began: *On the face of it, Deborah Watkins is every inch the tech-savvy, sussed out career girl, and her income topped seventy thousand last year. But far from being a solicitor or an executive in IT, Deborah works as a high-class call girl.* End of para; pause for the readers to absorb the shock. New para: *Deborah agreed to meet me in the bar of an upmarket West End hotel* ... Deborah, or whoever, was always a *high-class* call girl, with a *first-class* degree in English Literature, and the pieces always ended, *Deborah Watkins is a pseudonym.* Sally Wilkinson herself made up the pseudonyms, and quite possibly made up the people to whom they belonged.

Camilla suspected Sally of having a genuine, lurid imagination. She would read crime novels on her own in the canteen at lunch, and someday she might write her own crime novel, but she would never be as good at self-publicity as Polly

Mitchell. She was shy, or possibly inhibited by the darkness of her fantasy life. For example, she obviously fancied the chief sub, Mark, but never seemed to do anything about it. Right now, as Mark doodled, Sally was staring at him as intently as if she were drawing him, which she probably was – in her mind. Would Mark reciprocate an overture? Probably not at first. Mark was considered 'glam' by the ladies of the office, whereas Sally was mousy. But Sally ought to persist. She was more talented than Mark, and if she were ever to let loose her imagination in bed . . .

It had occurred to Camilla that she herself was eligible for the Sally Wilkinson treatment. She had her own true-life tale of woe that could appear under the headline: I MARRIED A . . . ' Married a *what*, exactly? Camilla had thought of commissioning from Dr Lewin a piece along the lines: 'How to tell if your husband is psychotic'. Of course, that was the main issue on any women's internet forum, but the Doctor might be a bit more authoritative. It was his turn to pitch now, and he was waffling on about mindfulness. Camilla let him waffle, because she might be needing him as well as her crisis deepened, as it undoubtedly would.

She said 'Yes' to whatever Dr Lewin had just proposed (Camilla had been thinking about Coates throughout) and the meeting would now close with a little morale-booster from Stephanie from advertising. The advertising, Camilla knew, was holding up very well, as were the ABC figures, so she would presumably be permitted to keep churning out this baleful 'human interest' for the foreseeable future, which meant she would be able to fund her longer-term plan, which was a little more drastic then her short-term one.

They all listened to Stephanie, then the meeting was breaking up. Lee Christian – heralded by his strong cologne or after-shave – was approaching her. He would embrace her at the start and end of every features meeting, and this time her response was a little warmer than usual. 'Lee,' she said, 'can I ask you a favour? It's sort of private.'

'You've got it, kid,' he said. They waited until everyone else had drifted away, Lee using the time to good effect by studying his reflection in the window glass, and smoothing down the side of his hair as he prepared to be important. Camilla turned to him, and said, 'This is strictly off the record, you understand . . . ?'

———

When the maid admitted me to my second day of tuition, I made a point of saying, 'Good morning, and how are you?'

'I am well,' she said, miserably.

In the parlour, Draper passed to me a series of typewritten lists. They were called 'sets', and there was no end of them – at least thirty. It would be as tedious for me to rehearse them here as it was for me to memorise them in the first place but, in short, each set was a list of ten objects likely to be presented to Draper by any auditor. The attempt had been made, not always successfully in my opinion, to group like with like. The 'first set', so called, comprised what I thought of as 'women's stuff', and was indicated by the question 'What article is this?' There were ten items in the set, and the words denoting the numbers (as previously outlined by Draper) would also come into play here, for each item in the set was numbered. Here was the 'first set':

1. Handkerchief
2. Neckerchief
3. Bag
4. Glove
5. Purse
6. Basket
7. Muff
8. Comforter
9. Head dress
10. Fan

'Now,' said Draper, 'I ask, "What article is this?" The first set is thereby denoted. I then ask, "Can you tell?" To what item am I referring?'

I looked at the first set, then groped through my notes for the number list, where I verified that 'Can' denoted number three. I looked back at the first set. 'A bag,' I said.

'Correct,' said Draper, who had been looking at his watch. 'That took you twenty seconds. It ought to be instantaneous. Say it was not a bag, but a handkerchief, in which case I might have asked, "What article is this?" followed by, "Tell me now". Do you follow?'

'I do.'

'I then ask, "Say the colour."'

A silence fell. Draper was eyeing me. 'It would be quite wrong of me to peek beneath the blindfold, I suppose?'

'There will be no question of that, Miss French.'

'I thought not. What kind of blindfold is used?'

'Your predecessor—'

'Mr Brooks?'

'Your predecessor favoured a rather silly spotted

handkerchief. In your case, I am thinking of black velvet, with perhaps a supplementary blindfold underneath.'

'And what form might this second blindfold take?' I asked.

Draper eyed me once again. 'Two pennies, perhaps, for your eyes.'

'You mean,' I said, scarcely able to credit what I had heard, 'two pennies, such as are placed on the eyes of a *corpse*?'

'Not pennies then, but some form of disk or medallion. The velvet would then go on top.'

'Unlike the majority of *corpses*, Mr Draper, I will be sitting upright, so any discs will naturally fall off.'

'We might find a way of securing them. It will be worth the effort to remove any suggestion of subterfuge.'

Another silence, this time engineered by me. 'I suppose,' I said eventually, 'your ideal associate would be a little blind girl?'

'Nobody would believe she was blind,' said Draper. 'Now, back to the first set, and the fan . . . *Say the colour.*'

I turned again to the materials before me. 'Say' denoted number one, and number one on the colour list was white.

'White,' I said.

'Correct,' said Draper. 'Now let us assume there to be initials.'

'Initials on the fan? That would be pretty irregular. You'd have to be an egomaniac to have your initials on a fan.'

'You would know all about that, Miss French.'

I eyed Draper narrowly. He was perhaps to be congratulated on having made his first ever joke. I then glanced over to the bookshelf, which looked different. It now accommodated only two volumes: *Physical Training for Men* and *How to Play Golf*. *Curious Things* and *A Tour of the American States* had gone. I must stop noticing things about Draper. There was nothing to be gained by it, and possibly a good deal to be lost.

'I give the following instruction,' he said with particular asperity (for he had noticed the direction of my glance). '"Tell the initials. Say."'

Back to the original code: the *letter* code, in which T corresponded to B, and S to C.

'B.C.,' I said.

Draper nodded; didn't seem *entirely* displeased.

For two weeks, I went to Providence Road every day – Sundays excepted – to be instructed in the codes. Whilst travelling on that branch of the Metropolitan Railway that goes under the river between Wapping and Rotherhithe, I would sit muttering to myself in a manner that must have seemed imbecilic to my fellow passengers, 'A is H, B is T, C is S, D is G . . .'

At the beginning of the third week, Draper said, 'We have an offer of a booking.'

'A booking? Are we ready?'

'The question is whether *you* are ready.'

'Where and when?'

'Friday, at the Rotherhithe Hippodrome.'

I was surprised at the booking – the shocking soon-ness of it – but not at the venue. The Hippodrome was Draper's 'local', only a few streets away from his house. He had interviewed me there; he'd played the hall often, I believed, with Brooks, and he was evidently on familiar terms with the management.

'They've had a cancellation,' he said, 'so it's a fill-in.'

'Early and late shows?'

Draper shook his head. 'On Fridays, the Hippodrome has only one performance, but it's a big one. About twenty turns. It's called the Friday Fun,' he added, and those two words did not belong in his mouth. 'We might put something on the bill matter to reduce expectations. Something like: "Special preview of a new turn." Of course, we must accept a modest fee, since we are introducing the act.'

'I'm not sure I'm ready.'

Draper folded his arms, making no reply. Did *he* think I was ready? He had never given me a single word of praise, but the booking might be in *place* of praise.

'Very well,' I said. 'I'll do it.' He nodded, and we turned again to the codes. But after a minute or so, I said, 'What is the fee?'

'Seven,' he said.

'Seven *pounds*!' I exclaimed.

'I trust that four-three will be an acceptable sub-division?'

'Oh,' I said, momentarily disappointed that I would not be getting seven pounds all to myself, which was extremely greedy of me, seven pounds being an absolute fortune. 'Yes. Three pounds will go down very well indeed. Just the ticket. Fairly made my day, that has.' *Do shut up, Kate*, I told myself, and finally I did.

'It will be payable on completion of a satisfactory performance, naturally.'

I nodded eagerly, thinking of how it would have taken me a month to accumulate three pounds when assisting in the classroom. I would be able to buy a week's groceries at

Rhodes's shop on Railway Street, where the vegetables were fresher than at the Co-operative, and the milk was nearly all cream. That would do The Dad a world of good, provided I could make him eat the vegetables and drink the milk. And I would be able to buy the steam machine.

I had gone off into a moneyed dream world, and when I floated back down to Providence Road, Draper had his watch in his hand. 'The letter codes,' he said. 'I am going to time you.'

———

Camilla was on the Piccadilly Line heading north. In the world above, dirty grey snow had begun a slow descent. She was wearing her John Rocha black wool cloche hat and too much mascara; also a grey wool-mix duster coat borrowed from the fashion department, 'slim and slouchy' according to Gigi Forbes. It was not necessary to fasten the belt; in fact, Gigi had expressly forbidden Camilla to do so. Some subconscious impulse had made her dress like one of those femmes fatales in a noir film; the sort that tangles with private detectives. The one she was going to see was called Anderson.

'I've known dozens of these guys,' Lee Christian had said, when they were alone in the boardroom after the features meeting, 'and a lot of them are dodgy. But Anderson's completely straight. One caveat though.'

Lee had then stopped speaking and started smoothing his hair, obliging Camilla to ask, 'What's the caveat?'

But she must be in thrall to him for a little longer. 'I'm not going to ask why you want a private dick,' he'd said, 'that's none of my business ... '

'What's the caveat, Lee?' Camilla had asked again.

'If it's tech stuff – hacking texts or emails – Anderson's probably not your man, and I'd put you onto a very sussed-out guy called—'

'I want somebody followed,' Camilla had said.

'Surveillance,' Lee said, nodding. 'That's Anderson's speciality.'

His other specialities, according to his website, which Lee Christian had produced on his phone, were in 'tracing and status reports', 'process serving' and 'litigation'. Anderson, who had an office near King's Cross, 'always worked within the law' (but then he wouldn't say otherwise on his website). He came recommended by the Chartered Institute of Private Investigators, or whatever the industry body was called, and was equipped with various certificates and a BA. Camilla had remarked on this to Lee Christian, who said, 'That's not the really interesting thing about him.'

'No?'

'Here's the kicker,' Christian had said, risking a kicking himself, 'he's a shepherd.'

'A shepherd!' Camilla had said in disgust.

Anderson – according to Lee Christian – had a share in a sheep farm 'up north'.

'Where up north?'

'Not exactly sure,' said Christian. 'In the countryside, obviously.'

Clearly, they had reached the limit of Lee Christian's knowledge.

Camilla was now crossing the black stone forecourt of King's Cross station, where various smokers were being gently snowed upon. The station clock said 10.15 p.m. She could see the McDonald's – at the end of a scruffy terrace, on the corner of York Way and Pentonville Road. Whether by accident or design, Anderson had suggested meeting in the one ungentrified spot in King's Cross. (Didn't the man know that the whole station was now almost entirely given over to restaurants and bars, with trains a mere afterthought?)

She entered the McDonald's.

'Mrs Coates?' somebody to her left immediately said. She had been picturing a primitive-looking man in a cross-stitched smock resembling a pregnancy dress – possibly carrying a crook. The actual person was perfectly plausible as a shepherd of the modern era. He was thin, pale faced, with a five o'clock shadow. He had dark, sparse curly hair, with remarkably pretty dark blue eyes. In fact, he was remarkably pretty in general.

'Hope you don't mind a McDonald's, Mrs Coates,' he said. 'I'm driving north later on, and I'm parked up just along the road. Also they're dog friendly.' A black and white dog was sitting meekly by him. It seemed a stoical sort of dog, unfazed either by the wafting, meaty smells of a burger bar or the shrill beeping of some kitchen alarm that had now started up. 'Fancy a coffee, Mrs Coates?' Anderson asked, quite loudly, over this beeping.

'Black, please,' she said, sounding unprecedentedly southern. She cleared a lot of McDonald's litter off a table and sat down. Clearly, Anderson was very northern indeed. Camilla tried not to be a regional snob. It wasn't a matter of where you came from but where you ended up, and any bright northerner would surely end up living in London. Anderson apparently lived in London only half the time, so the jury was

126

out on him, as far as Camilla was concerned. There was also the question of whether anything good might come from a recommendation by Lee Christian.

'I assume you think your husband has a girlfriend, Mrs Coates?' said Anderson when he returned with the coffees. As Anderson spoke, the dog tucked itself very neatly under his chair, and lay down.

'A *mistress*,' said Camilla, wondering whether he was an idiot after all. 'They're usually called mistresses in London. And yes, I do.'

Anderson poured a pouch of sugar into his white frothy coffee while saying nothing. But this wasn't a Coates-like silence. It wasn't the withholding of conversation. Here, simply enough, was a man who didn't say much. There was no point in countering his silence with a silence of one's own, and so for as long as the McDonald's coffee lasted (and it was enormous), Camilla talked – rambled really, in a most uncharacteristic manner, and with a slight resurgence of approval for Anderson, since he didn't interrupt, and twice cut off incoming phone calls. (He was obviously in demand *as a detective*, because a shepherd was presumably *never* in demand, however competent.)

What Camilla told him was at slight variance with her own private thoughts about Coates. On her way to see Anderson she had been formulating a list of her husband's attributes:

1. Good-looking and vain.

2. (the unfortunate consequence of 1) Lecherous and unfaithful.

3. Kind to his daughter (but too intense).

4. Charming and amusing, when not silent.

5. Prone to rage.

6. Civil towards his wife (but see 2).

She began showing Anderson some photographs of Coates on her phone. She made a point of not showing the many pictures of him with Lucy. Her speech, and her thoughts, ran on ...

Coates really was the most priapic of men. Camilla believed he'd recently had his teeth whitened twice in quick succession simply because he fancied the hygienist at their local surgery. 'She's much cleverer than Meredith,' he'd say (Meredith was the dentist), and Camilla believed he'd been encouraging the girl to make the most of herself and go into the law. Whether he'd got anything in return other than the whitest teeth in Chelsea, Camilla couldn't say, but he had obviously progressed elsewhere. When she had first started reading his emails (he was very reckless about his online security) she'd thought of walking out immediately. Then she'd considered a range of responses: outrage, phlegmatic acceptance, irritation ... boredom. When challenged, he would tell the most ridiculous lies, or wheel out one of his silences. It had then occurred to Camilla to reciprocate, so she'd 'taken a lover' herself, which had proved just as stilted an experience as the phrase implied. The lucky chap had been Simon Kendall, the well-known motoring columnist. But it turned out he really wanted to write novels, and was no good at sex. In the end she'd been fantasising not about having sex with Kendall, but about betraying him to Coates. What would Coates do? It was possible he thought that everybody – including Camilla herself – was entitled to have as much sex as possible. But on balance, a philosophical response was unlikely.

He had told her that when he was eighteen, he'd tried to kill a motorist who'd nearly (only 'nearly') knocked him off his bike. It had been on Great Portland Street. He'd got the man out of the car by ripping his wing mirror off. Then he'd hit him in the face with the wing mirror, and when he saw all the blood, that was enough to make him stop; but not to make him regret what he'd done, he'd been very clear about that. There'd been other road rage incidents later on, with Camilla in the passenger seat. She remembered Coates running along the side of a traffic jam on Waterloo Bridge to 'fuck up' some driver who'd done something wrong at the Waterloo roundabout. She didn't know what happened but he'd come back shaking, so that Camilla thought she might have an epileptic fit on her hands. He'd been a pupil barrister at that point, so if he really had fucked up the guy, that would have been the end of his legal career before it started. He *would* hit other men, she believed, and very often threatened to. Camilla's younger sister, Emma, had had trouble with a man who lived in her block of flats. The man had turned menacing, and Emma had come to Coates to ask about injunctions and restraining orders and so on. He'd asked Emma, 'Do you want *me* to have a word?' She'd said no, but he did have a word, and the next time Emma saw the guy, he had a broken arm; and she never had any more trouble from him. Coates saw himself as chivalrous, which was possibly why he had never shown any violence to Camilla, only a tendency towards sadism in sex, and unfaithfulness. When he was angry with her, it only ever took the form of silence. 'He doesn't even smoke in the house,' she heard herself saying to Anderson, at which point she decided to conclude her speech.

Anderson said, 'Why did your husband stop being a barrister, Mrs Coates?'

'Would you mind calling me Camilla?' she said, partly to buy herself time to come up with an answer. Her own question had in turn prompted the thought that she couldn't recall Anderson's first name. It came to her now: Stewart, which was 'Stuart' spelt the wrong way. The dog was stirring below the table. She glanced down at it, then glanced again. 'Your dog's only got three legs!' she said.

Anderson pretended to do a double-take of his own. 'Bloody hell, you're right!' he said.

'What happened?'

'Cancer,' Anderson replied, unexpectedly. 'But your husband?'

'There was a row in his chambers. He's not the sort to apologise and back down, so he walked out.'

She knew, or suspected, more than she was saying here, as Anderson had probably guessed. Even the dog had guessed, because he had now woken up, and was looking at Camilla with curiosity.

'You live on a farm, don't you?' she asked in an accusatory tone, which he detected.

'Somebody's got to, Mrs Coates. Otherwise there wouldn't be any food in this country.'

'A sheep farm?'

'Correct.'

'I believe that's a difficult way to make a living – farming sheep?'

'It'd be a lot easier if they weren't so bloody stupid.'

Now Anderson's phone rang for a third time. 'Do you

mind if I take this, Mrs Coates?' She nodded, and he began talking to someone about a gate that had been left unlocked, which was clearly a problem for him, but conjured a pleasantly bucolic scene in Camilla's mind. He said at one point, 'But you've got them in the field house now?' The answer – presumably yes – seemed to reassure him.

'What's a field house?' she asked, when he'd finished the call.

'A barn.'

'Do you mind my asking: who *was* that?'

'My sister.'

Camilla was pleased with this answer. She now thought of him as someone in a Thomas Hardy novel.

'You run the farm with her?'

Anderson looked at her for a while. 'She runs it with me.'

He was becoming attractive again, so she didn't really mind giving him her and Coates's address in Chelsea, and agreeing that the surveillance would start on Thursday, when Anderson would be back in London after what was evidently a flying visit to the north. As they discussed the fee – three days of surveillance would cost seven hundred pounds – she felt facetious and morally lax. For his own safety, she ought to have told him about her suspicions concerning Coates's sudden departure from chambers ... and there was the related matter of his mental state: the question of whether his number one characteristic in the List of Attributes ought not to be 'Good-looking' but simply 'Mad'. It was partly fear of seeming melodramatic that prevented her from mentioning to Anderson that, according to her amateur researches, her husband exhibited signs of both psychopathy and paranoid schizophrenia, which was almost incredible, since these conditions were unrelated. It would be like having measles and pneumonia at the same time, but there was a name for it: 'co-morbidity', so it must happen. By way of a possible response, she had prepared an evacuation plan for Lucy and herself. Whether it was implemented might depend on what Anderson came up with.

The coffees were finished, and when they walked out of the McDonald's, he shook her hand while standing alongside a car – a long, muddy hatchback. They were on York Way; the car was pointing to the north of England. The three-legged dog hopped into the back, nimbly enough.

'He's a sheepdog, I suppose?' Camilla said.

'*She's* a border collie, Mrs Coates, and she's also a sheepdog. Or she was.'

'She's retired, I suppose, because of the leg?'

Anderson nodded.

'So you bring her up to London, because she's got nothing else to do?'

'I bring her because she seems to like it, Mrs Coates.'

'Why?'

Long pause from Anderson as the taxis and buses roared past unnecessarily loudly, and the dirty snow came down with no hope of making its presence felt. 'I don't know, Mrs Coates,' he said, 'I really don't know.'

————

Coates was on Fleet Street – the St Paul's end of it. For five minutes, the bells of the City churches had been chiming ten o'clock in a shambolic way. Coates had the whole of this Thursday before him, not that he particularly wanted the day. He didn't know what he was going to do with it. Trouble was, he had neither the bike nor the car with him, so he was always likely to go for a drink. He began heading west, walking through the infuriating light rain that went neither up nor down but swirled pointlessly around. He tried to deny it to himself, but he knew he was heading towards El Vino's wine bar.

The place smelt faintly of cleaning fluids. He ordered a coffee and sat on a stool at the bar. He was the first customer. It was not time for drinking yet, but soon the under-employed criminal law hacks would be coming in for a morale-boosting white wine or gin and tonic. El Vino's was a lawyers' bar – almost exclusively now that the journalists had gone. It was outrageous that he should have even less to do than the under-employed hacks: that he had in fact nothing to do at all. He could sometimes sit for up to an hour in El Vino's before the memory of his banishment overwhelmed him. It was a miracle he had the bravery to do even that.

Two lawyers walked in: both fat and ugly, but sleek. He vaguely recognised them as Chancery types from Lincoln's Inn. They had come in for breakfast, to get a little fatter. They were not advocates, could not sway a jury; they just sat on their fat arses and read, for which they might be pulling down about three hundred grand a year.

Coates heard one of them say, 'I'm going to have to get rid of the Ferrari, it's really doing my back in.' Hearing that, he was forced to order a glass of white wine, and when he'd drunk it, he felt better in relation to the fat Chancery men: he had ten years on them; he would be back in gainful employment before long, and as one of them glanced over towards Coates, he felt he saw a satisfying apprehension. Perhaps he'd been recognised. Perhaps they'd heard the gossip about Parrish, and the good thing about being assumed to be the cause of Parrish's downfall was that Parrish had deserved what he'd got. Coates stared directly back at the Chancery man, and he turned away. Of course he did.

The door opened, and Coates turned and looked with equal directness and confidence at the new entrant: a pretty oriental woman in jeans and interesting grey suede boots. As far as Coates knew, jeans were banned in El Vino's, but an exception would be made in this case. She stood in the doorway, looking about with a slight squint – vulnerable, like the kind who might bite off more than she could chew. This was exactly Coates's type, but the type had remained elusive. He often thought it a pity that neither Camilla nor Jean realised that they were at variance with his ideal. They might give him a bit more credit for being nice to them if they did.

The woman smiled at him, which was as it should be. But then her escort came in: an inadequate bureaucrat in a bad suit, a Parrish type. He touched her arm, and she whispered in his ear. The scenario was deteriorating fast, because the man was now steering the woman towards the two Chancery QCs. So he was the solicitor – the pimp – and they were all set for a flirtatious conference. Coates quit El Vino's, but not quite fast enough to avoid hearing one of the fat QCs giggle with delight as the woman was presented to him.

The rain was congealing into a dirty white mist, from which a succession of buses loomed with a horrible, painful groaning. Since the night with the Yob, he had developed a hatred of double-decker buses. Somebody he knew might be on the top deck of any one of them, and looking out and down at him. Somebody he knew ... Jean. He still could not decide whether she had seen him on Millbank that night. But something had changed in her attitude towards him, and he had not heard from her since the night with that Vincent character – the Monday of the previous week. Coates stopped, wondering: did that Vincent character know what Jean knew? Had she confided in him?

Then he was heading west along the Strand. The oriental piece had stirred him up, and there was only one thing to be done. On the forecourt of Charing Cross station, he paused again, waiting to see if the Head of Chambers would have anything to say about his coming action; but there was no directing voice, only the profusion and confusion of the city – from which he could, and would, escape.

He entered the station and took two hundred pounds out of the ATM. *Do you wish to view your account balance?* the machine asked. 'No!' he said, and left the station with the money, heading towards Soho. On Charing Cross Road, he took out his phone and found a number in his contacts. He dialled, and a woman answered. 'Can you tell me your location?' he said. She told him, and he turned left.

He was feeling better now. The mist suited Soho: it gave the right glow to the already-illuminated signs of the bars and restaurants; there were no buses to speak of in Soho, and the *Evening Standard* wasn't yet on the streets. It turned up at about two, and he had to undergo the penance of buying a copy to see if the dead Yob had made the big time. There'd been no mention in its pages of his being fished out of the river, or of any police inquiry arising. Any such news, he had worked out, would appear on page four or five, the kind of gutter of the paper, where a rivulet of depressing London reality ran between the international headlines and celebrity glamour: bailiffs called in to well-known nightclub; two killed in hit and run; a breakout from Pentonville. His heart would beat fast as he turned through the gutter pages, and if the paper was Yob-free by page six, his day could resume. What bothered him was that the police might be keeping quiet for a reason.

He walked into the Coach and Horses. He liked this Spartan pub, with its wood panelling and single small TV, only ever turned on for the cricket. A few dapper, dark-suited alcoholics were in there, shakily manipulating their cigarette packets and mobile phones. He drank two glasses of white wine and went back out into the mist, heading for the specified location.

It was above a newsagent's. He rang the buzzer and was admitted to a staircase. A large, matronly English woman waited on the landing, holding a mug of tea. He hoped to God this wasn't the 'submissive beauty' the phone card had advertised. No, the girl was sitting on a bed in the doorway behind the matron. The matron showed him in, introducing him by saying, 'This gentleman would like a word.'

The girl was fiddling with her phone. She had quite good hands, but bitten-down fingernails. She wore a T-shirt and shorts – actual shorts, not French knickers – and she did look remarkably physically fit. She couldn't have been more than thirty, but it was too easy to imagine her a middle-aged, moaning wife.

'Do you like being tied up?' Coates asked her as the matron looked on. It was like when – prior to sitting down at a dinner party – you were forced to make small talk to your hostess's child before they were put to bed.

'I don't know,' said the girl.

'But you are submissive?'

'I like all sorts.'

He turned to the Madam, who was observing proceedings rather coolly, making no attempt to sell the goods on offer. 'Do you have any rope?' he enquired, and it was as if he were a customer in a ship's chandlers.

She took a sip of her tea. It was a horrible mug; a picture of a rose on it. 'I could go and buy some,' she said.

'Where?'

'A sex shop.'

Coates sat on the bed. 'But there are no sex shops left,' he said. 'They've all been turned into delicatessens.'

'There's a Harmony on Charing Cross Road.'

Coates frowned. 'Harmony? That's a kind of boutique, isn't it?'

'It sells fetish stuff. You'd have to come with me; I couldn't leave you alone with the girl.'

'Does it sell handcuffs?'

'I think so.'

'I'm not being handcuffed,' said the girl, looking up from her phone.

'I don't mind,' said the woman.

'You don't mind what?' said Coates.

'You can handcuff me.'

Coates looked at her. He was quite tempted; she was a handsome woman, in a way. Good skin – a lot of it, mind you. In one way, she was younger than the girl.

'Are you into S&M?' he asked.

'Yes,' she said, but there had been a fractional hesitation. He didn't believe her. It had been exciting for the moment in which he had believed her though. He quite admired her spirit, and she hadn't given up yet, because she said: 'Be a change to go with a cute-looking man.'

He slowly took a hundred pounds out of his wallet. Then he put twenty back, and gave eighty to the woman. 'It's been nice talking to you,' he said. 'But I have to go.'

'Ok. Do you want me to bring you off?'

Coates admired this woman's directness. 'All right,' he said.

So they went into the next room, and she did.

Walking back down the stairs, Coates felt reasonably good. He'd purged the feeling the oriental piece had brought on, and he'd managed to do so without killing anyone. Of course, in an hour's time he might regret not taking up the big woman's proposition. She'd offered to come out of retirement for him, so to speak. But no ... they had to be into it to some extent; otherwise it would not be chivalrous. Coates knew that while he was far from unique in his sexual tastes, they did put him in a minority. He knew that the women who didn't fancy him — and some of those who did — were wary of him even when they didn't know of those tastes, because there was something overbearing about him. But he would not be characterised as unchivalrous. He was a gentleman. He would not hurt a woman, a principle that some of them — Jean, for instance — seemed determined to test to breaking point. How? By playing mind games of which only they knew the rules: nothing ever stated. They implied, he was left to infer. But they should know he didn't like inferring. Life was too short, especially – the way things were going – *his* life.

The front door of the place was on a spring. It closed too quickly and loudly behind him. The promising woman upstairs was gone for ever, and the mysterious potential of the morning had dissipated. The rain was now normal, coming vertically down in a vindictive way. On the other side of the road, a black and white dog was pissing on the pavement, ignoring a perfectly good lamp-post. But there was something else wrong: the dog had only three legs.

Coates heard: 'Now pay attention, boy.'

The dog was being collected by a thin man in black who seemed to emerge from a doorway. They started heading north towards Oxford Street. The dog gave a sad glance back at Coates, but the man had been too determined not to look at Coates. Had he been holding a phone in that doorway of his? Had he been photographing Coates? What was he? Vice Squad?

'You fucking mug,' said the Head. 'He was interested in you, not the place.'

'But he's gone the opposite way.'

'That's because you clocked him, and he's scared. Now get on and think. You've seen that dog before.'

'But where?'

It occurred to Coates, as a woman stepped into the road to avoid him, that he'd said that out loud.

'What am I?' said the Head. 'Fucking Google? Get on the web and search three-legged dogs.'

Coates was on Shaftesbury Avenue now, and a lot of people were getting interested in him, but were they really present?

139

When the Head of Chambers came on, a lot of other things would fade away. Piccadilly Circus for instance – theoretically in front of Coates just now – was becoming nothing more than a sort of slowly turning hologram of a merry-go-round for tourists.

But Coates had found on his phone an article from *The Times*. He was a subscriber to *The Times*, and he knew he'd seen the article before, if not exactly *read* it. The thing was headed 'The Power of Three', and four people who owned three-legged dogs had been assembled to boast about how happy their dogs were even though they only had three legs. As if they would know. One human–animal pairing fit the bill. He was called Anderson, and he combined being a private detective from an office in London with being a sheep farmer in Yorkshire. So he was a journalist's dream all right, even without the three-legged dog. Coates had seen the dog in Milford Lane. Yes. Any private detective in Central London was liable to turn up in the Temple from time to time – they worked for the solicitors in and around the place, tracking down evidential leads – and so they would all have known what happened to Parrish, and the rumours about who was responsible. Or was this the very shamus that Jenkins had put on his tail seven months back? And was he coming back for more? Still investigating? Coates googled Anderson, and brought up an office address and phone number.

The Circus continued to revolve, wobbling slightly on its axis, in a way that was starting to make Coates feel slightly ill.

———

Cliff watched the Turk lining up to miss another red. 'Put your head down over the cue,' he said.

'What?'

'You might have a chance if you *aim*,' Cliff said. 'Your chin should be resting on the cue.'

The Turk lowered his head to the cue, took his shot. Well, he'd *hit* the red, at least. 'That don't feel right to me,' he said. Cliff potted a red, screwing back nicely for the blue, but this was lost on the Turk, who had a one-track mind, and no small talk.

'So a deactivated gun,' the Turk was saying.

'Will you keep your fucking voice down, *please*,' said Cliff.

Cliff brought any prospective client to snooker, or maybe to a boxing night – basically to work out how much of an idiot they were; how much heat they were likely to bring on him. So far, this Turk was failing the test. He was small, very dark and bald, except for his arms, which were incredibly hairy; he had a high voice that was half foreign, half cockney. He'd turned up carrying one of those little man bags. He wasn't gay or anything, just foreign: specifically Turkish; and he was a Turkish Turk, the Full Monty, not a Turkish Cypriot. Cliff knew the difference because his barber was a Turkish Cypriot, like Muzzy Izzet, ex of Chelsea. (Archbishop Makarios, on the other hand, had been a Greek Cypriot.) Any sort of dodgy Turk ought to have no trouble getting hold of a weapon from his own people. The Turkish boys were very tooled-up generally speaking, to protect their narcotics trade. But this man was not Turkish Mafia; he seemed to be a kind of freelance pimp. 'I have some few girls and I minds my own business,' he'd said, soon after they'd shaken hands. 'They good girls. One little cocaine line, heroin fing . . . one little joint, and they is out!' he had squeaked – yet quite bloody loudly – at the start of their first game. His name, apparently, was Behmen, or something similar, but he'd said, 'Just call me Benny, that way is all simple.'

He was lining up for another red: the wrong one.

'Don't know about your shot selection there,' said Cliff.

Benny looked up, and Cliff indicated, with the end of his cue, the red practically dangling over the top right pocket. Benny now addressed that ball with not a word of thanks, not even when he managed to pot the ball. He was now moving on to the brown instead of the salmon, which was nicely set up for right middle, needing just the slightest kiss. But fuck him. Benny missed the brown, saying once again, now in a whisper . . .

'The deactivated one. What kind of—'

'*Re*-activated,' said Cliff. 'Deactivated ain't going to be any good to you, is it? Because it's not going to fire a bullet.'

'Reactivated, yes,' said Benny, but he sounded doubtful. 'What sort of prices we talking about?'

Cliff potted a red, leaving himself nicely on the black, which he also potted. He suddenly realised that neither of them was keeping score. Well, it would just be embarrassing. 'Couple of hundred, but maybe you want something a bit sexier. What's your budget?'

'Budget?' said Benny.

'Money. How much have you got to spend?'

'Money is no limit!'

Now what sort of negotiating technique did we have here, wondered Cliff, taking another red in his stride and leaving himself with an easy black again.

Benny said, 'You don't . . . interested in what I want for this gun, right?'

'Come again?' said Cliff. He deliberately took on a difficult red, and missed.

'You don't want to know reason for it.'

Cliff, deciding this was a question and not a statement, said, 'Not particularly, no.'

Benny nodded, looked disappointed if anything. He was chalking his cue in the way beginners did; grinding the tip right into the hollow of the chalk. Cliff found himself feeling sorry for the little fellow.

'Sounds like you want to off somebody.'

'Off is kill?'

'Correct.'

'I tell you, man. I want to annihilate him. Annihilate.' He was proud of knowing the word.

'Who?' said Cliff. He might as well ask, since he was obviously going to be told.

'This man, he kill my son. So is like: no *way* can he live.'

'Obviously,' said Cliff. It was Benny's shot, but he seemed to have lost interest in the game. When he put the chalk down on the edge of the table, his hand was shaking. He's going to blub, thought Cliff. Bloody hell, he *was* blubbing.

'Can't have this, mate,' he said, walking over to Benny and taking the cue off him. 'Why don't we take a little breather? Go outside?'

The Turk nodded, sniffing like a little boy, and they walked out together, tracking past the normal people playing normal games.

In the car park, Cliff offered Benny a Marlboro Light.

There came the sound of breaking glass and shouting, but it was far off, and only to be expected anywhere along this stretch of the river. The wind from the river was blowing the big banner that advertised the snooker; it made a sound like the rigging of a sailboat, and Cliff should know, because he owned a sailboat. They retreated behind a container lorry to light up. Benny's phone rang, and he did the decent thing, putting the caller off: 'No, is fine but I am in a meeting about the thing so . . . Yeah. Is going good, really good. Bye.'

This guy's not looking for a modified starter pistol, thought Cliff. He's going to be in the market for a fucking Uzi.

'You got the old bill involved in all this?' said Cliff.

'Bill?'

'The cops. About your son.'

'They investigating, yes,' said Benny. 'They found my boy in the river with big hole here.' He indicated his throat. 'So they know is murder case, but not serious for them, and they is racists man, so my boy is not priority . . . '

'He was involved with the girls, was he?'

'He was involved as businessman, yes. He ran some girls, kept them off the street, off the drugs; what is wrong about that?'

'Nothing. Where did it happen?'

'Pimlico.'

Blimey! Cliff had been expecting Wood Green or Tottenham.

'So you're going after the killer yourself?'

'Yes. Me and my brother.'

'And you know where to find him?'

Benny finished his cigarette with three quick puffs; didn't inhale. He shook his head. 'This is big problem, no.'

'You got any idea?'

'I have a . . . sort of picture.'

'You mean a photograph?'

'Description,' he said with a sigh.

'It wasn't a drugs thing?' said Cliff, cautiously. The Turks were big into the heroin after all.

'It was not drugs. My boy is clean, I told you. He call this man out for his . . . He was sex pervert. He like to tie the girls and stuff.'

'That narrows it down a bit, I suppose. That kind of thing's not available in too many places.'

'It not available in my boy's place. A little bit of . . . play hard, yes, but then with special price, and this man want it cheap. He a rich guy, as well. For the rest of my life, I search for this man, my brother too. The minute we see him, he is finished. Annihilate.'

'So you'll be carrying the piece?'

'Carrying? Yes, always.'

'Vigilante patrol.'

'What?'

'Who's running the girls now?'

'Me and my brother. We look out for them always. They our friends.'

'Yeah?' said Cliff, because he was sceptical about that.

The Turk was holding the little bag. It was probably stuffed with cash. It had bloody better be.

'How about a little Glock?' said Cliff. 'Two of them. One for you and one for your brother. Three grand the pair and a bag of ammo thrown in.'

'Definitely. Where is?'

Cliff threw his cigarette stub in the general direction of the Audi.

'Boot of the car,' he said.

PART TWO

Starting time of the Friday Fun was half past seven. I had thought it best to arrive early, lest there be one of the fairly regular blockages or breakdowns on the Metropolitan branch that prevented the trains from going through the tunnel, or left them stuck in it for upwards of an hour. In the event, the journey was trouble free, and I felt slightly foolish as – with carpet bag in hand – I approached the theatre in full daylight at quarter past four. The Rotherhithe Hippodrome had been intimidating when I'd first visited it, for my interview with Draper, and it now continued its stand-offish behaviour, seeming, if anything, even more unnecessarily tall and imposing than before.

The front doors were chained shut (whereas one of them had been open on my previous visit) and my tentative ringing of the stage door bell at the back met no response. I returned to the front. The words FRIDAY FUN: NEW FACES AND OLD FAVOURITES appeared in large letters above the doors, but only one turn was mentioned by name: Marie Lloyd, the star. Copies of the bill itself appeared in glass cases between each set of doors. We were on fourth after the interval, and billed as DRAPER & THE MARTIAN GIRL. So Draper must have liked that suggestion of mine. There was no subsidiary matter, so he had rejected the idea of any disclaimer about this being our first show. The Dad had said not to worry: 'You have a great deal to gain, and nothing whatever to lose,' but I had a great deal to lose – in particular The Dad himself, who was in a bad way, and who had spoken something nearer the truth a few days before-hand, when he'd said, 'Food is getting awfully dear, isn't it?' Not that prices were rising at anything above the usual rate, but our funds were rapidly dwindling. He had further tried to console me – but achieved the opposite – by saying, 'It's a very small engagement, really.' In fact, it was no such thing: this was a chance to become the regular partner of a seasoned pro. I had ordered him not to attend my debut – on account of his health – and he agreed a bit more readily than I expected.

A clock chimed four – the clock of the Town Hall. I wished to defer the arrival of half past seven for ever. On the other hand, it could not come quickly enough, because then the torture of not knowing my fate would be over. I dare not imagine myself taking my call amid deafening applause; therefore I pictured myself receiving polite applause from the friendlier auditors, while the others studied the inside of their hats, or shook their heads in mortification. I glanced inside my bag, to make sure I hadn't forgotten anything. There was the black velvet blindfold, which Draper had obtained from some amenable seamstress of the locality (there had been no further mention of a second blindfold), and there was the dress I had decided on: a kind of sheer tea gown with sash, intended to give an impression of after-dinner sophistication, not least by virtue of the daringly low neckline.

I turned towards the road: Lower Road. The turn of a

corner or two would bring me to Providence Road, and Draper's house. I wondered what he could possibly be doing at that moment? Standing motionless before his small fire, perhaps. Perusing *Curious Things*? Or sitting at his table and typing? Either way he would not welcome a visit from me.

I must seek distraction in the streets round about, which ought not to be too difficult, for if the Hippodrome was asleep, Rotherhithe in general was bustling, and Lower Road itself was thronged with the traffic of the docks. A lot of tea was being carried, whether coming from or going to the river. A good deal of flour (signified by vehicle and driver being ghostly white) was being carried – and it was mainly *going*, whereas barrels of pickles were mainly coming. But the principal cargo in both directions was timber. If in doubt – the motto of the Rotherhithe carters seemed to be – then load up with timber. I began walking away from the theatre. In hopes of forgetting my anxiety, I would take a look at the riverside wharves.

I was really taking a leaf out of The Dad's book. When the possibility of a flat in Stanley Buildings had come up, he'd jumped at it, not only because they were 'Model Flats', well insulated and solidly built so the neighbours would not be disturbed by his music, but also because the block was, as he said, 'in the thick of the action' on Pancras Road, which ran between King's Cross and St Pancras stations. You'd think a musician would want quiet, but The Dad wanted *life*, so he picked a flat on the ground floor, with the traffic and the trams rumbling past the windows all day and night – and on Sunday too. There was in effect no Sunday on Pancras Road, which suited The Dad, who was prone to go into a 'depression' on that day. That was why he played the harmonium at a Sunday school on Busaco Street during the morning, and the piano at The Fox and Hounds on Pentonville Road in the evening. (Of course, he did not disclose the evening activity to the Sunday school people, and they were never likely to discover it for themselves, since they never went near a public house.) I had often thought my mother must have died on a Sunday.

As I approached the river, the buildings seemed to grow higher and move closer together, as if to say, 'Are you quite sure you want to come this way?' They seemed to guard the secret of the river; but I had a glimpse of it from time to time, with Wapping on the opposite bank, where stood a building resembling a sheared-off turret of a castle, which I knew – from having got off the tunnel-train prematurely a few days beforehand – to be a police station, the principal one of the river force. A blue flag flew from the roof.

The sky was darkening now, with smoky clouds converging. Even on the finest days, there would be little light in the alleys through which I now wandered, the tops of which were criss-crossed with bridges, like elevated railway carriages jammed in at crazy angles. Sometimes a thunderous noise came, as barrels were rolled down these inclines in some mysterious commerce between one building and another. I emerged on to the waterfront, and what at first looked like a purposeful black cloud coming fast around the bend of the river turned into a great flight of sparrows, which then appeared to be sucked with rapidity into the high aperture of a warehouse. This must have been a grain store, but I thought of it as a giant bird house, which with its steeply pitched roof and projecting jib it somewhat resembled.

I was woken from my reverie by a glance from a passing workman, which alerted me to the fact that I had possibly entered a territory where no respectable woman ought to be seen alone. I headed inland again, and drank a cup of tea at an eating house on Neptune Street. I had asked for a slice of sultana bread as well, but was too nervous to eat it. When I emerged once again, a slender crescent moon had appeared over Rotherhithe, and I knew the theatre doors would be open. I approached from the rear, seeing the words STAGE DOOR electrically illuminated in white, inside a blue glass box.

I opened the door and entered the theatre, which smelt of paint. Immediately to my right was a hatch, just big enough to display the beaming, rubicund face of the stage door manager.

'I'm Miss French,' I said.

'I know!' he said.

'Is Mr Draper here?'

The stage manager shook his head, still beaming.

'Marie Lloyd?' I asked, foolishly.

He shook his head again. 'She won't be here 'til five minutes before her call,' he said. 'And she might cut it finer than that.'

Obviously, because she might have been booked at three or four other halls this evening, and she would go between them in her own brougham. The stage door man directed me to the female dressing room, which was for every female except the star. It was a long room – a sort of red and green corridor of gas-lit mirrors – and quite empty. I sat down, and saw myself reflected to infinity in the mirrors before and behind. I changed into my tea gown and put on my make-up, with a lot of black around the eyes. That had all taken ten minutes. I then put the blindfold over my eyes to see whether it would smudge the mascara. It would not. That had taken up another thirty seconds. There came a knock on the door. It was the stage door manager again, handing me an envelope. A wire – and of course it was from The Dad, who shouldn't be wasting money on such things, or walking about in the cold night air to despatch them: *SLAY EM, KIDDER*, I read, and I found that I was almost crying, so it was a good job the stage door manager had already retreated to the stage door; a good job also that other turners began to appear.

The first to pitch up was one of a dancing troupe. She introduced herself as Emily and seemed very nice. The second to arrive appeared to be the first one all over again, which was a bit confusing until I recollected Which One's Which: identical twins who performed a dramatic interlude with some hapless man who couldn't distinguish between them. Soon the dressing room was full of loud and laughing females, and I began to feel less nervous – or rather, I felt ashamed of being so nervous.

When the half was called, I went out into the wings. It was far too early for 'standing by' but that's what I was doing. Backstage people loitered alongside me, including the call boy, who was telling a funny story to a man I believed to be the assistant stage manager – so it must be that every-one who was meant to be present when the half was called *was* present, otherwise the call boy would have been agitated. But where was Draper? Should I knock at the men's dressing room and ask for him? No, because that would be the action of a little girl looking for her father. What I did instead was position myself to one side of the men's door. Presently a fellow came out, and I arranged to be walking past the opened door. There, in a room full of laughing half-dressed males, was one fully dressed and not laughing, but sitting gravely before a mirror: Draper.

I stayed in the wings and watched the curtain rise and the lights go up to full as the chairman called the audience – of which I could see not a single member from my vantage point – to order, and gave his list of the treats in store, including 'mentalists supreme, Draper and Finch'. He'd definitely said 'Finch'. He had, in other words, made a mistake and nobody seemed to mind, which made me feel a little better even though I could tell the house was packed to bursting. (It was a matter of a great seething energy projecting down onto the stage and round the corner towards me.) I waited in the wings all the way through the first half, and right through the interval as well. I could not enjoy the turns, but just counted them down until some skinny acrobats swarmed past me on to the stage. Then Draper came out of the dressing room and stood beside me. He and I were to follow the tumblers, who were called the Nine Neros. It seemed a remarkably brief act, and in no time at all they were climbing onto each other's shoulders for their big finish. The littlest would go up last, and he would get there by jumping. Meanwhile, he was turning cartwheels in front of his chums, who had formed what looked like a vertical rugby scrum (it wavered somewhat) in readiness to receive him. Draper had said nothing so far; I heard only his rather heavy breathing. His stage clothes consisted of neatly pressed dark trousers, black frock coat, white collar very starched and a dotted tie: a bank clerk's outfit. He wore some eye make-up behind his habitual wire glasses. On the stage, the pyramid was stooping somewhat to receive the final Nero. Draper was pointing at me.

'Where's the blindfold?'

I had left it in the dressing room. Loud applause greeted the leap of the imp, and the acrobats' closing music struck up as I ran, clattering into a dangling fire bucket – and startling the call boy, who had been reading a newspaper. I entered the dressing room. Two spangled singers were occupying the entirety of my place: one sitting on the chair I had used, the other on the dressing table itself.

'Have you seen the blindfold?' I practically shrieked.

'*What* blindfold?' they both said.

But then the one on the chair coolly scooped the thing up from the floor where I must have dropped it. I ran back to Draper, passing the call boy, who said, 'Your number's up, miss,' and our music was playing. (Draper had supplied the part: a slow and dreamy piano piece, as befitting extra-planetary activities.) I hoped it was loud enough to drown out the desperate apologies I whispered as Draper received me on the edge of the stage and took possession of the blindfold, pocketing it with a graceful gesture quite at odds with the words he hissed in my ear: 'A single property to remember. A single *one*, and you can't do it.'

Draper himself had one property to remember, and he

had remembered it, because it was being placed on stage right then: the perfectly ordinary dining-room chair on which I was about to sit. We entered from stage left, and the chair seemed very far away as I approached it under the eyes of the three thousand, towards whom I could not resist giving nervous glances. The strange music continued to play, like a glittering rain falling; the black cloth showed a night sky dotted with stars. Draper had borrowed it from a magician. We had reached the chair. Like a host at a dinner party, Draper pulled it back for me, just as though there had been a table to pull it back *from*.

Only when I was seated did I have a proper look at the audience, and I fear I gave a gasp that must have been visible if it was not audible. In the stalls were ... far too many people; and the circle would surely collapse under the weight of its occupants. This theatre, I realised for the first time, lacked pillars: nothing was holding any of it up. I was just about to brave a glimpse at the gallery when the lights went down, and slowly tumbling smoke became visible in the spotlight that had been aimed directly at me. There were quite a few propped umbrellas. All these people had been in the real world more recently than me, and it must have rained in the real world.

Draper had retreated to stage left. The music stopped, and even though this was Rotherhithe on a Friday night, the resulting silence was almost total. My left leg hurt, I realised, as a result of the fire bucket smash. I scratched my knee, until I realised I was a Martian who probably didn't need to do that.

Draper said, 'You are quite comfortable I hope?'

I nodded.

'Please confirm,' said Draper, 'that you are quite comfortable?'

Quite ... comfortable. For a moment, I thought this must be the code for a set. The ninety-ninth set, perhaps, comprising some of the objects not included in sets one to ninety-eight. But no, it was a simple question. 'Quite comfortable, thank you,' I said, and I dimly realised – in the darkness – that my hesitation had somehow affected the audience, for all remaining muttering had now died away.

'Ladies and gentlemen,' Draper began, 'we commence with a quotation from the Roman philosopher, Cicero.' At this, some amused muttering did start up. 'It is the soul itself which sees and hears,' Draper continued, speaking with the infuriating slowness of a vicar reading a lesson, 'and not those parts of it which use, as it were, the *windows* of the soul.'

Somebody in the gallery shouted a word I am not going to relate. It began with 'B'. I myself doubted that Cicero had ever used the expression 'as it were'. There was some laughter, but also a shout of 'Give him a chance.'

'Some may profess,' Draper was continuing, 'to find in what follows a mere trickery. Others may see feats performed that are completely incompatible with inductive science. Others again may recognise a purely natural occurrence, as when two people say the same thing together. They are amazed and say, "That is strange, I was just going to say the same thing!" Suffice to say,' he continued, fishing in his pocket for the blindfold, 'what I see, Miss French sees, and what Miss French knows, I know.'

I had not heard any of this preamble before. I could only think that if Draper's aim had been to muddy the waters, he had succeeded.

'Our time is limited,' Draper was now saying, begging the question of why he didn't get on with it. 'Therefore I would ask that you have some articles ready, such as bank notes, business cards, envelopes with your address – of which Miss French will give the full name, the time of mailing; also the numbers of any cheques, or the initials or monogram on any odd curio that you may have in your possession. Everything will be minutely described by her on the stage. To assist us, may I ask you to be ready, and give us your whole attention, as the success of our demonstration depends entirely on the quietude of the audience.'

He was approaching me holding something that was not the blindfold. I thought at first it was a pair of spectacles; but the lenses were opaque. It would be the pennies on the eyes after all, or at any rate two brass medallions, somewhat larger then pennies, and with small holes drilled in the edges of them, and thin wire threaded through. He had entrusted me with the blindfold, but not with this device, which he knew I would have objected to as being morbid. But I could make no show of insubordination before the three thousand.

I tilted my head back to receive the medallions. Immediately before I closed my eyes, I thought I saw, in the half light, sailing ships engraved on them. Draper wound the wire quite tightly around the back of my head, with a sort of frightening expertise; I knew that my hair, carefully arranged into curling tendrils, must be badly disarranged, but Draper now smoothed it with his large hands. He had a great capacity for slowness, which I would never have guessed from such peremptory marks as he had uttered while educating me in mesmerism. A new sort of muttering had arisen from the audience, and I detected in it an impulse of concern.

Then came the black velvet on top; so stultifying that I thought at first I could not breathe. By holding tight on to the edge of the chair, I stilled my panic and rehearsed breathing in this new situation. Yes, the air – smoke-filled, citrus-scented and amazingly hot – came into my lungs and went out again, more or less in the approved-of manner, but I must work at it. I was perspiring freely.

I heard footsteps. Draper was walking away again, crossing the stage, then leaving the stage entirely. I divined that he must now be progressing along a row of seats, seeking the property of the auditors, like a kind of highwayman, and that the foolish auditors were yielding up their property while he said, 'Thank you, sir,' or 'I am much obliged to you, madam,' and was in general unprecedentedly polite. From behind the two blindfolds, I seemed to discern burnished, copper-coloured planets (sometimes with a touch of verdigris) approaching at great rates of rapidity from the black depths of space and exploding and dissolving into other planets. Their purpose, evidently, was to distract me by their beauty from all the knowledge I had gained in the course of my instruction. What number in the codes denoted *green*, for example? Was it number six, corresponding to six in the number list and therefore indicated by the question 'What?' Or was green number five, corresponding to either 'Will' or 'Won't'? If anything green was produced by an auditor, I was sunk, and The Dad was sunk, too.

'What have I here?' somebody was saying; and of course it was Draper, and he was saying it to me. I breathed in, breathed out, because staying alive must be the priority. Then there came a further demand: 'Won't you say?'

I had somehow expected that we would begin with an item from the first set ('What article is this?'). But we had leapt into the thicket of the much later sets.

'What have I here?' Draper repeated. He was not supposed to have to repeat the question. I must respond, somehow or other; therefore, I repeated the question:

'What have ... ?'

A sort of butterfly of puzzlement began to flit through the audience.

I was progressing mentally through the sets, ploughing through 'What article is this?', 'What *is* this?', 'What is here?', discarding treasure troves of watches, bracelets, chains, cuff links, cigarette holders. I came at last to 'What have I here?' But now I must descend through the numbers, which was akin to climbing down a ladder into a well, ever deeper towards danger and darkness, as I resisted the temptations of 'Say, or speak', 'Be, look or let', 'Can or can't'. I came at last to 'Will or won't.' I had arrived at number five – number five of the fifth set: opera glasses. This was Rotherhithe, not a very operatic place. But I staked my whole life on this unlikely article.

'Opera glasses,' I said.

I expected to hear whatever noise three thousand people make when they wish to express disappointment, because at the moment I said 'opera glasses', I knew it must be the wrong answer. The reaction, however, was something in-between: the butterfly of uncertainty on the move again.

Draper's voice came again. 'Speak up, please.'

A novel command – nothing of the sort had been rehearsed between us. Had I simply gone unheard? I must stake my life again; double or quit.

'Opera glasses,' I said, more loudly, and at that moment I fell in love with Rotherhithe, for the house 'erupted', as the journalists of *The Era* like to say. I was on the point of rising to my feet, turning to face those lovely Londoners and taking my bow, but Draper was pressing on amid the roar. 'Do you know the metal?' I did not know the metal. It was news to me that any metal was involved. But yes; opera glasses were not made of ivory or ebony, especially not in Rotherhithe, and Draper was giving me the all-important supplementary – 'Can you say the metal?' – by which I was guided to the special metals sub-set, and number three in that sub-set.

'They are, I believe, brass.'

By which remark, I froze Rotherhithe; brought time itself to a stop. (I learnt subsequently that Draper had turned to the auditor, a woman, who had verified by a nod of the head that brass was indeed the metal.) Then further acclamation, during which I began to breathe more freely. But I could not relax, for Draper was saying, quite bluntly, 'This article?'

On the basis of this information, I computed my way slowly to the seventeenth set, during which time the audience fell silent once more.

'Are you able to say what I hold?'

After further interminable thought, I recollected that

'Are' was number eight, which brought me to another object that surely did not belong in an East End music hall. 'It may be . . . it *is* a prayer book.'

Yet again, Draper had to raise his voice against the acclamation. 'Will you say the fabric?' He was directing me to number five in the special 'Fabrics' set.

'Leather?' I said. One ought not to say it as a question, especially given that a prayer book really only could be leather. (Buckskin or silk were outside possibilities.)

Draper was still talking amid the applause, and this time he was saying a good deal. 'Give me the name on the flyleaf. Hurry up. *See* this. Maybe you cannot? Do try.'

Finally, the wretched man stopped speaking and I could start working. We were now back in the territory of the letter code, in which G, the first letter of Draper's first sentence, signified D. 'Hurry up' meant repeat the previous letter. The first letter of his second sentence, B, signified I. Draper's 'See this' meant X (and it seemed very unfair that an X should have come up in my first performance). M meant O, and finally, D meant N, after which laborious calculation (it had taken me about a full minute, during which the house had again fallen silent), I pronounced 'D. Dixon.' Another eruption, complete this time with wonderful cheers.

'Do you know what this is?' the relentless Draper was enquiring. '*Do* you?'

We were in the seventh set, the fourth item.

'A coin,' I said.

'Say . . . ' Draper began.

'The year of the coin is 1889,' I said.

After a moment's hesitation, Draper asked the auditor to verify the dates. I heard a faint, female voice saying, 'Yes, the young lady is quite correct.'

Draper put his next questions firmly enough, but I knew he had been somewhat shaken by my giving the year of the coin, for I had *given it before he had asked it*. I had simply *seen* the numbers of the year, imprinted in a copper-ish colour (fitting for a coin) on the blackness of the blindfold, and I can only say that I had been impelled to declare the number by a sudden sense of confidence.

I identified four further items by the conventional method, but still too slowly. Draper then came over and removed the two blindfolds, and that was when we received our applause – when I gazed out on the auditors while still seated. As we took our bow, the applause redoubled. We had undoubtedly knocked them, but Draper was silent as we approached the wings. As we stepped *into* the wings, I immediately saw Marie Lloyd emerging from the star dressing room. A number of acolytes, male and female, had fallen in behind her, for she must have an entourage, even for this short walk from dressing room to stage.

Mrs Lloyd, who was sucking a lozenge, was simultaneously wearing a great deal of clothing and not very much. Her outfit was really just a mass of white silk underwear, with a giant flowery hat on top. Everything was in twos: big eyes, lined rather messily with black; long, crossed front teeth (behind which the lozenge steadily revolved), and then the famous décolletage. She was looking at Draper.

'Hello, cock,' she said.

Draper – mopping sweat from his brow with a handker-chief – didn't like that. 'Good evening, Mrs Lloyd,' he said. 'You're keeping well I hope?'

Mrs Lloyd was self-evidently keeping well, so she didn't bother to answer. Instead she was now looking *me* up and down. She bowed her head, rather graciously. 'Going on all right, dear?' she said. She turned again to Draper. 'She's much prettier than your last feed, I must say. What was his name? Brooks.'

Draper didn't like that either, for – I believed – two reasons: firstly, the use of the word 'feed'; secondly, the mere fact of Brooks's name having been mentioned.

'What became of him?' asked Mrs Lloyd, while commencing to crunch the lozenge. 'Brooks, I mean?'

'My previous *assistant*,' Draper said, emphasising the word, 'went to Australia.'

'Didn't come across him when I was there,' said Mrs Lloyd, swallowing the remnants of the lozenge. A young man who had been standing behind her now stepped forward, so that he was at her side. He had been eyeing Draper stonily, and this he continued to do from his new position.

Draper said, 'I don't even know if he's on the Halls, I'm sure. He has not thought it necessary to correspond with me.'

The young man spoke up. 'You and Brooks, sir, were on the very first bill I saw in Britain. It would have been in 'ninety-one, sir. Collins' Music Hall in Islington.'

The young man was dressed extravagantly (we will be coming to that), but did not seem extravagant in his person. His accent was American, or half-American, and quite soothing to listen to. But I had suspected that the first 'sir' of his speech had not been meant politely, and the tone of the second one had confirmed my suspicion.

'Yes,' said Draper. 'I have played Collins many times.'

'You got a good hand,' said the young man. 'The act was going along pretty nicely.'

'Not as far as my associate was concerned,' said Draper, and with a brief nod towards Mrs Lloyd he walked off to the male dressing room ... which was pretty irregular. You didn't leave the presence of Marie Lloyd; she left *your* presence. But if the lady minded very much, it didn't stop her smiling at me.

'I'm not surprised the other bloke went to Australia,' she said. 'It's about as far as he could go away from *him* ... short of going to Mars, where you're from.'

'I live in King's Cross actually,' I said, smiling back.

With a jerk of her head towards the dressing room, she said, 'But you've been reading Draper's mind, even so?'

'It's mainly a question of numbers,' I said, which I knew to be a strange remark, but the only one just then available to me.

'It certainly is, dearie. You're filling in aren't you? What is it? Ten quid joint?'

'Seven,' I said.

'That's what he's telling you.'

The call boy had appeared. 'One minute!' he said in a friendly, joshing way to Mrs Lloyd, who said to me:

'What's the split of this seven? Four-three in his favour?'

I nodded, rather ashamed, even though I had been delighted about the arrangement before.

'See,' Marie Lloyd said, 'I can read minds as well, love;

and I can tell the future. When you've got a book full of dates, he'll be riding in his brougham, and you'll be on the top deck of a bus with the penny soldiers. And as for any expenses that come up: transportation of properties, agent's fees . . . You do have an agent?'

'Mr Draper does the agenting for us.'

Marie Lloyd hesitated. 'I nearly said something very rude just then, darling,' she said. 'Get yourself a good agent. It won't be very difficult.'

'You don't think so?'

'You're not stone deaf, I take it? It wasn't a warm reception you got tonight, darling, it was an *ovation*. Do you think Draper ever got anything like that when he was working with old whatsisname?'

'I don't know, I'm sure.'

On the stage, W.P. Dempsey, a singing comedian, was taking his call.

'Did you watch our turn, Miss Lloyd?' I was emboldened to ask.

'No, but Art did.' She indicated the young man, who was dressed, it seemed, for holidaymaking. He wore white flannel trousers, a white shirt with high-standing collar and a green and white striped tie of what looked to be good silk. Instead of a waistcoat, he wore, beneath his dark lounge jacket, a cummerbund with his watch chain strung across it. So it was a rather formal holiday, perhaps. He was smoking a small cigar, which he now carefully extinguished in the fire bucket I had clattered into, which hung below a NO SMOKING sign. He gave a brief bow and extended his hand for me to shake. 'Arthur Wakelam,' he said. 'You were very good, Miss French. Not rapid, except in one instance, but good. I've seen countless mind readers and you were something a little different in that line.'

It was my fault, having fished for a compliment, to have ended up with something rather less.

Mrs Lloyd interjected again: 'Art said the people liked you because they thought you a bit nutty, dear.'

'Charmingly eccentric, I *think* I said,' Arthur Wakelam corrected her. But he wasn't embarrassed, merely polite. He was certainly very at home here, backstage at the Hippodrome – seemed to be in his element. He must be in the business somehow.

On the stage, the Chairman had been announcing 'the culmination of our evening, to say the very least!' In other words, Mrs Lloyd. Dempsey must have gone off the other side. The call boy was simply staring at Marie Lloyd and pointing at the stage with right arm extended, like a human signpost. One of the prettiest elderly women I have ever seen came up to her now and started yanking her bustle about, which rather violent attention Miss Lloyd ignored. A good dozen or so of the turners were spilling out of the dressing rooms to watch her from the side.

'He makes out,' she said, indicating Arthur Wakelam, 'that you guessed one of the objects before the code was given.'

'But I'm sure I must have that wrong,' Art Wakelam said, smiling.

'Four for Draper and three for you?' Mrs Lloyd was saying, as she finally moved towards the stage. 'It should be the other way about, darling. Better still, ditch him altogether! Do you have a sister?'

'No.'

'Get one,' she said, over her naked shoulder. 'The Martian *Girls*. Two for the price of one! She mustn't be quite as pretty as you, but there's not much chance of that.'

And she was on the stage and singing, while the auditors tried to drown her out with cheers and applause. Meanwhile, Arthur Wakelam was holding out a business card. *Selwyn & Wise*, I read, *Theatrical Agents*, and below this in smaller writing, *Arthur Wakelam, associate*. The office was on Piccadilly Circus, and if that wasn't dashing enough, the telegraphic address was *BRAVISSIMO, LONDON*.

'I keep a desk in their offices, Miss French,' he said. 'Most people call me Art. Fix an appointment by telephone, or just drop by, any weekday before four.'

I ought to have thanked him, but couldn't, in the first place because he had turned aside in order to whisper to the elderly party, Mrs Lloyd's dresser; secondly because, when I looked along the line of turners watching Mrs Lloyd from the side, I perceived Draper, his collar open and his tie hanging loose. Having gone into the dressing room, he must have come out again, and he was watching me, as though I were the star, and not Miss Lloyd. But now the pretty, elderly person (who was also remarkably small) was beckoning me down to her level. She was indicating my bodice. 'The *décolleté*, dear,' she said, 'is only beautiful if the substance is there. And remember you are a young girl from Mars. You don't know our earthly ways. You are naïve.'

That was certainly the case.

*

Jean's own Friday evening had been less momentous. Having spent most of the day writing, she was rolling a cigarette and watching the river through the hole in the Monster. It looked black and ruffled, like crepe paper. The moon occupied a ragged, white hole in the cloudy night sky. As she applied the lighter to her cigarette, the email counter on her Mac moved up from 2765 (she did wish she could find the Mark as Read option) to 2766. Email 2765 had come through at 4 p.m., from Brett at Tobin's Supper Rooms, in response to her request for a meeting. He had replied that he would be away for the next few days, but he'd suggested a week on Sunday: 19 November at 6 p.m. When in London, he was always at the Rooms until six on Sunday, doing 'admin'. Jean had agreed to the arrangement, even though that would be leaving things rather late. She was sticking to the idea that a face-to-face was the only way to break the news of her cancellation, and she would be looking her best to sweeten the pill for Brett (if he was not gay, which she suspected he was).

This new email would be from the very un-gay Mr Coates. Wherever he was, he would be slightly pissed at this point on Friday evening, and so liable to get in touch. Then again, he'd managed to avoid doing so on the previous Friday. In fact, come Monday, it would be a full fortnight since she had heard from him – an unprecedented hiatus. Perhaps it really was all over between them, which would be good in a way but also bad, because she wanted another Sunday afternoon of messing about on the mattress, in that French film-like way, with the bottle of good white wine on the floorboards, and the cigarettes burning in the ashtray. She opened the inbox.

The email – oddly, given that it was 7.30 p.m. – was from the British Theatre Memorial Fund. Like all their emails it was very polite, yet unsigned. *Dear Jean,* she read, *We are delighted to be able to tell you that the work on the lift in our building is complete, and you are very welcome to come in and view archive material on any afternoon (1 p.m.–5.30 p.m.) in the coming week. Please make a booking using the link below.*

Jean immediately made bookings for Monday, Tuesday, Wednesday, Thursday and Friday, after which she felt this had been rather greedy of her; but she'd reached the point in her writing where she needed further nuggets of hard fact about Kate, Draper and Art Wakelam to steer her towards a vaguely accurate denouement. She wasn't looking for strict historical verification – that, she knew, would be impossible to come by – but she sought *human* truth: she didn't want her characters' actions to be too disparate from those they had actually performed.

She felt she was on track so far, thanks to the nuggets she had already discovered, and a mysterious sense of being externally guided in her writing. Certainly she had never written anything as quickly as her Martian Girl screed. And she had enough for at least one more instalment, before it would be necessary to refuel at the archive. She was idly looking down the list of recent emails. That morning, there'd been one from her mother, who lived (with Jean's father) in Brighton, which was about the right distance away. The gist of it was 'It would be lovely to see you.' It would be 'lovely' for her mother to see Jean about every five weeks, whether or not that was actually the case. Jean had replied immediately to the summons: it would be lovely on her side as well, but she had withheld

171

a date. She wanted to get the Tobin's business out of the way first. There was still nothing from Vincent. Pretty soon, it might be more appropriate to be worried on his behalf rather than irritated at his silence.

Jean opened the Martian Girl Word file, which kindly informed her that she'd closed it only half an hour before. She might do a bit more on it now but, given the time of day, she would need wine. She walked to the kitchenette and poured herself a glass from the chablis in the fridge. She returned to her table, took a sip, then returned to the fridge and brought the whole bottle back to the table, because who was she kidding really? As she sat down, a sudden sound made her jump – that sound of something slotting into place, for better or worse. A text. She walked over to her phone, which was in purdah beneath the cushion on the sofa. It was from Coates: *Meet Sunday, usual time?* Good, she thought, the French film is *on*. What she ought to do now was wait two hours before typing the offhand reply, *Okay, if you like.* Instead she called Coates, who amazingly enough picked up.

'I got your text. You're not going to the country then?'

'Nope.'

'It's just that I haven't heard from you for a while.' Her first remark had been redundant, and this latest one was a non sequitur . . . so the silence that greeted it was probably justified.

'Well,' Coates said after a while. 'I haven't heard from you either.'

'But you said *you'd* call *me*.'

'So that's what you were waiting for?'

'Is that so illogical?'

'It's rather literal minded.'

'Where are you?'

'At home.'

'I'm at home too. What are you doing?'

'Nothing.'

'I'm not doing anything either.'

Intermission; Coates might have been smoking.

'I hope this call isn't costing you too much,' he said, eventually.

'You needn't worry about that; I have unlimited free talk time in the evenings.'

And they both laughed, to some extent.

'I'm going to have to go,' said Coates.

'Okay. I'll see you on Sunday.'

'Yes,' he said. 'Good. I'll bring some wine.'

It was a while before Jean could get back to work. She was pleased about the call and anxious at the same time. But that, surely, had always been the Coates effect?

'Well?' asked The Dad from his chair by the fire when I got home.

'Oh, I think we were tolerably ... tolerably creditable, you know,' I said, removing my gloves and putting more coal on the fire, which The Dad would keep too low, so as to save money for spoiling me with extravagances, such as the sending of the wire that evening, for which I now thanked him. 'But you really shouldn't have bothered, Dad. Shall I put the kettle on? I could just do with a nice cup of tea. I got rather hoarse, you know, during the turn. I should take a leaf out of Mrs Lloyd's book. Marie Lloyd, you know. I was chatting to her a bit after I came off. She was sucking a sweet of some kind. I don't care for *boiled* sweets, but I might try to get something soft from the chemists. You know, those sort of heavily medicated jelly babies.'

The Dad stood up, with some difficulty, from the fireside chair, and I tried not to think of him making his painful way into the telegraph office of the station, as he must have done five hours previously. 'Kate,' he said, taking hold of my shoulders, 'kindly shut up, and tell me: you knocked them, didn't you?'

'I don't see how I can tell you if I'm to shut up,' I said, and he eyed me until I began to nod my head, probably while grinning in a somewhat inane manner. 'Perhaps we did, a little bit. It was a pretty good hand, anyhow.'

The Dad nodded sagely. 'I knew it all along,' he said, but I did not believe that was true. When worried he would not play the piano, and the lid had been down ever since I'd told him of my approaching debut. What he would do was cough, and there'd been a good deal of that lately. He kissed me on the cheek and went over to the china cabinet, where he also kept his medicinal whisky. But it was a bottle of wine that he produced – claret, as it turned out – and he also brought out two brand-new wine glasses, our previous two being somewhat cloudy and chipped. He had also laid in some shortbread biscuits, and two very fine oranges, a special combination of which we were both very fond.

'I will say this once and once only, Kate,' he said after the toast. 'Of course, I am rather biased in your favour, but I have thought, ever since I watched you dance the maypole aged six, that you had a great natural grace that deserved to be seen by thousands. You have had a long hard struggle, but I think you are achieving your true destiny.'

I frowned. Did he mean that I was a true mesmerist? A clairvoyant? The thought had occurred to me when I had seen the vision of the coin. It had never occurred to me that clairvoyance was a real thing. If it was, why might I not have the gift? But I didn't want the gift, and so had put the vision down to some sort of beginner's luck.

'The true commodity,' said The Dad, 'is not singing, dancing, or telling jokes. It's charisma, dear – *presence* – and you have it. Now, tell me about Marie Lloyd.'

Of course, he loved her almost much as he loved Dan Leno. He had seen her on many occasions in many Halls; and here was the slight strangeness of The Dad: the paradox, you might say. Marie Lloyd was a rather wild person, often in trouble for indecency, and once or twice with the income tax people. So you might have thought he would disapprove of her on moral grounds, but the only indication he gave of this was to say that I ought not to have referred to the lady as *Mrs* Lloyd: 'It's rather unwise to assume that she is married at any given time. Her husbands come and go pretty quickly.' Therefore 'Miss' was a safer bet. I mentioned her entourage, and the name of Art Wakelam slipped out. The Dad had not heard of him, but suggested he must be a 'scout' with a particular connection to the agency of Selwyn & Wise: that was quite a normal arrangement.

'Ought I to go and see him?'

'Of course you must, Kate; and you know very well that you *will*.' He eyed me, smiling. 'Really dear, you must not be so fey.'

He did like to apply that word to me. I was closing the curtains on the rattling carriages of Pancras Road, and the dark, fuming station beyond, when The Dad said, 'Draper must have been very pleased.'

I turned from the window. 'I don't know about that really.'

'Well, we know he's a rather funny man.'

'Yes,' I said, 'while not being in the least amusing.'

(He had been as good as his word about paying, however, even if he had done it in a rather offhand way: leaving the three pound notes in an envelope at the stage door.)

The Dad ought to have been standing up at this point, and redistributing the coals in the grate so they would burn slowly through the night. But he remained seated. I'd had the idea all evening that he was keeping something back. I glanced over at the hat stand, which was in the parlour, since we had no hall, and there was The Dad's rather dinty brown bowler – only it was less brown, and more black, than it should have been: the effect of rain. His mackintosh, hanging beneath, was similarly discoloured. If I hadn't been so caught up in the success of my debut, I would have noticed these clues immediately – and now everything else told the same story. Too much coal left in the scuttle. The Dad's neat-combed hair. He would always comb it when he came in from the rain, and he had done so lately.

'You went somewhere else, didn't you, Dad? Apart from the telegraph office?'

'I looked in at the Slack, love.'

'Oh,' I said.

176

The Dad made so few expeditions these days that they were all accounted for. He would announce them, and I would advise against on grounds of his health. The Slack Horse was a famous turner's pub near the Hackney Empire. It was officially the *Black* Horse, but a bit – in fact two bits – of the letter 'B' had fallen off the sign years ago. But the point was: the Slack was an hour away, when you took into account the walk to the North London Line, the wait for the train, and so on. So The Dad had gone out, contrary to my advice. I had half expected him to do that – but in order to see me at the Hippodrome, not merely for a drink. This was all wrong, but The Dad was perfectly relaxed.

'Ran into Sid Barley,' he said.

I took him to mean that he had visited the Slack with the specific *intention* of seeing Sid Barley, who practically lived there. The Dad had often told me that if the Slack Horse were ever to close, then Sid Barley's life would come to an end (or indeed *begin*). Although The Dad was very far from being a toper himself, he liked Sid because, having once worked as a 'super', or stage hand, at the Hackney Empire, he was well up on the gossip from the Halls.

'I was asking him what he made of Draper,' said The Dad.

'Oh yes?' I said, and I'm afraid rather coldly. For financial reasons I was stuck with Draper whether I or The Dad liked it or not. Therefore, I did not welcome any close examination of his character.

'Sid,' The Dad continued, 'had heard he was back working. He was pretty surprised when I said it was with you. He said he didn't know *what* to make of friend Draper. He's a solitary chap evidently, seldom spotted in the backstage bars, but he would be seen tippling on his own occasionally. Champagne – that's his drink, according to Sid.' The Dad was now looking up at me and smiling. 'I said "That's a good sign, Sidney!" and he agreed that Draper must have a few quid put by. Always drove a hard bargain with the managements. But Sid thought he'd retired, after the break-up with Brooks.'

We were coming to it now, The Dad leaning forward in his chair. 'I said, "What do you reckon about that business, Sidney? Brooks going off to Australia?" He said when he first heard, he couldn't believe it.'

'Why couldn't he, Dad?'

'Brooks was always well turned out; carried a silver-topped cane, and he'd wax his moustache whether he was performing that day or not. What struck Sid, when he first heard he'd gone to Australia, was that it would wilt. The moustache, you see, love, because of the heat.'

He was smiling again, perhaps picturing the sagging 'tache, but I am afraid it was very definitely the far-distant smile of an old man.

'But when he thought about it a bit more, love,' The Dad resumed, 'Sid could sort of see the logic. As far as he knew, Hugh Brooks and Draper had never really got on, forever bickering about money, so why wouldn't Brooks go off? The turn was pretty successful. He'd have accumulated quite a bit of cash, even if Draper was taking the lion's share, and Brooks had no family to keep him here. Not exactly a ladies' man, if you see what I mean, love? But then Sid came back to this business of Brooks always being so nicely turned out. The one time Sid had a proper chat with him, it was about suiting. Always went for the heaviest weight of cloth apparently – fourteen ounces and upwards.'

'Why?' I said.

'Two reasons. Firstly, a heavier cloth holds its shape better; secondly, he said he felt cold something shocking. "Bad circulation, it must be," he told Sid. "I'll often be shivering in the middle of summer; and I must always have a fur lining in my boots." So the way Sid looked at it, Australia, with its terrific heat, must have been quite a draw for old Brooks.'

I nodded.

'Anyway,' said The Dad, as he rose from his chair. 'Sid knows a fellow who was probably the nearest thing Brooks had to a friend on the Halls. Chap by the name of Alfie Dale. Does imitations of comedians, and sings a bit. Sid told me he'd get hold of him and quiz him about Brooks.'

'Nice of him to go to the trouble,' I said, relieved that The Dad's speech was apparently over.

'It's not really much trouble,' said The Dad, 'being as Dale's very often in the Slack.' He was coughing a little – but only a little – as he began separating the coals of the fire. The really important thing, I decided, was that The Dad mustn't worry about me.

*

That was the Friday night. On the Saturday morning, I went directly to Marylebone to buy the steam machine, which did look suspiciously like a kettle, in spite of costing eighteen shillings, and which The Dad received with amusement rather than falling on it gratefully as a life-saver. I could not persuade him to use it on either Saturday or Sunday.

At about six on *Monday* morning, I was lying half awake in bed when I heard The Dad get up and go out. He would often step into King's Cross for a breakfast tea and a bun in the dining rooms on Platform One; but this time he came back after only five minutes. I was waiting for him in the parlour. It was raining, and in spite of the shortness of the walk, he was soaked through.

'Dad,' I said, 'why didn't you take your brolly?' Rapid walking was bad for emphysema. Walking in the rain could be disastrous.

What he carried instead of a brolly was a newspaper: *Theatre & Music Hall Review*, which came out on Monday, whereas *The Era* came out on Friday. Without removing his sodden topcoat, he sat down with the paper at the table. I could hardly bear to watch as he turned, coughing badly, to the review pages. He found something, read it quickly (all the reviews were of one or two sentences only) before pushing the page towards me. I knew it must be good, because he'd stopped coughing.

Mr Joseph Draper and the Martian Girl, I read, *elegant mystifiers, made a highly successful debut on Friday. Their mind-reading and thought transmission performance is extraordinary and bewildering.*

The Dad had walked through to the scullery, to begin the breakfast. 'Of course,' I shouted after him, '*The Review*'s like *The Era* – a turners' paper! Nice to everybody!'

'It's generally not rude,' The Dad agreed from the scullery doorway, with a packet of celebratory bacon in his hand, 'but some of the compliments are pretty backhanded. You'd soon complain if you were put down as "solid in support", or "not unimpressive".' He eyed me shrewdly for a while. 'I can see you're pleased,' he said, 'so don't bother denying it.'

Much is heard of feminine intuition, but The Dad had a good deal of the masculine variety. Soon enough (I was reading the review over and over) I heard the sizzling of the bacon. Persuading The Dad to take a proper bronchitic's breakfast of porridge and cocoa was quite hopeless even though I had laid in plentiful supplies of both.

*

When, two hours later, I turned up at Providence Road for the resumption of my training, I expected Draper to confront me on the subject about which he had surely *meant* to confront me until Marie Lloyd had intervened, namely my pre-emption of the codes in the case of the coin. But his manner was somewhat changed, and he was rather watchful, as the maid showed me into the parlour. Draper was sitting at the table, and he had the *Theatre & Music Hall Review* open before him. 'A red letter day, Miss French,' he said, indicating the review. 'I'm not sure I want to be "extraordinary", but it'll do to be going on with. Sit down, please.'

'I'm sure we can become ordinary with practice,' I said, and he gave in reply a thin smile that complemented the thin wire of his glasses. He also held my gaze for slightly longer than usual, seeming to imply a question, but since it *was* only implied, I could not answer it. There were a number of letters and a couple of telegrams on the table besides the paper, and when the tea came (it was a little hotter and stronger than usual, as was the fire in the grate) we broke off from the lesson – which had been somewhat more politely conducted than those hitherto – and he said, 'We have received a number of offers, Miss French. I assume you would be agreeable to some fill-ins starting next week, and there is the possibility of a week on the south coast.'

'Oh, where?'

'Various places – on a tour.'

'But that'll be lovely. Won't it?'

'Unfortunately, no. It's for the second week of December, and the Halls will be half empty.'

'Why?'

'People are saving up for Christmas presents and panto-mime tickets. Even so, I think I can get us forty pounds.'

'But that's a fortune.'

'Fifteen of which will be for you. There will be a good deal of paperwork on my side.'

'Well,' I said slowly, trying to think as I spoke, 'that's quite all right. The Dad ... my dad, I mean, was on four pounds a week in his last year in employment. And he was years working up to that.'

'Just so,' said Draper. He then showed me one of the letters. It was addressed from White's Club in St James's. The writer was offering five guineas for the chance to prove our act a sham. Draper informed me that he would not be deigning to reply. 'By the way,' he said, 'what did your father work as?'

'He was in the police for a while,' I said.

Which Draper might not have heard, for he was reaching

for his watch. 'Today,' he said, 'I mean to time all of your responses.' No mention was made of Marie Lloyd or Art Wakelam, and certainly none of my predecessor, Hugh Brooks. One way or another, I had made a new impression on Draper.

*

For Draper and I, the dates began to flow, our book began to fill, and we were performing most nights as 'fill-ins'. Very soon, I had accumulated twenty pounds, of which I gave fifteen to The Dad, who put it under the lid of the piano stool, which he thought a secure place, because the piano stool did not appear to *have* a lid. I encouraged The Dad to spend the money on whatever he wanted, but he seemed reluctant to do so, aside from taking a couple of rather mysterious journeys by cab.

Draper furnished me (at retail price) with a *New Railway Map of London and Suburbs Showing Each Company's Line in a Separate Character* – but not so separate as to make one readily distinguishable from another. After long and close study of the map, the lines I needed did emerge from the black tangle. The one I principally used was the North London. I would catch its trains – which seemed, like McVitie's Biscuits, to originate in Willesden Junction – at Camden Town station, a little way north of King's Cross. They would then dawdle through Islington in a slow and dispiriting sort of way, invariably on viaducts and under heavy rain. I would sit alone in the dusty compartments, or almost alone, breathing in the smoke, or just the smell, of some strange man siting opposite, for there were neither non-smoking compartments nor non-smoking *men* on this train. They would slump in their heavy, wet coats and smoulder like so many damp bonfires.

The North London took me to the Silvertown Empire, where we performed three times in that month. This Empire attempted to cheer up the poor people of Silvertown, in which a remarkably high number of offensive trades were concentrated, it being sufficiently far east of the places where the rich people lived. My *Gazetteer* spoke of 'important chemical manufactories', but what I saw from the train were massive blank-faced buildings, whose chimneys put a kind of greenish fog into the night sky and (as one discovered immediately on stepping down from the train) an acrid smell of something burning that was not meant to be burnt.

We had good audiences at Silvertown (two thousand in the gallery alone) and appreciative, possibly because the beer was amazingly cheap, or the people were just so grateful for any light relief, poor things. The North London was also the line for Poplar and the Queen's Theatre, where we played twice, billed as Draper & French: Transmitter and Receiver, with 'Martian Girl' left out of account. If you stopped going east at Dalston Junction, and changed and went south instead, you ended up in Shoreditch and its Queen's Theatre, where we played four times.

The other important railway was the one coming out of Fenchurch Street, the London, Tilbury & Southend, which I would get to by taking the Metropolitan from King's Cross to Aldgate, then walking for five minutes. This was the line for Whitechapel and the Pavilion Theatre, where there were flambeaux – that is, burning torches along the front of the gallery – even though the Pavilion had burned down four times. In Whitechapel also was the Wonderland theatre, where I shared a dressing room with Mademoiselle Lativa, the snake manipulator, and her snakes, which she kept in a sort of laundry basket. We played the Pavilion and the Wonderland four times each.

The London, Tilbury & Southend is a somewhat brighter line than the North London, with more people and more advertisements, especially for Fisher's Kwikchange Suitcase, 'extremely strong and extremely light', and a tonic called Zoto's which 'Absolutely Prevents Seasickness'. There was no mystery about either of those, since this was the line for Tilbury Docks, where the ships to Australia sail from. And so my predecessor, Hugh Brooks, would presumably have gone to Tilbury, thence in the general direction of Gibraltar, then through the Suez Canal, and ... my geography wasn't up to what happened next.

Three weeks to the day after our debut, we received a review in *The Era*. *The Martian and Draper*, it began (it seemed beyond anyone to get the name of the turn right) *are developing an extremely interesting line in mentalism. The lady, a most attractive performer, seems to alternate between nervous hesitancy and quite phenomenal speed as she divines the identity of the objects produced by the audience. If there is less here of the slickness normally associated with the telepathic art, there is a great deal more than the standard allowance of mystery.*

The show in question had been given at the Whitechapel Pavilion, during which I had, as at Rotherhithe, pre-empted Draper's giving of the code, identifying a muffler and giving its colour, an out-of-the-way shade of pale lilac. As with the year on the coin presented at Rotherhithe, I had *seen* the thing: seen the muffler, I mean, snaking along in the darkness of the blindfold. As at Rotherhithe, I had detected a shocked hesitation in Draper's patter, but he had not mentioned the incident afterwards, just as he had not at Rotherhithe.

On the evening of the Friday on which that write-up appeared, we were booked at the Queen's, Poplar. Before the first house, Draper said he wanted 'a quick word, if you don't mind, Miss French' and he took me into the crush bar of that theatre. At half after five, it was far from crushed, but populated by half a dozen early arrivals for the early doors, and smelling strongly of carbolic. As we sat down, I was braced again for recrimination concerning my 'guesses' at Rotherhithe and Whitechapel, but a number of surprises were in store. Firstly, and before any waiter appeared, one of the half dozen drinkers came up to us: a young fellow with a rather experimental moustache. 'Are you French and Draper, the mind readers?' he enquired. I was about to affirm the surmise and to thank him (although strictly speaking, he hadn't yet said anything to be thankful for), when Draper gruffly said, 'Alleged.'

'I'm sorry?' said the young man.

'Alleged, pretended. Miss French and I are *pretended* mind readers.'

'It's not genuine telepathy?'

'It is a talent,' said Draper, 'that anybody may be able to develop over time, even you yourself quite possibly.'

The young man was plainly disappointed. As he retreated, I said, 'Rather a shame to demystify matters in that way, wouldn't you say, Mr Draper?'

He flashed one of his smiles, which made up in rarity value what it lacked in naturalness. 'I think perhaps we are at the stage in our professional relations at which first names become appropriate, Kate. Now what will you have to drink?' I had assumed we would not be drinking – that he had selected the crush bar for our talk merely because it had tables and chairs. 'I think perhaps a little champagne,' he said, and when the waiter came over, he specified, 'A bottle of the Pol Roger.'

'A bottle!' I exclaimed, and my reward for looking a gift horse in the mouth was that Draper said, 'Very well then, half a bottle.'

It arrived, rather buried in a bucket of ice. As the waiter popped the cork, Draper appeared to be watching my reaction.

'Glass of fizzle!' he said, which was almost a joke, almost humour.

'Indeed,' I said, foolishly.

'A toast?' he suggested, and I nodded, rather dazed.

'To Draper and French,' he said, adding, after we'd taken our first sips, 'for whom the future is beginning to look slightly more promising than I had dared hope.'

'Do you really think so . . . Joseph?'

'The book is filling up, Kate. I received by this morning's post several new offers, and I propose to raise our lowest.'

'Er . . . what?' I said, ever so graceful.

'I am required to wire our lowest offer. I propose going up to fifteen pounds per night.'

'Seconded!' I said.

'I trust that nine-six is an acceptable split?'

'At six pounds a night, I am on velvet!' I said. But even as

187

I spoke, I thought of Arthur Wakelam, and an image came before me of that gentleman sadly shaking his head while pronouncing me a very poor *négociator*.

'We have also had some private offers,' said Draper, producing from his pocket book a very beautiful little missive. It was written on a white card lined with black, at the top of which was a small black crown. I remarked on this.

'I believe it is a coronet,' said Draper.

'But still!' I said.

The address, written below in an elegant (but somewhat illegible) hand, was number 11 Rue something followed unmistakably by the exciting word 'Paris'. Lady Somebody presented her compliments to Mr Draper and would be glad to know at his earliest convenience if he would be likely to be in Paris in the near future. In any case, she would be very much obliged to Mr Draper if he would let her know whether he and Miss French would be willing to give a . . . something beginning with 's' . . . in a private house in Paris before a most distinguished company of friends. Could he kindly let her know *when* he could do so and what his terms would be? Lady Something would be grateful for the earliest possible answer.

'But that's absolutely wonderful!' I said.

Draper did not appear to think so. 'Lady Sinclair is in mourning,' he said, 'as signified by the black border. Her son died recently in a sailing accident off the Riviera. It was in all the papers.'

'But that's absolutely terrible!' I said.

'I will be declining her offer.'

I sipped some champagne while revolving the matter. 'But might not our performance cheer her up a bit?'

'She requires that we conduct a séance.'

'Ah. I see.'

And he looked at me. 'I hope you do, Kate. She, like that young man of a moment ago, thinks we are genuine. She thinks that you in particular, Kate, are genuine. And we have another.' He fished again in his pocket book. Here was a more ordinary piece of stationery, but the writing was very fine, perhaps rather too fine, appearing to have been produced by a needle dipped in violet ink. I read the address: *The London County Asylum, Hanwell*. With trepidation, I read on: *First, please allow me to congratulate you on the eminence you have achieved by your remarkable stage presentations. Although I have not myself attended one of your performances, I have seen them highly praised in print . . .*

'This person is very kind about our act,' I said, looking up.

'He is a lunatic,' said Draper.

I had been rather hoping he was one of the doctors, but evidence of a disordered mind was soon disclosed as I read on:

and I am convinced that you practise genuine telepathy for the legitimate purposes of entertainment. It is not always so used, however. Of course it is well known that hearing voices is a sign of insanity, but this condition, when found in some unfortunate individual, is but the malicious infliction of the science of telepathy by the doctors and nurses who practise it in order to recruit for the asylums and so achieve for themselves a permanent means of subsistence.

189

The poor man appeared to believe that the doctors and nurses – *acting out of sight, in a different part of the asylum* – were inflicting voices and visions upon him by means of a 'phreno-magnetic' influence.

I handed the letter back to Draper. The plaster statues adorning the front of the bar suddenly looked rather unhygienic and tawdry; the red carpet, I now saw, was dotted with cigar ash, and one of the sash windows had suddenly become rotten. We turners were surely the most trivial people in the world. A cue missed by the band, a forgotten line, a poor hand at the end of a turn . . . we counted all these gigantic misfortunes; we had no understanding of true misery.

'I must write back to this poor man,' I said, but Draper shook his head.

'It would be dangerous to initiate a correspondence, Kate. We would soon be receiving letters from all his . . . fellows. Any mesmerist is likely to be taken for a psychic, or medium, or whatever the term is. Would you care to see the proof of that?'

'You've just shown me the proof, Joseph.'

'Further proof, I mean.' He passed over another letter – an educated hand, but very hard to make out. 'This comes from a member of the Psychical Research Society in Kensington. They ask whether we would be willing to give a demonstration under laboratory conditions.'

'And would we?'

'Of course not.'

Silence for a space. Draper topped up our glasses, then sat back, looking at me for a while. The smile came. 'In our very first performance, Kate,' he said, 'you supplied the date on a coin before I had given the code. You did something similar at Whitechapel with a muffler.'

Well of course, he'd been leading up to this all along.

'You were no doubt encouraged to make your first leap in the dark by the fact that any coin will be eighteen-something, and quite likely eighteen eighty-something, given that relatively new coins are commoner than relatively old ones. And you were perhaps a little over-excited, it being your first performance?'

I decided to treat the question as rhetorical.

'And then the muffler ... ' Draper continued. 'It was a chilly evening. You'd heard me speaking to the auditor; you knew she was a woman, and only a woman would have a lilac muffler.'

'*Pale* lilac,' I reminded him.

He nodded. 'All lilacs are pale, are they not? I supposed you had glimpsed it in the audience, when we walked on.'

I kept silence. Perhaps he was right?

'Kate,' he said, leaning forwards, 'I confess myself mys-tified as to—'

'As to how I guessed correctly, you mean?'

'As to how you dared push your luck so far – to speak plainly.'

He required an answer; it was only fair to give him one, insofar as I was able.

'I don't really understand it any more than you do,' I said. 'In both cases the answer appeared before my eyes as a sort of little picture.'

'And where did the picture come from? Perhaps you will contend that you are actually reading my mind?'

'Certainly not,' I replied, indignantly. 'You are by-passed entirely. The pictures were put before me, I think, by the auditors.' It's a strange turn of events, I thought: one supposed mind reader assuring another that she could not read his mind.

He frowned. 'But how can you know that, Kate?'

I wanted to say that the images had been propelled to me by a certain generosity of spirit, a quality lacking in Draper. 'It's a mystery,' I said.

'Now please don't start talking about the collective unconscious, or telepathy, or some such thing,' Draper said, sitting back and looking at me again, perhaps almost with kindness, like a doctor with a patient.

'I believe it's called the para-normal,' I said.

'Yes, by people who are ab-normal.'

He seemed quite pleased with that. It struck me that he was happier than I had seen him, perhaps because of all the offers we were getting – albeit from these abnormal people – or perhaps because we had finally broached the matter of 'visions'.

'I do not know how the images appear,' I said, 'but that is not really the question.'

'And what *is* the question?'

'*Why* they appear.'

'You think there might be some important reason?'

I realised the discussion was heading into dangerous territory, so I shook my head, as though disowning, in a very blockheaded manner, my preceding remarks.

The crush bar was filling up. We would have to go backstage very soon.

'Kate,' Draper said, 'we have made quite a hit in our four

weeks, but there is something I would like you to understand, and I hope you will agree that I speak with the voice of experience.'

I agreed.

'Any suspicion, accidentally conveyed, of genuineness in the act is bound to prove fatal. Do you see why, Kate?'

'Not completely, Joseph. Of course, we mustn't encourage the poor people in the asylums, but ... '

'It won't *play*. People want to see the *trick*; to try to understand it, see how it's done. There are many credulous people quite happy to believe there is genuine mentalism on any given music hall bill, and once the thought is formed, they write off that turn, dismiss it out of hand, because there is nothing to guess at. We mustn't have them thinking you really are from Mars. People will become quite bored of the act, do you see?'

'You mean they'll write me off as just another – what's it called? – extra-terrestrial?'

'Once they think the secret is beyond them, they'll stop paying attention to the act.'

'It's paradoxical,' I said.

'It is, Kate! Of course, it won't stop them asking you if there really *are* green oceans and lakes in your homeland!'

'And electric ships sailing on them!' I said.

'Then we are agreed, Kate?' he said. 'No more wild guesses?'

'We are agreed, yes.'

And Joseph smiled his best smile yet.

*

Jean and Coates had concluded a fairly satisfactory tussle (she thought) on the mattress on the floor. After the hiatus of the past three weeks, normality had apparently been restored, with the American Spirits and bottle of wine on the floor beside them, rain and wind in the darkness beyond the window. But things weren't quite the same. Coates seemed tired – not his usual sardonic self – and when he asked, 'How's the mind-reading show coming on?' the question seemed dutifully polite.

Jean thought it was time to put him straight on this, so she said, 'I don't think I'm going to go ahead with the one-woman show. It doesn't work.'

Coates frowned, while sipping wine. Then he looked up, smiling – a new, rather silly smile. 'Why not?'

'Because it needs two people.'

'I suppose so, yes. The mind reader and the person whose mind was read. Like you and me.'

'What?'

'That's just a for-instance. But you're dropping it?'

She nodded. 'I'll go to Tobin's and cancel the booking. I think I ought to do it in person, wouldn't you say?'

'Yes, if you can get your money back.'

'That's partly the idea. I'm hoping the chap there . . . Brett, he's called—'

'Yes, he would be called Brett.'

'I'm hoping he'll be susceptible to charm. I've made an appointment to see him at six o'clock on Sunday, so we would have to finish early. That's if you were coming here, I mean?'

No answer from Coates, but the peculiar smile remained.

'Of course, it's your money, so if I *can* get it back, I'll give it straight to you, and even if I don't get it, I'll—'

'I don't want the money,' said Coates.

'That's very sweet of you,' she said, climbing on top of him, 'but quite irrelevant.'

They started messing about again. When this second tussle was well under way, Jean happened to say, 'I'm going to do it as a novel instead. Do you want to read it?' Coates made no reply, and Jean suddenly found that she was working on him rather like a paramedic trying to revive a corpse. 'What's wrong?'

'Give it me then,' he said, after a while.

'It's not printed out. You'd have to read it on the screen.'

Already regretting her offer, she went over to her table and brought the laptop back to the mattress. She logged into the Martian Girl file and handed the machine over.

'Of course, you'll have to skim,' she said.

But he began *reading* – and not even lighting a cigarette or drinking wine. After a while, he put on his boxer shorts and shirt, and took the laptop over to the table, where he continued reading.

'Do you want to finish the wine?' she said, lifting the bottle from the floor.

No reply, so she poured herself some. 'Are you sure you're not just reading all my emails?' she asked, in a hollow-sounding voice.

No reply.

Jean downed the wine. Needing something else to do, she picked up her phone and began texting Rasta Donald at The Space, asking whether she could come in and buy him a drink. She wanted to explain something to him. What she wanted to explain was that she would not be going ahead with the show, and was sorry to have wasted his time, but she didn't say that. Then she heard Coates say, 'Wait.'

'*What?*' said Jean. He was still sitting on the chair by the table, and looking down at his knees. Jean found that she was breathing fast. She must get this man out of her room. Meanwhile, she tried to say something normal. 'I'm sorry?'

Coates was now studying the dark sky through the window. He said, 'He's going to kill her, obviously.'

'Draper's going to kill Kate? Are you all right, by the way? He's not *necessarily* going to kill her.'

'What does that mean?' Coates said, addressing his reflection in the window.

'Well, even though this is a work of imagination—'

'Is it?' Coates said to the window.

Jean stood, began dressing. 'Why don't we drop the subject? You obviously didn't think much of it.'

He still hadn't really moved. 'You've got this private investigator – this detective – at King's Cross,' he said.

'*What* detective?' Jean said. (He must mean old man French, she thought, but he'd been a policeman, not a detective.)

'*You* know,' asked Coates.

It seemed she was in the dock. 'I was about to say,' she said, talking too fast, 'that this is a work of imagination, but I'm being guided – prompted – by what I find out in the way of historical facts, snippets of mentions in the theatrical press mainly, and that's sort of ongoing. I've got this archive that might tell me more about what really happened, but meanwhile, in another archive, about the school she went to, I found out that Kate's father had been a policeman for a while, and they lived at King's Cross.'

Then she remembered about Holmfirth & Watford. Was Holmfirth – the comedy detective impersonated by Anderton – the one he was referring to?

Coates was saying, 'He's going to kill her because he thinks she can read his mind, and he killed someone else.'

Jean did not respond, and was proud of herself for not doing so. She watched Coates in profile as his lips formed about three silent words. At last, he turned and looked at her, and she realised she didn't know him. Something was going to happen, and then it did: a terrible clanging . . . which resolved itself into Jean's phone ringing by the bed. The caller was Rasta Donald. He'd got the message that she wanted a chat, and he was both available and on her side of the river, for once.

'Yes,' she said, 'come over now if you like. That's great, see you in a minute.'

Coates was getting dressed, and Jean's words came out unnaturally. 'That's the guy from The Space. He's in the area, and he's coming over. Sorry, but you seem to be going anyway.'

'Yes,' he said, still not looking at her.

'Bye, then.'

'Bye,' he said, and he turned and opened the door.

'Where are you going?' she said. He said something else – again, no more than about three words, but she couldn't make them out because of the noise made by his closing of the door. He knows it's good, Jean thought, and he's jealous. He's going down in the world and I'm on the way up, so he can no longer be paternalistic and patronising.

But his pride ought to have stopped him behaving like that, so she was wary of her own conclusion.

Coates was out in the street with the main door of the block closing behind him.

The Head of Chambers was protesting: 'What are you coming out for, you dope? Get back in there and do what you've got to do.'

'She's expecting company,' said Coates.

'Fuck that, it's a bluff.'

'I thought it was going to be all right,' said Coates, crossing the road. 'I thought she'd dropped the whole thing.'

'She ain't going to *drop* it, boy.'

Coates was walking directly towards the power station. At the last minute before hitting it, he turned so that he was walking along the side of it. The walls towered twenty feet above him; then came another twenty feet of grey windows followed by more bricks. Coates felt very small in comparison with the building, and the wind was hitting him hard. Amid its blustering, he heard, 'I don't know what the fuck you're playing at, but you're not leaving this street. You've no secrets left, boy. It was all there in black and white. The voices in the head (which is a right bloody cheek), the shamus at King's Cross with nearly the same name ... Draper's you, isn't he? The clue's in the fucking name: people are draped in coats. And she knows what you did with the Yob, *and* where you put him. You were meant to be shitting yourself every time you saw the word "river". *And* they'll bring Parrish into it, you can bet. It's a forty-year touch, if you've got forty years in you. But you know all this; I don't know why I'm having to tell you.'

As Coates walked, fighting the rain and the wind, the

words 'But how can she know?' came out, followed by the answer: 'They've had you tailed, boy – surveillance. The women in your life are getting together to fuck you up, so here's the plan: you do her back there, then you do the other two. And then it's off to King's Cross to do the bloody shamus. Clean sweep, boy, sweep *clean*.'

'I'm not doing Lucy,' said Coates, who found that he was walking in the middle of the road.

'Fair enough,' the Head was saying. 'The kid's an innocent party, she'll be better off without the fucking mother anyway.'

'And why the shamus?'

'Why the shamus? I despair of you sometimes, boy. You've got to take out every fucker who knows what you've done.'

'Yes, but . . .'

In the middle of Lots Road, Coates was trying to get things straight for himself, while thinking and possibly talking. His wife had put a detective on him. Somehow Jean had got to know about that. The two of them might have talked about him; compared notes, in the interests of staying safe in the presence of this nutcase . . . or maybe Jean had employed the detective? But no, because she didn't have the money. It was always the wife, not the mistress, who put the tail on the husband. That was traditional. And he knew *something* had been going on with his wife. The marriage was clearly over, it was just that no one had so far mentioned it. But why was Jean telling him – through the medium of her silly little story – that she knew all this?

A car went rapidly past Coates tooting its horn, as the Head gave the reply: 'No point her knowing everything unless she *tells* you she knows.'

'But what does she want to get out of it?'

'Something. Power. But she's not going to get it, because you've got the power, boy. Only thing is, you don't have much time.'

It was Sunday; the end of the week, the end of the world. And the end of the road. There was a pub there: the one he'd met Jean in. He walked too rapidly up to a blackboard mounted beside the door. *Pick of the day,* he read. *Red onion and goat's cheese bruschetta.*

'Would you mind telling me what the fuck's going on?' enquired the Head.

'You've got to clear off now,' said Coates, as he entered the pub. 'Bruschetta and red wine,' he said to the barmaid. No, that was wrong. But the girl was smiling, so maybe not too wide of the mark. He clarified the order, found a table near the window. He tried to think about the way he was seeing things, but it was only possible to say *what* he was seeing. Through the enormous window of the pub he saw the dark sky over the river, and a new triangular tower with lights on the top. Those lights would come on every night until the tower met the same fate as the old power station: hollowed out or destroyed. Most likely destroyed, because as architecture it was shit. One night would be a last night for that tower, but not for a long time. It was different in his own case, and he must make the most of the nights remaining, because the nights were obviously more important than the days for someone like him. Things could happen in the nights. For example, the woman who'd been staring at him since he came in. Yes; return the compliment. She was a small person, bouncy; tight jeans, white trainers and fluffy blonde hair. Cheerleader type, flicking her hair around a lot. That was

200

always a sign. She was with some other people who obviously didn't matter to her, and certainly not to him.

He took out his phone as she smiled at him. He called the flat and left a message for his wife to say he was sorry and he'd be home late, and he hoped she'd had a good time in the country. In the circumstances, it was *extremely* polite. He sent his love to Lucy and only to Lucy. The Head had been quiet since he'd come in here, but it was necessary to square things with him. Not wanting to look like a total madman with the cheerleader eyeing him, he pretended to make another call. The Head came on straight away. 'Am I right, boy one? Do we have a deal?'

'You're dead right,' he said. 'Because I don't want to be banged up for life.'

'*Really?* Because the way you've been carrying on—'

'And I have the right. Nothing I've done – nothing – has been my own fault. If people had left me alone, I'd have left them alone.'

'You definitely would have, boy one.'

'I quite like the look of this piece on the opposite table,' said Coates. 'So I'm going to go now.'

'Right you are, boy. Better than perving about with those red light girls. I'll check in again tomorrow ... which is going to be the day of action, right?' Coates closed his eyes, because his glass of wine was behaving strangely.

'Tomorrow,' the Head repeated, 'which is going to be the day of action, right?'

'I don't know,' said Coates. 'I'm thinking next Sunday for Jean. She's off to that theatre. Tobin's. It's in the middle of nowhere, so good opportunity.'

'I don't know that you've got a week, boy.'

Some loud music came on, and Coates knew the Head had gone for the time being. His food arrived, and he had some more wine. The Cheerleader was into the music, nodding to the beat, and often looking over at Coates. He found a spare newspaper on the bar and began to read. The pub was on the corner of Lots Road and another road, and he would see taxis with illuminated signs passing the windows in one wall, then the windows of the other as they turned the corner. These taxis were marking the time, like a second hand sweeping round, and eventually the bell went for last orders. The Cheerleader was coming up to him.

'*You're* weird,' she said. She was zipping up her coat.

'You don't know the half of it,' said Coates.

'Well, I'm off,' she said, when the zipping was complete.

'That's a shame,' he said. 'Do you want a last drink?'

'All right,' she said, and she unzipped her coat.

As they were finishing the wine, the pub was almost empty. 'Do you know anywhere to go dancing?' she said.

'The honest answer to that is no,' said Coates, who wouldn't have known a place to go dancing even if it hadn't been nearly midnight on a Sunday.

'I do,' she said, and they went out and stopped one of the taxis. She told the driver an address in south London. 'That's my place,' she said, turning to Coates. 'I lied about the dancing.'

'Good,' he said, smiling, but he was smiling to himself in the rain outside the pub because none of that last part had really occurred. It was the kind of end to an evening that had been possible once, but no longer. The cheerleader had left the pub an hour before, and she'd obviously been pretty freaked out by him, kind of clinging to the no-mark male by her side. Which was fair enough really, in the circumstances.

––––––––

Camilla was heading towards her second meeting with Anderson. King's Cross McDonald's again; Tuesday again; but this time, instead of snow, a dirty wind was charging about the forecourt of King's Cross. She had tried to deflect Anderson from McDonald's, suggesting his office instead, but he hadn't been keen.

'I thought you might like a coffee,' he'd said, in his flat-toned voice.

'Don't you have a coffee machine in your office?' Camilla had asked.

'No.'

There was no use trying to elevate proceedings. Looking at the McDonald's signage (*We can bring the food to your table*; Toilets for Customer Use Only), she realised it set the right tone for what was bound to be in store. Anderson was already present at the table they'd used before. There was no interesting dog this time, and Anderson himself looked less interesting. He was still pretty, but in a weak way, and the wind had made him look balder. He was really just a boy with thinning hair; and he seemed worryingly suited to McDonald's. Between him and this place there existed a ... co-morbidity, which was Camilla's new least-favourite word. When bad met worse, you had co-morbidity.

Anderson had on the table before him a coffee, a mobile phone and a white A4 envelope.

'What's in the envelope?' she said.

'My report on the surveillance. They're best not sent electronically. Do you want a coffee?'

'No. I mean, no thanks. How did it go then?'

'Mrs Coates, your husband has a girlfriend.'

'A mistress, yes. I thought so.'

'... Unless a young woman called Jean Beckett is a friend of the family?'

A rhetorical question, but the name seemed to snag. 'As a matter of fact, I think I do know of her. If it's the same one, she's a freelance journalist. She once pitched a feature idea to me. I'm glad I rejected it.'

'Your husband—'

'... It was about women in pubs: whether they should go into them on their own, and how they should behave. I rejected it because the author was bound to come over as slatternly whether she really was or not. I looked her up online and found a picture. She's attractive in a slightly alternative way; and I realised I'd seen her before, and it *was* in a pub. She'd been playing the records – DJing – and my husband had gone up to her. They'd talked, and I wondered at the time if anything was being arranged.'

'He spent three hours at her flat on Sunday.'

'Where is the flat?'

'Lots Road, Fulham.'

'That's where the pub was.'

'The door number's in the report.'

'In case I want to go round and kill her, you mean?'

'Two days before that,' said Anderson, 'on the Friday—'

'Yes, I do know that Friday is two days before Sunday.'

'I know this is difficult for you . . .'

'Not in the least; it's just that I actually like taciturnity, which I thought was a trademark of yours.'

Anderson eyed her. She would not apologise. She did not like him, and she was starting to think he was a bit thick. He had come to her, after all, from Lee Christian.

'On the Friday, your husband visited a prostitute.'

'Where?'

'In Soho.'

'How very unoriginal. The address is in the report, no doubt.'

'Yes. He didn't spend very long there.'

'Is that meant to be consoling?' Anderson did not have the maturity – the worldliness – to broach these facts in the right way. Really, she ought to turn the whole saga over to Sally for one of her lurid my-husband-is-a-swinger sagas; and this thought prompted a question. 'Do you know what kind of prostitute this was?'

'They offer a variety of services at that address, I think.'

'All-rounders, eh?'

'I have pictures if you want to see them?'

'Why not?'

So he moved his phone towards her, and there was her husband, ringing a doorbell. But the scene was presumably Fulham, not Soho. Anderson withdrew the phone.

'Some of these are printed out in there,' he said, nodding towards the envelope.

'You don't actually have one that shows him with the girl?'

'Which girl?'

'Jean Beckett.'

Obviously thinking her a glutton for punishment, Anderson slid the phone back towards her. He whisked through the photographs of her husband ringing the doorbell, and then came one of the door being opened by a woman.

'I don't think the entry system was working properly,' said Anderson. 'So she had to come down and let him in.'

In the next one they were kissing on the doorstep – a greeting kiss. The woman appeared to wear pyjamas, but when Camilla looked harder, they were T-shirt and leggings. So here was proof of the affair and, incidentally, proof of the indestructible good looks of her husband. Naturally there was something haggard and tragic about him. Those looks might have been parlayed into any career: politics, broadcasting . . . in addition to reaching the top in the law. Instead they had earned him this tryst on a dark rainy afternoon in Fulham: the place that was not Chelsea. Camilla looked again at Jean Beckett. She was quite pretty but quite big; didn't know what to do with her hair. Something of the unmade bed about her: a sexy but kind-looking person, you would have to say, if you weren't Camilla.

'Afterwards,' said Anderson, 'he went to the pub at the end of the road.'

'On his own?'

Anderson nodded, and that was the saddest thing of all, Jean thought.

'He looked a bit dazed. He was walking along the middle of the road.'

'Drunk?'

'I think so.'

'He didn't come home until about three that night.'

'*Was* he drunk?'

'Probably. I was in the spare room.'

'Where is he now?'

'Not sure. He was still asleep when I left for work yesterday. At lunchtime – lunchtime yesterday – he texted me to say he was staying with a friend for a few days. Someone who was going through marital troubles and needed a bit of moral support. I wonder where he got that idea.'

'A lie, presumably.'

'There's no presumably about it.'

She asked to see the Soho shots as well, and there was her husband, standing in front of a newsagent's she vaguely recognised, and which looked garish on a dark day. She could well believe there were red light premises above it. As for Coates, he seemed to be surveying the building – valuing it, like an estate agent. Anderson was flicking through the images.

'Wait a minute,' said Jean. 'Can I see those last ones again?'

In these, her husband was different. He looked angry, and appeared to be staring directly at the picture-taker.

'This was when he came out,' said Anderson.

'Where were you when you took these?'

'Me? Across the road, and slightly round the corner.'

Thinking this a very undignified place to be, Camilla asked, 'Are you sure he didn't see you?'

Anderson shrugged. 'Doesn't really matter if he did.'

'It might if he sees you again.'

Anderson pocketed his phone in a complacent manner. He seemed to have a special place for it in his wind-proof coat.

'I was going to ask,' he said, '. . . what do you want to do?'

'I'm going to divorce him.'

'About the surveillance, I mean.'

But Camilla was thinking about the marriage that was ending, as though viewing photographs taken by some other detective who'd been following them on a longer-term basis: Coates and herself dancing at the Magdalen College ball to Orchestral Manoeuvres in the Dark, both with incredibly bouncy hair. It was 1998. They'd had an off-on arrangement throughout the three years, but when she'd left the university, she'd left with him. It was like the end of the party: collect your Coates. And he was a considerable prize to come away with, making up (almost) for the just-missed First of her finals. He was a bit of rough really – scholarship boy from some unmemorable place in south London – but with the looks of an Old Etonian thoroughbred. Together, they had bravely exchanged the mellow cosiness of Oxford for a bleak, roaring road in Camberwell, where they'd had their first flat. Some images from that time would have been of at least passing interest to the Drugs Squad. Later, the fulcrum of enjoyment had moved to an earlier point in the evenings: the two of them putting Lucy to bed in their new flat, where something of the lambency of Oxford was regained, with the garden square, the lit fire in Lucy's bedroom as Coates read her a story still in his barrister's subfusc, with his 'story juice' (glass of wine) on the bedside table, while Camilla rounded up the toys – which was really just a pretext to listen. The stories were always slightly in advance of Lucy's comprehension, but that didn't mean Lucy didn't enjoy them, and Coates wasn't always pushing her. Sometimes he did the opposite, indulging her most primitive whims. He would let her jump up and down on her bed as if it were a trampoline, and he had, at Lucy's request, filmed her doing it on his phone, so Lucy could watch it back in slow motion. The bed had broken, which was why all *that* came out, and Camilla had shouted at them both. Later on though, Coates had bought a hundred-pound bottle of wine to apologise, and cooked the one thing he could cook, a meal testifying to his extreme raciness: steak, done almost rare in brandy with fried potatoes. Later, they'd both watched the film of Lucy jumping. 'Hasn't she got lovely hair?' Camilla had observed, watching the slow looping of her ponytail. 'Every day's a great hair day for Lucy,' Coates had said, with a great satisfaction that was not entirely self-satisfaction. Camilla was amazed to find that she might be about to cry.

Anderson was watching her. 'Nobody likes what they see when they lift up a stone,' he said.

An agricultural metaphor, possibly; a rural one, anyhow. As a shepherd, he would often be lifting up stones – out of pure boredom, possibly. She definitely hated him now. If he was any good, either as a detective or a part-time farmer (she would not henceforth romanticise him as a shepherd), he wouldn't need two jobs.

'There's something else,' said Anderson.

'I see,' she said. She knew what was coming: the fulfilment of this McDonald's horror.

'I do some work for solicitors,' said Anderson. 'They put work out to PIs – evidence gathering. A couple of solicitors I work for are based in the Temple. Obviously, it's mainly briefs who work there – barristers – but there are some solicitors as well. I've got a mate who does a lot for them, and for other solicitors *near* the Temple.'

'What's he called?' Camilla asked, which was just a delaying tactic. She didn't want to know.

'He's called Martin.'

She hated the sound of this person.

'A year ago,' said Anderson, 'he was asked to look into the circumstances of an assault that occurred in the Temple, or just outside it . . .'

Camilla thought back over all those news articles from a year ago, each one at the same time too long (telling her everything that confirmed her suspicions) and too short, not giving her enough information. 'Unknown assailant . . . a probe has been launched . . . life-changing injuries . . .'

'A solicitor called Parrish was nearly killed in a lane coming off the Embankment,' said Anderson. 'Martin reckons your husband did it.'

'You realise that's slander?'

'It's not slander if it's true.'

Was it really true that Coates had attacked this Parrish?

Naturally the idea appalled her, but she worried that it did so for the wrong reasons: if it turned out she had married a genuinely dangerous man, then she would look a fool; and *he* was a fool too, since he'd not covered his tracks.

She asked Anderson, 'Why would he attack Parrish?'

'Over a professional dispute, Mrs Coates.'

But sex must be at the root of it.

'Who asked Martin to look into it?'

'The head of your husband's chambers.'

'A man called Ivor Jenkins?'

'That's it. He wanted to see if there was any evidence.'

'Wasn't it the job of the police to find that?'

'It was the job of anyone minded to take it on, Mrs Coates.'

'But don't the police specialise in that sort of thing?'

'Yes they do, but Mr Jenkins had formed an unfavourable opinion of the investigating officer.'

'On what grounds?'

'On the grounds that he was a fucking idiot, Mrs Coates.'

'And what did Martin come up with?'

'Not enough to convict.'

'It was only circumstantial evidence, I suppose?'

'There's nothing wrong with circumstantial evidence, there just wasn't enough of it. I've put a summary of the investigation in there,' he said, nodding again towards the envelope. They both stood.

'Where's the dog?' asked Camilla.

'Up north,' said Anderson, in an almost parodically northern way. Well, she was jealous of that dog, being two hundred miles away from London; and she was jealous of Anderson too, since he was evidently heading that way himself once again.

They agreed they would speak by phone in the coming days, and she told him he could no longer take it that her address was still her address.

———

In the first week of December we performed every night, Monday to Saturday. My familiarity with the codes improved, and the speed of my responses, but they were made by the conventional method, with no visions occurring, which was just as well.

I had not wanted to antagonise Draper, who I still couldn't think of as Joseph, although I *called* him Joseph, and he called me Kate, and perhaps thought of me as Kate. He would look directly at me more often, sometimes indeed for an uncomfortably long time. Once, at the Hackney Empire, I thought he was about to take my hand as we waited in the wings before going on, but it was perhaps just that our hands had coincided as I smoothed my palms against my skirt in a somewhat nervous fashion, and he reached into his pocket to verify the presence of the un-transparent glasses. He had also taken to paying me directly, pressing the money into my hands with a meaningful look. I did not find his advances – if these were advances – roman-tic, so much as controlling; or perhaps a mixture of the two.

When we played at Silvertown in that week, The Dad was in the audience, with a pass for the stalls I had provided. He had not wanted to come because of his cough, which he feared might bother his neighbours in the audience and distract me, but I did not hear him cough, and he generally did not cough when he was happy. As Draper and I left the stage, I mentioned that my father might be 'coming behind' in a minute. 'Very good,' said Draper, 'do give him my regards.' In other words, he had no interest in meeting any relation of mine.

The Dad did come behind, to marvel at the bright, happy chaos of the dressing room and to shake hands with some of the other turners. We then took the train home. In the rattling compartment, which we had to ourselves, he told me that our opening music was Nocturne No. 1 by Chopin. He then said how much the audience had liked me.

'*Why* do you think they liked me, Dad?'

He shot me the look that said I was fishing for compliments. This was a fault of mine apparently, and it was tied in with my feyness (if that is a word). 'There's not much mystery about why the male auditors like you,' he said. 'As you know very well.'

'But Dad,' I said, 'I'm not Samantha Dare.'

... she being one the many female turners who showed a great deal of leg. Having taken the advice of Marie Lloyd's dresser, I had gone the opposite way, and so performed with Draper in much the same clothes I had worn as a trainee teacher: simple white blouse, a black skirt with a wide belt.

'No,' said The Dad, 'you're not Samantha Dare. You have a more winsome appeal, which you have calculated to a tee. You project a sort of vulnerability, something to do with your eyes being covered up in that way. You have your mother's very pretty eyes, as you have often been told. You're not telling me the man Draper hasn't thrown his hat into the ring.'

'If he did it would be thrown straight out again. Fortunately, he seems wary of me.'

'Very wise of him,' said The Dad.

'He is not a very attractive person, is he?' I said, and The Dad shook his head, smiling. 'Oh, he's respectable enough, I suppose. I mean, he's *bespectacled* enough.'

The Dad said, 'Did I tell you I bumped into Sid Barley again?'

Now it was The Dad's turn to be disingenuous. 'No Dad, you did not.'

'Hardly worth mentioning, but he'd had a word with Alfie Dale.'

'In the Slack?'

'Obviously in the Slack, love. Sid never goes anywhere else. Apparently, Alfie had a letter from Hugh Brooks.'

'When?'

'Couple of years back. Said he was very happy out in Australia.'

'Where in Australia?'

'He's travelling about, apparently.'

'I wonder how his moustache is holding up?'

The Dad smiled. 'I'll bet he's given up on the fourteen-ounce cloth.'

We came to a station, or it came to us.

'He probably has one of those hats with corks hanging off it,' I said.

We stepped onto the platform beneath the one gas lamp that served Camden Town, which was adjacent to the one luggage barrow, both of which were next to the sign reading FASTEST WAY TO CITY with its arrow pointing east, indicating the viaduct, tracks, signals and telegraph wires ... None of which cumbersome means of communication were required between The Dad and me.

'It's good, isn't it?' he said. 'That Brooks is happy out there, I mean?'

'Yes, Dad. I'm very pleased for him.'

*

In the second week of December, we embarked on our seaside tour. We set off from Charing Cross station in a special train – or rather two specially booked carriages of a perfectly *ordinary* train – and there were two men with a cinematographic camera to record the event for a bioscope. We all had to wave our discounted tickets in a silly way, and Draper was at first very unwilling to do it. For a turner, he was oddly reluctant to be *seen*, although the reason he gave for his moaning was that the bioscopes would eventually kill off the Halls, so why should we help them? I had no objection myself. But I privately considered that any film of music hall artistes boarding a train would have made a dull show compared to bioscopes I had seen, such as *Catching a Shark*, *Coaling a Battleship*, and, best of all, *Berlin Motor Race*.

The tickets we had waved were for Ramsgate, where we would begin our tour with two nights at the (very small) Grand Theatre. Draper sat opposite me on the train, and after a little more fuming over the impertinence of the film-makers, he resumed his rather strained friendliness, as first exhibited during our conversation in the crush bar at Poplar. We shared a compartment with an elderly magician called Incognito, who slept throughout the journey, affording Draper the chance to criticise him – 'a comedy magician: neither fish nor fowl' – and the other members of the troupe. There were about twenty of us, including an American female shooting act called the Vivians. 'A *shouting* act, if you ask me,' was Draper's charitable comment, and we could, admittedly, hear their rather animated conversation from two compartments along. He added, 'I don't much care for Yankees, Kate – a very brash people,' which I took to be a reference to Art Wakelam as much as the Vivians. There was a Madame somebody-or-other – a French woman with a talking parrot whose name I could neither remember nor pronounce when I did remember it (the woman's, I mean). Draper said, 'She's about as French as I am, Kate. Hails from the Midlands.' There was also the all-male Camille Trio – a comedy bar and equilibristic act who, said Draper, 'are far more concerned with the other sort of bar' – and there were a couple of patterers called Rich & Rich, 'who are decidedly *not*, Kate. Rich, I mean, and you will see why if you watch their act.'

Most of the company were somewhat on the decline, if not the actual 'skids', whereas Draper and I were on the up, and he had ensured that we appeared on the bill in biggish writing, going on just before the interval – so we were second top really. The actual bill topper would be different in every theatre. They would be coming, said Draper, 'by special arrangement, direct from the Hippodrome Leicester Square, or some such humbug'. He had seen the projected list of these supposed stars, and pronounced them 'second-raters to a man', about which he was obviously quite pleased, since the laurels might then all come our way.

He seemed to know a lot about trains and he asked if I'd ever been on a Pullman, which is a luxury train. I said no, and he said I ought to try it, now that I was moving up in the world. He said, 'They'll do you a nice quarter bottle of champagne,' and he was obviously even keener on quarter bottles of champagne than he was on halves. After Canterbury, I began feigning drowsiness, to escape his depressing conversation, and the possibility of his speculations about what *I* might do in a social way becoming what 'we' might do ... because he would keep leaning forward, in a way that suggested he was about to take my hand. Between Canterbury and Ramsgate, I would occasionally open my eyes to see him making notes in his pocket book.

The second time this occurred, he said, 'I have great plans for us, Kate, great plans.' As we approached our destination I fell genuinely asleep, and when I awoke suddenly, with the slowing of the train, I caught him staring directly at me, with an expression of puzzlement.

The jerk of the brakes that had woken me had also roused Incognito from his slumber. As he blinked awake, he said, 'What's the fastest express train of all?'

'Is this a joke?' said Draper, standing to bring his case down from the luggage rack.

'The train of thought,' said Incognito.

'Very good,' I said.

Handing me down my own bag, Draper said, 'You can manage that all right? I'm not paying for a porter.'

*

In the event, I do not believe we were very good on that tour, and if we had ever been reviewed, I might have been in real danger of being 'solid in support' or 'not unimpressive'. There were no slips, but then again I received none of the flashes or visions about the articles brought forth from the audience, and so made none of the sudden pronouncements – the 'wild guesses' away from which Draper had warned me. The lack of the visions was possibly due to my being more experienced somehow. Or if my theory – which seemed increasingly fantastical – was correct, and the visions were projected from the audience, it might be that the few people who turned up to see us on this tour were quite indifferent (being half asleep) as to whether my performances were successful or not.

217

There were a dozen dates in all, and most of the theatres were given over to rehearsing forthcoming pantomimes. We spent most of our time going *between* the dates in the slow, if rather luxurious, trains of the London, Chatham & Dover, the London, Brighton & South Coast or other, equally grandiose outfits. Our diggings were all in tall houses of faded stucco, like the make-up of raddled clowns. My memory is a jumble of lounges and promenades (sometimes called Winter Gardens) stuffed with dusty plants and flowers, the window glass always steamed up, which was usually just as well, given what lay beyond – namely empty beaches with gigantic green waves rolling furiously towards them, gathering volume inexorably, only to smash into black stone harbours that were always too slimy to walk on, even if one had wanted to do that. Some excursions were laid on. We went to castles on cliffs, or watched giant sea creatures dying in blurred aquariums. But I was uneasily aware that Draper would also be watching me, and I felt he was working up to something that I could not bear to think about.

On that first night, at Ramsgate, I managed to fall in with the Vivians as the dinner gong was sounded (we would eat early, before the show). Since there were five of them, they asked me to make a sixth, and so a round number, as might be accommodated on any large table, and this turned out to be a repeatable arrangement. The Vivians – none of whom was called Vivian – were all from either Ohio or Kentucky; they were very kind (if loud) and they called me 'Doll'. Draper would dine with Incognito, remaining largely silent in the face of his barrage of jokes. The comedy-magician was a very insensitive and incurious man, which is why, I believed,

Draper was willing to put up with him. There would be no enquiries about his former partner, and no question of having his mind read. It had occurred to me, during a rainy afternoon in the lounge of a hotel, that my own improved relationship with Draper was down to two things. Not only had I foresworn any future 'guesses', I had also reassured him that my psychic inspiration, if any, came from the auditors and not from his own mind. Could I read his mind? To this extent: I believed he intended to ask my hand in marriage.

He was laying the ground by seeking out bookings for our act, and spent a good deal of time sending telegrams, telephoning, and writing letters. I myself wrote a good many letters, all to The Dad. Only once – no, twice – was there anything worth writing about.

At the Brighton Theatre Royal, I saw the person considered by The Dad to be the greatest limelight man in the world, namely Dan Leno. It was three in the afternoon, and he was walking through a bit of business while half dressed as Mother Goose. He was sharing the stage at the time with some gas engineers, who were doing something to the sun burner.

I had just walked into the wings when I saw him. He wore an ordinary suit, with a pinafore on top. He was 'on the book' – holding the script, I mean – as was his co-star (a man I did not recognise). The director looked on from the front row of the empty stalls. There were the makings of a set, denoting a crazily disarranged parlour, and a door flat was repeatedly being flown in and out. As I looked on, Leno lay down his script and walked – in a somehow musical way, a dancer's walk – to the front of the stage, where he knelt down. He beckoned the director, and some whispering took place while Leno's co-star very patiently lit a cigar. Leno then returned to his script, and when he saw me in the wings he did a wonderful little five-second dance that I have replayed many times over in my mind: a kind of little clog dance, except that he wore ordinary boots. His expression remained mournful throughout; but I wished I could have transmitted this to The Dad by the Astral Plane, or some other supernatural means recommended by the College of Psychics, because The Dad had particularly liked Leno in his Northern days, when he would include clog dancing in his turn. (The dancing went by the board once Leno became *the* top-lining comedian in London.)

The director was now shouting from the stalls: 'Property master! Clear away all this stuff and get me a kitchen table, two frying pans and a dozen large potatoes!' There was shouted assent from somewhere backstage, and the director returned to his seat. Picking up his script once more, Leno spoke some lines as Mother Goose, and the other fellow spoke some other lines, in among which was a clearing of the throat, occasioned presumably by the smoking of the cigar.

'Here,' said Leno, 'something wrong. My next speech doesn't fit in.'

Their voices echoed in the all-but-empty theatre.

'But you've turned over two pages,' said the other man, exhaling smoke.

'Oh. Sorry, governor,' said Leno, and it was perfectly charming that Leno – 'the funniest man in the world' – had called the *other* fellow 'governor'. He wasn't quite satisfied, however. 'No, you see, it has to be wrong because my cue is you laughing.'

220

'I did laugh,' said the other.

'Was that a laugh?' said Leno. 'I thought you had the croup.'

Two people laughed properly at this: the director, sitting in the stalls, and me. Leno turned my way again, and I approached a little way towards the stage, because he did look such a kind man, and when you saw his eyes, it was very easy to see how he could impersonate Mother Goose in her beautiful phase. He also looked rather tired.

'Hello, my dear,' he said. 'Are you with the tour that's going on here tonight?'

I nodded, too overwhelmed to speak.

'And where are you next?'

'The Empire,' I murmured. 'At Hastings.'

'Now Hastings is a lovely spot, dear. If you've never been, go again.'

All of which I faithfully related to The Dad, together with most of the following . . .

On our second night at Brighton, I received a message in the dressing room just before the end of the show. It was a short note, but became more exciting as it went on, and the name at the end was perfect culmination.

Dear Miss French,

You were perfectly entrancing tonight. Might I see you in the Gulp Bar for a short professional conference (and a glass of champagne)?

Yours ever,
Art Wakelam

The Gulp Bar at Brighton was famous, and I had not yet been in it, even though it was backstage – being for the exclusive use of turners and their friends – and indicated by numerous hand-painted signs propped up in the laby-rinthine back corridors, and always reading THIS WAY TO THE REFRESHMENT ROOM. But everyone knew it as the 'Gulp Bar' and certainly nobody was *sipping* their drinks as I went in there. In fact, the place – painted white and with a tapestry of Brighton seafront behind the bar – was populated by almost our entire company, including Draper, who stood alone at the bar. He turned to me as I entered, and I nodded towards him, trying to convey that he must make do with the nod, and that I would not be coming up to him ... for there, in the middle of the throng, was Art Wakelam, wearing a lovely suit coat of midnight blue with black turnovers. Word had obviously leaked out that he was an important scout, and the poor man was besieged by a whole gang of the turners, in particular the night's bill-topper, W.P. Dempsey. Art Wakelam broke through the press to shake my hand, and to congratulate me again on my performance.

'But you didn't come all the way here to see me?' I said, in an entirely disingenuous manner.

'You were the one I *wanted* to see, Miss French,' he said. It was quite a romantic answer, I thought, but also quite legalistic. Obviously, his main business was with others, and he was claimed once again by W.P., who was sozzled, and began singing his (quite) famous closing song for Mr Wakelam's particular benefit. It was a take-off of 'The Man Who Broke the Bank at Monte Carlo', entitled 'The *Bank* that Broke The *Man* in Monte Carlo': 'As I tramp my feet, up Regent Street,' Dempsey was softly singing into Art Wakelam's ear, 'You can hear the folks declare/ He must be soft up there ... '

In response, Art Wakelam was smiling and nodding, while looking my way.

'He must be soft up there ... ' Dempsey was repeating. He kept going back to the start of the song, by way of emphasising its brilliance. 'Best five pounds I ever spent,' said Dempsey, when he'd finally left off singing. Draper, I noticed, had moved towards the door. I hoped he was leaving, but if so, he was doing it by degrees.

'It's a very droll number,' said Art Wakelam, before breaking away again, this time making good on his promise to buy me a glass of champagne. 'Miss French,' he said, handing it over, 'may I buy you dinner this evening?'

I must have looked shocked, which I was. I hoped I did *not* look tremendously pleased (which I also was); but then he withdrew the offer. 'No,' he said, 'probably best if ... Look here, what are you up to tomorrow?'

'Not much,' I said, 'and I'll be doing it in Hastings.'

'I can easily drop into Hastings on my way back to London,' he said.

Whether this really would be easy, my knowledge of the railway map of southern England did not allow me to say.

'There's only one pier at Hastings,' Art Wakelam said, which piece of topographical musing seemed quite irrelevant until he added, 'How about if I see you at the entrance at midday?' In the moment of agreeing to this proposal, I glanced over towards the door, hoping that Draper would have gone through it, or – if he had not done so – that he would not be staring balefully in my direction. I was disappointed on both counts. Art Wakelam had followed the direction of my glance. He reached out and touched my hand. "Til tomorrow,' he said, with a note of anxiety in his voice.

*

Art Wakelam – in expensive tweed greatcoat and Derby hat – was as good as his word, as I had known he would be. The midday sky above Hastings had been washed clean by recent rain as we intercepted one another in a remarkably easy way at the pier entrance. We discussed the idea of ascending a zig-zagging cliff walk on the edge of town that would take us into a large park, then to a seaside village Art knew of. He put all the arguments in favour, then all the arguments against, and I let him run on, just because I liked the sound of his voice. After 'zigging' for a while, then 'zagging' for a similar distance, we came to a bench, where we sat, looking down on some fishermen in great, backwards-pointing oilskin hats. They were stringing up nets – putting them out to dry – between poles stuck in the shingle, and so creating a great spider's web across the beach.

'Awfully picturesque, aren't they?' I said. Art Wakelam eyed me, smiling, perhaps thinking this a rather 'fey' remark.

'They are from a distance,' he said. 'Do you mind if I smoke, Miss French?'

I said I didn't in the least, and would he please call me Kate.

'I meant what I said about your turn yesterday, Kate,' he said, and it was lovely to hear him say my name – like coming home after a long, tiring journey that had perhaps lasted my entire life.

'Oh, we were nothing above ordinary,' I said, and like the fellows down on the beach, I was fishing – in my case for *compliments*.

'*Draper* was ordinary,' said Art. 'He is so matter-of-fact, whereas you almost make me believe in all that psychical stuff.'

'I believe Draper thinks I can read his mind.'

'And can you?'

'No. I presume there must be openness and generosity for anything like that to occur. Which is why I sometimes think I can pick things up from the audiences. Or perhaps I just can't resist making wild guesses.'

Art merely nodded, blowing smoke.

'Might I give you a word of professional advice, Kate?'

'You think I should leave Draper.'

'You have read *my* mind.'

'Hardly,' I said. 'Miss Lloyd advised me to leave him when I saw her at the Rotherhithe Hippodrome, and I presumed you were in agreement.'

'I was, Kate, and I am. He's not a man to be crossed.'

I frowned, while contemplating the fishermen down below. There were great puddles on the beach, which they seemed to make a point of walking through rather than around. 'I haven't crossed him,' I said.

'But you will do. The praise in the reviews is all for you; he must see that you will ask for equal pay.'

'He can always say no, can't he? Then he can look for another Brooks.'

'Brooks wanted equal shares, Kate. Look what happened to him.'

'He emigrated to Australia. It's a land of opportunity, you know.'

Art Wakelam dropped his cigar stub and put his boot on it.

'Why don't you just say it?' I continued. 'You think Draper murdered Brooks, and means to do the same to me.'

'All I want is to make you pause for thought.'

'Well, the word "murder" does tend to do that to a girl.'

'I didn't say "murder" exactly.'

'You're right, that was me. But it's what you mean. It's really very kind of you to worry on my behalf. Shall I seek to reassure you?'

He turned to me and smiled, rather sadly. 'Yes.'

'First of all, I am not as stupid as I look – nearly, but not quite. Second, Draper has been quite kind to me. At the Queen's, Poplar, he bought us a whole half bottle of champagne to share. And he is responsible for my earning more than I ever did as a pupil teacher, or a singer or dancer, and come to that more than my father ever did as a detective sergeant.'

'Your dad was a cop? He's still around, I hope?'

'We share rooms together at King's Cross. But will you not interrupt me while I am reassuring you? We are doing pretty well at the moment, Draper and I, and you are kind enough to say that is down to me. In that case, why would he kill the goose that is laying the golden eggs, if I may so refer

226

to myself? As for Brooks, I don't doubt Draper had a falling out with him, but I hardly think he would continue on the music hall stage if he had actually killed a fellow turner.'

'Perhaps not.'

'And it's not as though people haven't had letters from Brooks in Australia.'

'Have they?'

'Certainly.'

'*Who* has?'

'A friend of a friend of my father's, for one. A man called Alfie Dale. He's on the Halls.'

'Yes. I've heard of Dale. He has a reputation as a solid pro.'

'Lastly,' I said, no doubt to the relief of my companion, 'I do not intend this to be a longstanding arrangement between him and me. I do not wish to be known as a mere accessory of another. I mean to strike out on my own very soon.'

'As what, Kate? Not that you wouldn't be brilliant at *anything*.'

'Oh, a comedy-serio-tragedienne, or something in the musical line, possibly all three combined with a little dancing and club swinging. I have made a great many sacrifices to get where I am, chiefly of The Dad's money. Now I mean to press home my advantage.'

The fishermen were now all smoking pipes on an upturned boat.

'How would you like me to stand you lunch?' Art enquired.

'It's enough for me that you can stand me at all,' I said, 'the way I go on about myself.'

'Oh, I like the way you go on about yourself,' he said, rising and offering me his arm.

'But won't *you* do it for a while?' I said. 'Go on about *your*self, I mean.'

As we descended the cliff path I learned a little about him. He had been born in America, in New York, which explained his un-place-able accent, and perhaps his openness of character and flamboyant waistcoats. As a boy he had lived in New York and London in what sounded like prosperous circumstances. His late father had been a successful lawyer, and Art himself had studied law for a while at an American college, but he then 'chucked it' in favour of the world of the theatre, which had always fascinated him. He had always been 'a free-lancer', at first being the eyes and ears on the London scene for American agents and theatre managers, but now working principally for Selwyn & Wise, of Piccadilly Circus.

Over lunch of Dover sole in a seafront dining room, we left the subject of Draper behind. Art mentioned the new Euston Palace of Varieties, which was being built around the corner from Pancras Road. 'They've practically finished it,' I said. 'The Dad ... my dad, I mean, was given a special tour. In the dome is a painting of sort of French shepherds at twilight, dancing in a wood hung with Chinese lanterns, as French shepherds tend to do, you know. The whole auditorium is gold and café au lait, and it has more paintings inside than you'll see in an art gallery. They had a professor from the Belgian Academy in to supervise.'

'But it's the sixpennies of the working classes that'll make it pay,' said Art, who was also very interested in The Dad, and about how he could be both a policeman and a musician.

'Well,' I said, 'he's always been able to play anything on sight, despite having no encouragement that way from his own folks, and he would play at any Police Concert going.'

Art told me about a Police Concert he'd been to. 'The whole thing was quite violent. A display of shooting ... a comic boxing match; and a lot of "God Save the Queen".'

'Yes, because they always play it at the beginning *and* the end. It's as though they never think he really *will* save her.'

It was a very jolly lunch. Afterwards, I accompanied Art to Hastings railway station, where he'd left his portmanteau. The London train was waiting, and before he climbed up, he gave me his card (again) and said I must come in to Selwyn & Wise at midday on the coming Thursday, which was the day after the termination of the tour, and if Draper tried any 'funny stuff' in the meantime, I was to wire him, or preferably telephone immediately, to which I replied that there never had been and never would be anything 'funny' about Draper. I waved to Art as the train departed, feeling silly, sad and happy all at once. Despite living next to that gigantic terminus, King's Cross, this was the first time I had seen anybody off from a station, never having been separated by any great distance from the man who had been the most important person in my life up until then, namely The Dad.

The way to my diggings took me back along the front. The light was beginning to fade to a rather alarming violet colour, and a sea swell was getting up. The fishermen had gone from the beach – home to their houses for a good tea, I hoped, rather than out into the waves. I was passing the choppy waters of the model boating pond when I saw a figure in the bandstand. Draper, wearing a long grey coat I hadn't seen before. Had there been somebody, similarly attired, hanging back on the zig-zag walk? He approached me rapidly.

'I have been telephoning to London, Kate, and I have news.'

He waited until I asked, 'Good news, I hope?'

'We have an offer of the Friday Fun again.'

'Which Friday?'

'The coming one, Kate: the sixteenth.'

I had a busy week in store then, what with the tour running 'til Wednesday, and my appointment with Selwyn & Wise on the Thursday. Behind Draper, a gigantic green wave was rolling in.

'We have become great favourites with Mr Briggs,' he said. (Briggs was the assistant manager of the Rotherhithe Hippodrome, and the brains behind the Friday Fun.) 'He proposes to bring us back for four weeks from the middle of January.'

'Good,' I said, because I knew that work was always hard to come by in January. But the thought of another four weeks with this peculiar man . . .

'I suggest, Kate, that we take a holiday between the Friday Fun and the start of those four weeks.'

I eyed him. 'A *paid* holiday, would that be?'

His smile came. 'Why not, Kate? I'm sure we can come to an arrangement. I mean to go north in that time.'

'Yes,' I said. 'Why?'

'To secure bookings, of course. I have appointments in Bradford and Manchester, and will be taking the night train north immediately after we come off on the sixteenth. And, Kate . . . '

'Yes?' I said, rather rudely, for I'd had about enough of his constant 'Kates'.

'I mean to raise our lowest again. I haven't settled on a figure yet, but I will be sure to let you know the moment I do. Shall I walk you back to your digs?'

His great hands came up; I took a half step back, and they went down again. 'That's quite all right,' I said, 'I'll see you at seven at the theatre.'

I left him lingering near the bandstand, and looking uncertain as another wave rose behind him. Perhaps Art Wakelam and I were being too hard on him. Might it be that Draper was merely shy?

*

I took the bus to Piccadilly Circus, and discovered on alighting that I was directly outside the offices of Selwyn & Wise. I immediately recognised the names, since they were depicted on the window glass of a door in white letters, which floated somewhat haphazardly in the yellowish beam of a lighthouse. Below was a foamy turquoise sea. The doorway was in-between a tobacconist's and a newsagent's, both of which I had often noticed before. Even though we were in December, these two premises had their stripy canvas awnings fully extended, to shade people from the bright sun, and the weather seemed all the more incongruous given that there was an early Christmas tree in the window of the tobacconist's, to which cigar boxes and pipes were affixed with pretty red ribbons.

There was an electric bell. It rang with a very modern, somehow American sound. After a while, a young woman came down.

'My name's Kate French,' I said, 'I have an appointment with Mr Wakelam.'

'Yes, Art's here,' she confirmed, and she stood aside to let me in. She was friendly, and distinctly 'liberated', since she was wearing quite a lot of make-up and smoking a cigarette. The street door gave on to nothing more than a staircase, so I began climbing it, with the young woman following.

'I'm Liz, by the way,' she said, but it didn't seem that anything needed to be done about this – no handshake or anything was required. She continued casually when we reached the offices, which were, I believe, a 'suite': the word was strongly suggested by the similarity to a hotel suite, with all inter-connecting doors open, and brightly coloured carpets. Yes, there were typewriters on each of the two big, oak desks in the main room, together with many telephones and a rather beautiful golden machine called, I think, a stock ticker; but there was also a comfortable couch with not only cushions but a blanket, and a drinks cabinet with a great parade of alcohol on top of it. The sunlight raying in from the wide windows was rather unnecessarily supplemented by electric standard lamps with pretty, fringed yellow shades. No fewer than four doors opened off this central room, and I could hear murmurs of conversation from two of them. One of the telephones was ringing, with a weary sound that suggested it had been ringing fruitlessly all morning. Meanwhile, Liz had disappeared. She had perhaps said, 'Have a seat, dear,' I couldn't quite recall. The couch did look very tempting. I was tired, not having slept much lately. The tour had arrived back at Charing Cross station at seven o'clock the previous evening, and some of the turners (the Vivians and Rich & Rich especially) had thought it a good idea to go into the station hotel for a goodbye drink.

As we stepped off the train, I had asked Draper if he would be coming.

'Don't you think we've all seen quite enough of each other?' he said.

'I daresay that's true,' I said, and he seemed in that moment such a perfectly ridiculous individual that I felt pity for him rather than anger. I certainly did not fear him at that moment.

As I walked away from Draper along the platform, he called after me, 'I did not mean that you and *I* have seen enough of each other, Miss French. It was not a personal remark; only that I find the company of these shooters and tumblers rather tiring.' As he spoke, those same shooters and tumblers were coming along in a happy throng behind him. I waited for them at the ticket gate, having decided to join them for 'just the one', and Draper and I parted with a stiff shake of the hand. His behaviour towards me had been mixed throughout the tour. His traditional reserve had been maintained, but there had been those occasional, rather alarming indications of regard, as just then on the platform. It was as if he didn't quite know what to do about me. But I knew what I would be doing about him. I would be leaving his employ, under the guidance of Art Wakelam, the moment we had completed our month at the Rotherhithe Hippodrome.

Just then I heard Art's voice coming through one of the open doors. 'Parisian duettists,' he was saying, 'one lady, one gent.' Then came the brisk striking of a match.

'Who does the quick changes?' enquired an older, more cautious voice. 'Both of them?'

'No, that would be rather confusing. Only her.'

Cigar smoke began curling through the doorway, dissolving in the sunlight of the room.

'And what does he do while she's doing the changes?'

The next words were obliterated by the loud striking of another match, and prolonged coughing on the part of the older man, who possibly then poured himself a glass of water, or had one poured for him by Art.

'Then there's Sylvia Loyal,' Art was saying, when things had calmed down. 'A very nice-looking lady who presents pigeons with her mother. I know you don't like animal acts, Bill, but they're absolutely necessary for the variety.'

'Or for clearing the house, perhaps? Let me think it over. What about the lady orchestra?'

'As soon as that's ready, I'll tell you.'

I began inspecting the photographs of turners arranged around the walls. They were all expensively framed, and signed. In one of them, six men in leotards were entirely obliterated by their own signatures. I recognised Samantha Dare, half naked as usual; and there was Lottie Collins, who had scribbled the title of her great hit, 'Ta-Ra-Ra-Boom-De-Ay'.

'And Regia?' the questioning voice was saying. 'I can't remember about her.'

'She's pretty easy to remember, in that she plays twenty-five different instruments and costs twenty-five pounds.'

'Oh,' said Liz, reappearing from a second doorway and indicating the first. 'Do go in. I thought you already had done.'

So I approached the open door, to see a room in which cigar smoke and strong sunlight were doing battle. With a gratifying exclamation of 'Kate, my dear!' Art stood up and escorted me into the room. The other man stood too, but more slowly, and Art Wakelam introduced him as Bill Wise. He was a big man with a big bundle of cigars on the desk before him, like sticks of dynamite. After shaking my hand, he pocketed two of them, then put on his coat. Art did likewise, adding a third check pattern to his ensemble, for his trousers and suit coat were disparate . . . yet somehow all was harmonious.

We crossed sunny Piccadilly Circus, quite untroubled by the swirling traffic, as Art sang my praises to a smiling (but perhaps slightly bemused) Bill Wise. 'Miss French holds the audience absolutely. There is not a cough: not a match is struck.'

We entered the golden portals of the Criterion restaurant. I had been to the theatre in the basement (if that is the word for so palatial an auditorium) but never to the dining rooms above, which I knew to be among the most luxurious in London. It was presumably home-from-home for Bill Wise, who ignored the fawning waiter showing us to our table in favour of asking me, 'You obviously have a great mastery of those mesmerical codes?'

'She does,' Art cut in, 'but sometimes she pre-empts the codes, in a manner highly mysterious.'

A bottle in a silver bucket arrived. Bill Wise nodded towards it, saying, 'This all right with you, my dear?' and Art held it up for me to read the label, just as though I was in the habit of distinguishing between one bottle of champagne

and another. I read THEOPHILE ROEDERER EXTRA
RESERVE CUVEE VINTAGE.

Bill Wise, pouring the champagne with an experienced
hand, said, 'Well, dear, we see you in the star dressing
room,' and it was just about the first thing I'd heard him
say that was not a question, so it was as though he had
firmly *decided*.

'With Mr Draper, you mean?' I said, continuing arch.

'Decidedly not,' said Art.

'But he has taught me all I know.'

'What you have cannot be taught, my dear,' Bill Wise
said, removing the wrapper from a cigar.

'Besides,' said Art, 'who do you suppose taught Draper?'

'Not Brooks?'

'Of course.'

'And it seems Draper gave him hell in return,' said Bill
Wise, lighting his cigar and sitting back. 'Art has some
pretty dark theories about friend Draper,' he continued. 'For
myself, I don't know ... But whatever occurred between
him and Brooks, there's no doubt that Draper's a pretty bad
lot, and you're better off without him.'

'But a mentalist must have a partner,' I said.

'And here she comes now,' said Art, rising to his feet.

I should have guessed, because we had been shown
to a table for four. A willowy, rather beautiful person
with the most enormous green eyes was approaching our
table. She seemed slightly nervous, and rather grave, but
with a fetching, slow smile. She was introduced to me as
Winifred McClure, singer, actress and tragedienne. She
had also assisted a magician, The Great or The Mighty

236

somebody-or-other; his name was lost in the excitement of the introductions. Here, it seemed, was my new partner, and we were down to business straight away, with accompanying draughts of champagne.

'Winifred has been learning the codes,' said Art.

'The Rochelle system,' she said, in a gentle Scottish accent. 'I hope I have the right one?'

I nodded graciously. 'Just so.'

'I have not mastered it quite yet, but I think I have some time left before we start together.'

'I mean to finish with Draper at the end of January,' I said, and Art was frowning somewhat at that, as though he had a different idea. I took another sip of champagne, which must have been going to my head because I caught up Bill Wise's box of matches and addressed Winifred: 'Now let us say, my dear, that the auditor handed you these?'

'Ah,' said Winifred. 'Fourth set. I say, "What is here?" and a box of matches is number nine, so I say, "Now." So put the whole thing together and it's "What is here . . . now?"'

'That's quite right,' I said.

'I'll *tell* you what's here now,' said Art Wakelam, beaming at Winifred and me. 'A bill-topping double act.'

'Mesmerelda and Clare Voyant!' I suggested, foolishly.

Art was shaking his head and smiling. 'The Martian *Girls*!' he said, and he raised his glass in a toast.

'To the Martian Girls!' we all cried; but I could tell that another question was forming in the mind of Bill Wise.

'One possible difficulty . . . ' he said, turning to Art. 'Our two ladies hail from the red planet, yet Winifred here is a

237

head taller than Kate, and looks generally a good deal different. How to account for the discrepancy?'

'Oh,' said Art, 'I think we can take it that there's a good deal of variation in Martian females, but it's variation on a theme of *beauty*.'

'Or,' said Winifred McClure, lightly touching my hand in a conspiratorial way, 'we could let slip that I have a little Venusian blood in me.'

Then came the charming, slow smile that I knew would go over beautifully in Rotherhithe or anywhere else. Bill Wise sat back satisfied, and it appeared that all was quite settled, even before the menus had arrived.

*

After lunch, back on Piccadilly Circus, we embarked on what I thought would be a comprehensive round of goodbyes. But when Art Wakelam had stopped a hansom for Winifred McClure, and put her into it – and as Bill Wise raised his hat one last time prior to strolling back to his office – Art turned to me: 'Kate, I would like to show you something: a shop, not too far; we won't need a cab.'

As we crossed the Circus, he took my hand, which might have been to protect me from the traffic, but he *kept* hold of my hand as we headed into the narrow streets to the north and east of the Circus. It did occur to me, in a conceited sort of way, that he might be taking me to some pretty little jeweller's, where I would be invited to take my pick of the engagement rings, except that this changeable (but always kind) man now wore an expression of anxiety, and made little further effort at conversation, save for an occasional 'We go left here,' and 'Not far now.'

It wasn't going to be a jeweller's because we had gradually descended, so to speak, from the grand swirl of Piccadilly Circus to the tighter confusion of semi-respectable streets and alleys. Finally, we came to a little square called Paved Court, and here Art Wakelam let go of my hand.

'Now ...' he said, surveying the shops that bounded the small square, which was pretty but also rather scruffy. In spite of its name, there was a defiantly rural aspect to it: one of the shops sold flowers, with many of its wares in tubs on the pavement. There was a horse trough in the middle of the square, which accounted for the rather large quantity of manure about the place. At first glance, this seemed a bookish quarter, with a lot of literature in the shop windows and in the penny boxes outside; but there were printers' shops as well. One window was bordered with notices reading CHANCERY BILLS, ANSWERS, APPEAL CASES, finally summarising the whole with LAW PRINTING. Another advertised OLD DEEDS AND PARCHMENT PURCHASED – a rag merchant's evidently. The next-door premises belonged to FOX & CO. THEATRICAL SIGN PAINTER AND WRITER. ARTISTIC TRANSPARENCIES OUR SPECIALITÉ.

'Joseph Draper was seen here last week,' said Art Wakelam. Thinking at first that his gloved finger was indicating Fox & Co., I said, 'Presumably he was after some bill matter for our turn?'

'No,' said Art. '*That* place.'

He took my hand again, and led me towards the premises he had indicated. Above the bowed window was written

239

D. COLVIN. STAMPS. I knew from Art's demeanour that I ought to be worried, but I could not quite see why. In the window was nothing more troubling than an arrangement of cancelled postage: colourful – that is to say foreign – stamps, for the most part still attached to the cards or envelopes they had once transported.

'It is a shop for philanthropists,' I said. 'Sorry, I mean *philatelists*. If it had been the first, Draper would never have crossed the threshold.'

'But wouldn't you be surprised to learn that he's a philatelist?'

'Not particularly. It seems a dull enough pursuit for him.'

'He was seen to emerge with a brown envelope.'

'By whom?'

'Liz, in the office. She was buying flowers three doors along. She's aware of friend Draper, naturally. She's a regular at the flower shop, and she's got to know something of this place. The fellow who runs it is a lag.'

'A what?'

'A recidivist. A gaol bird.'

'You mean an *old* lag?'

'I don't think he's particularly old.'

'You are not quite a Londoner, Art,' I said rather haughtily. 'If you had been, you'd have said an *old* lag.'

'Kate,' said Art Wakelam, 'the man who operates this business is a forger.'

'Of stamps?'

'Of postal markings. You said Alfie Dale had had a letter from Brooks in Australia. It's my hunch it was sent from London by Draper, with a forged Australian postmark.'

'Brooks being dead?'

Art nodded.

'But then they would be over-stamped with a London mark.'

'Oh, I don't know how he managed it exactly. Maybe there are two marks even on genuine letters from Australia. Or maybe Draper delivered the letters personally.'

I nodded. 'I'm sure Draper has learnt to forge Brooks's signature, but he won't risk handwriting the whole of a letter. I think he types them, Art – on his typewriter.'

Art Wakelam was a great *doer*, but we didn't do anything in Paved Court except stand in silence for a minute before D. COLVIN. STAMPS. During that period several people passed by the window, and one gent stopped to scrutinise the merchandise, but nobody went in, and I was not surprised, for I was now conscious of a great evil radiating from this colourful window. Presently, Art took my hand once more and led me fast away, saying, 'What's this about staying with Draper until the end of January?'

I told him about the two weeks at Rotherhithe.

'You must leave him before then. Immediately, in fact.'

'We are booked tomorrow at the Friday Fun,' I said.

'Then that must be your last performance with him. But do not on any account tell him in person. Write to him the next day, or send a wire. Do you understand me, Kate?'

As we turned a corner, he stopped and took both my hands. 'You must give me your word on this, Kate.'

I gave it.

'Thanks, dear,' he said, and he kissed me briefly on the lips.

241

*

Jean had been rolling a cigarette as she read over her manuscript. She now lit the cigarette and looked through the
window. A lorry – important in relation to the Monster – had
arrived, and the yellow-jacketed men were having a conference in the vicinity of it. That it was Saturday morning was
perfectly obvious from the weather: the sun challenging the
greyness in honour of the weekend. A long walk along the
river and into town was called for – unwind after the week's
exertions. She'd been working ever since Coates had quit the
flat in such strange circumstances on Sunday evening. She had
in effect run away to 1898 and taken refuge there; and Coates
had not tried to get in touch, so it was obviously all over, and
just as well. She'd heard nothing from Vincent either, in spite
of a follow-up email hoping he was well. His silence worried
Jean, but also irritated her because she'd had Vincent down as
someone who liked and in some way needed her.

She'd been working hard but also decadently, sustained by
the adrenaline of the discoveries that had filled the pages she
was about to read over. She had been taking taxis between
libraries and archives, smoking excessively when not in a
library (as though it were obligatory to smoke outside them,
just as it was obligatory not to when *in* them) and living on
takeaways. She hated authors who said this sort of thing,
but . . . she really *had* written as if the narrative had been dictated to her, and the realisation that her denouement ought to
be written in the third person (which meant she would have
to go back over the earlier parts and put *those* into the third
person) had not slowed her momentum. Kate was just as present to her as 'she' as she had been when 'I'.

It was a funny sort of evening in Rotherhithe, Kate thought, as she approached the Hippodrome with carpet bag in hand. The Lower Road traffic was as busy as if it had been the middle of the day, and while the sky was dark, thin white clouds lingered in it. And there was something sun-like about the moon, which was both full and orange in colour. (It struck Kate as being an imposter moon; the real one no doubt sulking in some obscure corner of the sky, over Deptford way.) The days had been racing by at speed, and it seemed they were no longer checked by the nights. It was hard to believe that only a matter of weeks had gone by since she had first walked into the Hippodrome for her interview with Draper. On that occasion, they'd had the place to themselves. Now, at a quarter to seven, East Londoners in their hundreds were already streaming towards the open doors of the Friday Fun.

Kate diverted off Lower Road to approach the theatre from the stage door at the rear. Forty-five minutes until curtain up. The first time she'd been on this bill, she'd turned up four hours early – and the building had seemed to be twice the height back then. She was now an experienced 'pro', and when she'd quit the flat, The Dad had said, 'Bye, love,' as casually as if she had been going off to a stint of pupil-teaching.

As she passed the little window of the stage door keeper, he called out, 'Evening, Kate!' (they had already gone through the 'Miss French' phase), and this time he added, 'Wire for you!' and passed her an envelope. She thanked him and took it with her to the dressing room, opening it in leisurely fashion. She had plenty of time. As on the seaside tour, she and Draper would be on immediately before the interval. The wire was from Art Wakelam: *Will be in Circle Bar post interval. Good luck!* Art had told her that a business meeting would prevent his coming, but he evidently did not trust her to make a clean break from Draper. He needn't have worried about her *intention* to make the break, but she had been hesitating over what to do if Draper were to suggest another 'glass of fizzle' after their turn, and the prospect of being trapped with him in some quiet bar (there were three in the theatre) while the second half went its raucous way in the auditorium, had been the cause of some anxiety ... But now she would be able to say, 'I'm so sorry, but I have a prior engagement with Mr Wakelam,' which would put him off most effectively. An expression from her days in the north came to her as she stepped into the dressing room. Draper wouldn't *like* it, but he would have to *lump* it.

On entering the dressing room, she was greeted by those jolly shootists, the Vivians. Kate said a friendly hello to all five, and there was a quick bout of cheek kissing, after which they went back to their preparations amid a tangle of grease paints, cold creams, rouges, brushes, silken gloves, jewellery and guns. One of them – the leader, Eleanor – was sitting at a mirror, but not looking at herself. She was squinting along the length of a shotgun that had beautiful pearl inlays in the wood. She then briskly *snapped* it, or appeared to, but it didn't quite break in two, and she stuffed two bullets (perhaps not called that, since things called cartridges were also involved) into the two holes revealed by her violent action. She immediately ejected those bullets or cartridges by some complicated means, as though the sight of them disgusted her, and they flew onto the floor. She picked them up and handed the gun to either Amy or Muriel (Kate still wasn't sure of the names), saying, 'I don't like that much, stick to the Colt.' Not all of the guns were real; or they didn't fire real bullets – certainly not the ones used when they walked on stage, shooting in all directions to the accompaniment of some very riotous piano music. But the Vivians would not be on until the second half.

Kate could hear the overture for the show, a piece rather sternly entitled 'Now is the Time For Fun'. She was putting on her make-up quite automatically as she heard the applause for the opening turn. A big hand always created a slight quaking of the mirror glass, which was sometimes accompanied by a flickering of the electric light, but this no longer troubled her in the slightest. She was not thinking of her coming performance, but of Art Wakelam . . .

*

. . . who was just then descending the steps that led into the ticket hall of Baker Street station. Ahead of him and below was a great throng of supposed travellers, many of whom – to his irritation – showed no signs of interest in any train. They were standing about, smoking, conferring with their fellows, reading newspapers or examining their watches. 'Something wrong?' he asked the attendant at the ticket gate.

'Spot of bother on the Extension Line,' he said.

Art nodded thanks, just as though this meant anything to him.

' . . . so they're a bit slow coming in from the Cross,' the man added. He was trying his best to help, but Art Wakelam had never grasped the intricacies of this Metropolitan Railway. He had it down as one of those phenomena you had to have been in London for longer than he'd been in London to understand. He was waiting for it to be made more like the railways of New York or, for that matter, Baltimore: to be 'electrivised', in other words. (And this was apparently in prospect; some men from New York had come over expressly to do it.)

As Art fought his way down a further staircase towards the platform, he encountered a crowd of still greater density. His ticket was for first class, but the sign reading FIRST was too far distant along the platform and there were too many second and third class candidates in the way. Beyond the throng, the tunnel mouth looked dark and empty.

Art thought of cutting his losses and going back up to the street to hail a cab. Now that a chance for a clean break had occurred, it was imperative that Kate must take it, yet Draper would surely try to keep hold of her. What man in his right mind would not want to? And a man not in his right mind would also want to . . .

He was about to fight his way back to the surface when he saw a glimmer in the tunnel. The engine – that absurdly self-satisfied contraption – was slowly approaching in a red halo made by the burning of the fire inside it. On emerging, it belched a gout of black smoke, which tried its best to escape – running rapidly along the centre of the brick roof in search of an aperture – before giving up and settling on the heads of the people waiting to either side. Disgusted anew at this, Art was on the point of leaving again when a platform guard shouted from amid the crowd, 'New Cross train!'

New Cross wasn't '*the* Cross' (there were many crosses to bear on this line): that was *King's* Cross. New Cross – as Art had ascertained by tracing his finger over a railway map prior to setting out from the offices of Selwyn & Wise – was somewhere in south London, and the trains that went there went to Rotherhithe on the way. At some easterly point, these trains escaped from the main loop of the Metropolitan in order to begin trundling south, making for New Cross via the under-river tunnel which ran between Wapping and Rotherhithe. This being an obscure and specialist train, there were not many takers for it. He climbed up into a third class compartment, sat down and . . . nothing happened. He was alone in the compartment; the crowd on the platform might have been a hundred miles away. He unbuttoned his top coat and sat back on the seat of dusty crimson velvet. He looked up at the ceiling, which was dirty but colourful, and *lumpy*: a design of flowers had been incorporated into something that was not plasterwork, but papier maché, possibly. It was now twenty to eight, and for the third time, he thought about quitting Baker Street station. There was no point in being on the right train if the right train wasn't moving.

The door opened and a man came in, accompanied by the sound of the platform hubbub. He put a big leathern bag on the seat opposite Art's. He then returned to the door, which he had not closed. In fact, he was holding the door open for – as it turned out – another man, who also carried a large leathern bag of a similar kind. They were not much older than Art himself, but somewhat out of condition, and there was a good amount of puffing and blowing, and wiping of brows with handkerchiefs, as the pair settled down into their seats with their bags beside them. They were good bags, Art thought, which was to say, the leather was of good quality. Their boots were good as well: black, high-laced and well polished. Their suits were not so good, and nor had their handkerchiefs been. The knots of their ties were insufficiently generous. The men, both red faced from the exertions involved in reaching the train, had still barely spoken. What they were doing instead was staring at Art's boots. But now a whistle was being blown, and the train was creaking away, so let them stare: Art was rather proud of his boots, as he was of all his attire. It was a quarter to eight. He ought to make it to Rotherhithe station by half past. A brisk walk would then take him to the Hippodrome by a quarter to nine, which was about when the interval would start.

*

By ten past eight, the train had crawled as far as some station Art didn't know the name of. There'd been some initial slamming of doors, but now the platform, coloured yellowish by the gas, presented a still life. Among the jumble of advertisements – Marigold Flake Cigarettes, Waltham's Brown Stout, Remington Typewriters – Art saw only one notice that implied railway proprietorship: *Through tickets are issued from this station to all parts of London.* The train's progress had been incredibly slow since Baker Street. The engine had ceased to be a confident thing, but groped its way through the tunnels as though for the first time, marvelling

248

at the twists and turns and the occasional appearance of a different darkness – the moonlit sky, revealed by some aperture – followed by a return to a greater gloom even than before.

His two companions in the compartment were talking. The slightly redder one was saying, 'Well, in some of our shops the parts for turning in are left on the patterns, with holes at the right distance from the edges of course, for pricking the turn in.'

'In our places,' the slightly less red one said, 'the pattern was always cut exact to the fitting.'

'But then the cutter has to prick very close to the edge, and not all of them are up to it.'

'Very true is that,' said less red. 'Very true indeed. We found that to our cost.'

Art had reached two conclusions about the men. Firstly, they were boot-makers of a middling-to-superior kind – the owners of boot-making premises rather than actual crafts-men. Secondly, they were slightly drunk.

'It's harder and harder to get the men for the bespoke trade,' the redder one was now saying. 'But the customers know that: they *know*, when they get one of our boots, that it's a rather special article.'

'Oh,' said less red, 'I hope you haven't been doling them out one at a time, old man. Better say, "*When* they get a pair!"' Which joviality prompted the redder one to produce a hip flask from his suit coat. He took a belt on it, passed it to the other. Art Wakelam resented their joviality.

'Where *is* this, sir?' Art said to the redder man.

'Aldgate East,' he replied.

'And why the delay?'

'Can't say exactly. They might be changing over the foot-plate men. They sometimes do that here.'

'We've just passed the junction, you see,' less red put in. 'They often have a new pair to take it on from here.'

As he spoke, the engine woke up again, and they were moving. Art immediately liked the men better, and felt ashamed at having been so peremptory.

'Couldn't help overhearing,' he said. 'You're in the boot-making line?'

'*Bang* on,' said the redder one, and he took his pocket book and handed over a card which revealed him to be E.B. SULLIVAN, BESPOKE SHOES AND BOOTS, of Union Road, Wapping. 'This is Mr Ken Parker,' he said, indicating his neighbour, who handed over his own card. Parker's shop was in Shadwell, which didn't interest Art, but Wapping did. They had come into another station.

'Whitechapel St Mary's,' said Mr Ken Parker. 'Another junction coming up now.'

Art said to E.B. Sullivan: 'Theatre's my line. I used to know a fellow – he was on the Halls – who lived at Wapping. Name of Brooks: Hugh Brooks. He was always pretty well turned out ... I wonder if he was a customer of yours?'

'Hugh Brooks? Certainly was – we'd do him a pair of Balmorals about once a year.'

They were still moving, shaking past the black brickwork of the tunnel.

'What *was* he on the Halls?' asked Sullivan. 'Singer?'

'Mesmerist,' said Art.

'Eh?'

'Mind reader.'

Sullivan nodded.

'He went to Australia,' Art said flatly.

'That's what somebody told me,' Sullivan said.

'Who?'

'His landlady. He had diggings on Paradise Street. She went away for a couple of days and when she came back he was gone. He left a note and half his belongings, which he said were hers to sell if she wanted.'

'In lieu of back rent?' asked Art. He was beginning to feel far too hot.

'No, he paid the back rent – the cash was there with the scribbled note. He never paid *me* though. We'd finished a pair of Balmorals for him the week before, as he knew very well. He'd always been a regular payer, and seemed a pretty straight-up-and-down chap, so the whole episode was a bit . . . '

'It's a *mystery*,' Parker put in, as if that were an adequate explanation.

The train had stopped in a station: Wapping. 'Here's us,' said Sullivan, and he and Parker were standing. 'That business with Brooks,' said Sullivan, 'it's one for Sherlock Holmes.'

'The Adventure of the Mind Reader's Shoes,' Parker supplied. '*I'd* read it,' he added, grinning at Art. And they both shook his hand before quitting the compartment.

The train moved off again. It was lonely in the compartment without the boot-makers. Why hadn't he damn well taken a cab? Art took out his watch: twenty-five past eight.

*

At twenty-five past eight, Kate stepped into the corridor. 'Knock 'em, doll!' she heard from one of the Vivians as she closed the dressing-room door behind her. Draper waited in the wings ahead of her. She could see his surprisingly broad back. She moved into place alongside him, and by way of greeting he muttered something, and adjusted his spectacles using both his large hands. On the stage, some tumblers were tumbling. There were about nine of them but they were not the Nine Neros. They were rather *better* than the Nine Neros, possibly.

'They're good,' said Kate.

'They're over-running,' said Draper.

As the tumblers took their call and came off, Draper was consulting his watch. He was still consulting it as the rowdy tumblers' music gave way to their own lonely-sounding theme and the stage lights dimmed, making the effect of the starlit sky. 'The mysterious Martian Girl . . . ' the Chairman was saying, in a sort of reverential hoarse whisper, '. . . and her assistant, Mr Joseph Draper.'

Even in the half light, Kate could see that Draper was frowning: 'Did you tell him to say that?'

'Certainly not,' Kate replied, in her own hoarse whisper, as Draper took her hand and they stepped out of the wings. With the music giving way to applause, Draper led her to the chair. When seated, she adjusted her skirt, composing herself in the way that she knew fascinated the audience for some reason she could not fathom. She could feel the deepening silence: they were always anxious on her behalf.

Draper said, 'You are quite comfortable?'

Kate nodded.

'Please confirm that you are quite comfortable.'

She confirmed again with a nod, realising that, in spite of being about to venture onto the Astral Plane or some such place, she was in imminent danger of yawning; and she did yawn, after a fashion, but with her hand over her mouth.

'Some may profess,' Draper was saying, 'to find in what follows a mere trickery.' (He had dropped the stuff about Cicero.) 'Others may see feats performed that are completely incompatible with inductive science ... Now,' he continued, fishing in his pocket, 'what Miss French sees, I see; and what I know, Miss French knows.' He turned towards Kate, who tilted her head back, like a patient on the dentist's chair. Draper lowered the heavy spectacles onto her eyes, the ships rolling broadside towards her, and commenced to wind the soft blindfold around them, sealing her darkness as he asked the auditors to have their bank notes and pocket books and tickets at the ready for her to describe in minute detail. But even that last part no longer caused her undue anxiety.

*

Very cautiously, the train moved through the brick tunnel. Then the tunnel became stone, but the train pressed on. Art listened to the slight swirling of the gas. There was an indicator in something resembling a cigar box above the opposite seat, where boot-maker Sullivan had sat. The name of the next station was supposed to appear there but the indicator was in dereliction of duty, because it read, quite

253

irrelevantly, *Baker Street*, which was half a dozen stops ago. The principle seemed to be that, if the indicator couldn't be correct, then at least it could proclaim the name of the principal station of the Metropolitan Railway. Art nearly smiled as the train began picking up speed. Whatever the truth about Draper's dealings with Brooks, he would soon be with Kate, and he planned to *remain* with her.

Art loved this city of London. It was music hall writ large: a place of drunken but admirably swaggering leonine men and beautiful yet wayward women, all walking in and out of strange effects of light, and operating with irony – such a rare commodity in the States.

The train had stopped.

Art stood, and opened the window of the compartment again: a brackish smell came in, and he thought he could hear dripping water. A different sort of watery noise came from the direction of the engine: it was somehow contriving to make the sound of heavy rain. But the heavy rain was distant and the dripping water close. The hot white fog of the engine began drifting towards him as he leant out of the window, and with it came a coal taint, but the brackish smell was the dominant one. Art closed the window and sat down. He knew perfectly well where he was: he was under the river.

It was twenty-five to nine.

*

She could hear the clattering of Draper's boots as he descended to the stalls. After a brief negotiation with an auditor or two, he enquired, 'What article is this?'

254

First set: women's stuff.

'Will you say?'

'Will' (or 'won't') was number five, denoting, in first set, a purse.

'A purse,' she said, and it was quite amazing that people were kind enough to applaud.

'What article is this?' First set again. 'Tell me.'

'Tell' signified the number ten, and number ten in first set was a fan. She said so, earning more applause. Evidently it was not one of those fans supposedly in existence that bore insignia (requiring use of the letter codes) because the subject of the fan was now dropped, and a new question was put ...

'This article?'

Seventeenth set.

'Are you able to say what I hold?'

The 'Are' keyed it to number eight, a prayer book.

'Will you say the fabric?'

Not unless you give me the number code, thought Kate.

The number code was duly given: 'Pray tell?'

'Pray' was number seven: buckskin.

Kate said so, and there was applause ... followed by a hiatus. She could hear a kind of rumbling from the front of the stalls. Draper was perhaps moving from one line of auditors to another, and the audience was becoming restive; there were other footfalls, people heading to the bars. Well, it was nearly interval time, and some people needed to have the interval drink the moment they started *thinking* about the interval drink. Kate heard Draper's rather ragged and weary shout from the stalls:

'Now, what is this?'

Ninth set was indicated.

'Do you know?'

Number four: 'An umbrella.'

'Say the fabric?'

Number five: 'Silk.'

Applause, fairly desultory. As it faded away, that was some new element; another rumble, a single loud footfall. Then, from Draper, a half-whispered reproof, 'If you would hold on a moment, sir, this lady was ... ' and a kind of whispered conflab had commenced. 'But if I might ask you to wait your turn,' he was saying, but Kate did not feel like waiting because the darkness before her eyes was relenting and the gift was being given more generously – and surely with more reason – than ever before.

'The gentleman presents a cane,' she said, naming the first item she saw in her mind's eye. 'It is of ebony with a silver top.' Because it was all so beautifully clear.

She had silenced everybody, but when the auditors real-ised what had occurred – namely that the answer had been given with exceptional speed – thunderous applause ensued, into which Kate was still speaking: 'The gentleman presents in addition a pocket book ... ' She waited as the pocket book of her mind's eye was opened and the owner's initials dis-closed. 'Inside are the initials H.L.B.,' she said, but she had not been heard, and there were shouts, as the applause died down, of 'Say again!' and 'We didn't hear.'

A dead silence succeeded these shouted remarks. Why was Draper not speaking? All excitement now gone, Kate repeated the words she had spoken, but this time slowly and with a sense of dread, realising she ought not have uttered them in the first place:

'The gentleman presents in addition a pocket book. Inside are the initials H.L.B.'

The silence continued, until the voice of somebody who was not a professional speaker – the voice of an auditor – said, 'That is quite correct,' and the ovation thundered down like an avalanche. When something like quiet returned, Draper was speaking in a small and weak voice: 'What may this be?' No image presented itself in the darkness, but Kate knew they were in the second set, and when Draper followed up with 'Let us know, please' he was signifying the second item of the second set: a bracelet. In other words, things had gone back to normal, and so they continued until the applause for the end of the turn, and Draper was removing the velvet band from around her temples. He lifted up the heavy spectacles, but he was already turning away as he came into view. He was looking towards the wings and heading rapidly that way. They were supposed to walk off together, but he was not waiting; she had the idea he might be going to be sick, and for all these and many other reasons, she knew that the silver-topped cane and the pocket book marked H.L.B. had been the property of Draper's previous partner, Hugh Brooks.

As she walked towards the wings, the spotlight followed her, and so did loud applause, for the auditors were commending her miraculous deductions of a moment ago. When she reached the wings, the stage became instantly dark behind her, and Draper stood before her, in relative illumination. His hands were by his sides in an unnatural

257

way, as though he intended to use them but had not decided what for. She could not read the expression on his face, but he was about to speak. She did not want him to speak, however, and in an attempt to deflect him, she summoned the call boy, who was loitering at the far end of the corridor. The call boy was called Jack, so she said, 'Jack!' but she didn't know what else to add. She hoped he would advance, coming in between her and Draper, but he remained small in the far distance, and his voice was also small as he said, 'Yes, Miss French?'

She was aware of a great, happy rumbling from the auditorium as the auditors flowed from their seats and towards the bars. Art Wakelam ought to be waiting – *would* be waiting – in the Circle Bar, and now she would go to him. She put her head down and simply walked past Draper, brushing his suit coat and saying 'Good evening,' because something had to be said after all.

'Kate,' he said.

She turned towards him. 'Yes?'

'It is necessary that we speak.'

'But I am going up to the Circle Bar, just now. And you are going to the north.'

She was standing next to the call boy, who looked rather fearful. He said, 'Is there something I can fetch you, Miss French?'

'Jack, would you go up to the Circle Bar, and tell Mr Wakelam ... you know Mr Wakelam, don't you?'

Jack nodded.

'Please tell him I will be there in five minutes.'

'Yes, Miss French.'

She looked again at Draper. He still didn't know what to do. She turned swiftly into the female dressing room, where Draper could not follow her. The Vivians were now clustered at the far end, sitting in a circle, dressed like lady cowboys. They were in deep conversation with three other lady turners, two of whom wore togas: Jean did not know their names, but she knew they performed songs and danced in a sort of Ancient Roman skit, along with two men, who were no doubt at that moment adorned in their own togas in the male dressing room across the corridor. Also involved in the conflab – or half involved, for she had a copy of *The Era* on her lap – was a woman dressed as a man: a very clever male impersonator called Lena Bishop. Nobody appeared to have noticed Kate's arrival. They all seemed very far away, as Kate put on her coat and collected up her portmanteau. The place next to hers, she noticed, was cluttered with all the guns of the Vivians. When Kate stepped out of the dressing room, Draper was gone, but Jack was there.

'No sign of him, Miss French.'

'Oh, thanks, Jack,' and she gave him a coin, which turned out to be half a crown.

'That's too much, Miss French,' he said. Then, as she approached the stage door, he said, 'Are you not going up to the Circle Bar?'

But she was out in the street. It was not necessary to step out into the street in order to reach the Circle Bar, but there was something she must do. She turned the corner and came to the front of the theatre. The weird orange moon continued to illuminate the scene, which was emptier than before. The white ragged clouds had been blown away by a new, cold wind; the traffic had declined, and all the people were inside the theatre. But not quite all, for the doorkeeper stood smoking outside the front doors, and a small man stood on the opposite side of the road, watching and waiting. He wore a brown coat and a brown Derby hat, and he held a cane. A cab was coming from the right. As it approached Kate, it slowed down, but not for her. Fifty yards to the left, Draper – in black coat and bowler – stood with arm outstretched. The cab stopped, and he climbed in. He was sticking with his plan of going to the North, it appeared.

The small man with the cane watched Draper's departure, then – as the cab headed off – he crossed the road towards Kate, walking with a rather scuttling motion. 'Miss French,' he said, in a rapid, constricted voice, 'I knew you would come out.' The man was not only small, but small-featured, like a ventriloquist's figure.

'And you are?'

'Peter Wilson. Hugh Brooks was my uncle.'

They had begun walking away from the Hippodrome.

'I read about you in the theatrical papers, Miss French, and I knew you had an exceptional gift.'

'A gift?' said Kate. She was thinking about how she'd known something was amiss with Draper when the cane had been presented to him by Wilson. She could tell by Draper's hushed and panicked speech. What object might provoke that reaction? She'd known that Brooks always carried a silver-topped cane. As for the pocket book ... that might be said to have followed naturally. What man didn't carry a pocket book, and that of a dandified fellow like

260

Brooks would have been embossed with his initials. And perhaps she was unaware of having learnt his middle initial on some previous occasion?

'I suppose,' Wilson was saying, 'that as well as knowing what the articles were, you knew to whom they belonged?'

'Hugh Brooks,' said Kate.

'And you can tell where we're going just now?'

'To the river.'

'Correct. You are quite obviously a genuine psychic.'

'Oh, it's difficult to avoid the river if you walk in this direction.'

'You are too modest, Miss French.'

He spoke with a precise formality, as though English were his second language, which it was obviously *not*, since he had a cockney accent. He was merely one of those elusive types who'd graduated from one social class without finding a secure berth in another.

'Why did you bring the articles?' she asked. 'You see, I must ask, because my psychic abilities – if any – are limited to occasional bursts of inspiration that only ever occur on the stage, and not when I am at large in the world.' They were crossing the big road that, in conjunction with Lower Road, formed a capital 'T'. There was little traffic at the junction: only a dray cart approaching from far to the left. 'You didn't bring them to test me, I suppose?'

'No,' said Peter Wilson. 'I brought them to test Draper, and you saw with what result. Well, you did not *see*, but he failed the test, Miss French. The villain nearly fainted when he saw this cane.' He held it up. 'My uncle carried it everywhere with him, and he used it on stage as well. There's no mistaking it. You'd think it would be a horse's head on the top, but it's a swan's, quite distinctive. You'll know where I found it, I daresay; and you'll know where I found the pocket book.'

'I would guess in the river, or on the edges of it.'

'Right again. Miss French, you are a marvel.'

But this was all quite logical and un-marvellous.

They were now passing the church that marked the start of the territory of the Thames. It was strange for Kate to be walking alongside a full-grown man who was smaller than she was. Wilson said, 'Here's another item I had about me, Miss French,' and he showed her – briefly and with great pride – a small revolver, before replacing it in the inside pocket of his top coat. 'I have never broken the law in my life, Miss French, but I was very tempted to shoot the man down from my place in the stalls. Draper killed my uncle, Miss French, and he put him in the river. You knew that, I suppose.'

'I *believe* I did,' said Kate.

The little man stopped. They had entered an alleyway. 'Then why did you enter a professional association with such a person?' he asked, quite mildly.

'I needed the money at the time,' said Kate, walking on, 'and I wasn't *entirely* sure what he'd done.'

She formulated in her mind, but did not speak out loud, a fuller defence. If she had suspected Draper, and banished the suspicion because of the money, then she believed she had been justified in doing so on two counts. In the first place, most of the money had gone to alleviate what were likely to be The Dad's last months. Secondly, she had been

262

biding her time: waiting to find the purpose of the revelations that had come to her on stage.

Wilson said, 'I've been keeping cases on him ever since my uncle disappeared, Miss French. There's nobody else to do it. Hugh Brooks had only a small handful of friends, but nobody with what you might call a permanent interest. I'm his only relative except for his sister – my mother – and she hasn't got all her wits.'

As they walked, Kate was trying not to look down at him, but it was hard to do otherwise.

'What line of work are you in, Mr Wilson?'

'I'm an upholsterer; I have my own small shop. But that doesn't signify in the least, Miss French.'

They crossed an echoing square bounded by tall sea captains' houses – dead sea captains, going by the darkness and silence of them. As they traversed the square diagonally, they heard footsteps approaching: two men in shovel hats came up. One of them spoke: 'Do you want a boat?'

'No, thank you very much,' said Wilson, and the men continued on their way, to his evident relief, quitting the square by a gap between two of the houses. Kate and Wilson left by another gap.

'We must walk down here,' Wilson said, and they turned into another alleyway. A clock was chiming a quarter to nine.

*

Ten to nine. The interval would have started five minutes ago, and Kate would be at Draper's mercy.

Among Art's many unspoken fears was that Draper

263

would ask Kate to marry him, as a means of controlling her and buying her silence. He pulled down the leather strap to open the window again. The river smell came in once more. Then he opened the door and jumped down onto the black gravel. He commenced walking, with the high train to his left and a series of transverse stone arches to his right, beyond which presumably lay the line heading in the opposite direction; but it was too dark to see. The gas light from the high windows of the carriages did not throw that far. He was approaching the engine, which was making a seething noise, because some sort of mechanical process had to go on even when it was stationary. There was an additional, louder seething. It was like being in a great cistern. He was wondering what the driver and fireman would have to say about seeing a pedestrian trudging by (his hat would be about level with their footplate), when the engine made a great crunching noise, followed by another, and another, and then it was dragging the carriages away, leaving Art alone in the tunnel, although he could now see the light at the end of it that signified the platform of Rotherhithe. What bothered him a little, however, was the green signal light that the departure of the train had revealed.

*

The alleyway seemed to begin as the result of an accident – for no better reason than that two great warehouses did not quite touch. They walked along it. The alley continued between high walls before intersecting at right angles with a cobbled road running parallel to the river. Beyond the cobbled road, the alley continued, in the form of steps running into the water, giving the impression that some disaster had occurred – some inundation – but this was only high tide, and the river had an easy look to it. On the opposite bank stood the building that resembled a castle turret: the police station. At that moment, not only was the blue flag flying from the top (very clear in the moonlight), but a blue lamp was also blazing above the door. In the middle of the water, a steam launch was going away towards the sea. 'The police,' said Peter Wilson. 'Off on patrol.'

Kate watched them go. Their boat was nearly all chimney, and its black smoke, spinning upwards, revealed the sky to be merely dark blue. On either side of Kate, and on either bank of the river, the great wharves were deserted, the moored steamers and barges immobile. On some of the jetties, red lamps burned, perhaps as a warning, perhaps as an invitation that was not being taken up.

The right-hand wall of the alley, at this terminal point, was made by a low building. A blurred glow – orange and red – projected from the back of it onto the water. 'The Spread Eagle,' said Wilson, raising his cane towards it in a rather dismissive way. 'This,' he said, turning to the much taller building on the left hand side, 'is the Thames Tunnel Mill.'

This mill was new, and – being made of pinkish bricks dusted with white – rather Christmassy. Most of the windows were open, and delicate clouds of white flour floated out from the top ones. This must be the source of the white-dusted wagons Kate had seen before her first performance at the Friday Fun. She could see from the bottom of the alley that the mill gave directly onto the water, and red-painted derricks projected from it on that side. There were small balconies at some of the windows (or high doors) that pierced the mill, which were located both on the riverward side and also above their heads in this damp alley. The noise of the mill – a muffled pounding – leaked out from the apertures. Suddenly, Kate's companion shouted, 'Mr Eugene Roberts! Hello there!' and a man stepped onto one of the balconies above them. 'Down in a minute!' he called, amicably enough.

After half a minute, he was approaching along the alleyway, obviously having come out of the mill by some unseen door on the landward side. He wore a long white dust coat and a sort of white forage cap. The light coat fluttered in the gentle breeze rising up from the river, and he lifted the forage cap towards Kate. Wilson introduced him as Mr Eugene Roberts, and he was a pleasant-looking, amused-looking fellow, perhaps in the late fifties – twice Wilson's age, anyhow.

'This is Miss French,' said Wilson. 'She is an associate of Draper's.'

'Not a *friend* of his, I take it?' said Roberts, shaking Kate's hand.

'Not exactly,' said Kate.

'She performs with him on the Halls,' said Wilson. 'She has an inkling of what he's about.'

'And is she another witness?' Eugene Roberts asked Wilson.

'She might yet turn out to be,' said Wilson. 'I don't know everything she's seen. I've only just made her acquaintance.'

Roberts removed his hat and ruffled his hair, even though he didn't have much of it. He was smiling. 'I do hope you *will* turn out to be another witness, Miss French,' he said. 'It's rather lonely being the only one.'

'Would you tell Miss French what you saw?' said Wilson.

'Very happy to oblige,' said Roberts, turning again to Kate. 'It's my party piece, you see, Miss French. Mr Wilson here has asked me to tell the tale so often that I have it down pat.' He smiled again, and Kate smiled back. 'As you might have guessed, I work in there,' he said, indicating the mill, 'generally at nights. It's hot work, and every couple of hours, I'll step out onto a balcony for a quiet smoke. I was doing just that one night five years ago.'

'Saturday the ninth of October, 1893,' Wilson cut in.

'I'm still not *quite* word perfect, you see,' said Roberts. ' ... It was about midnight sort of time and I was out front, looking over the water, when I heard a bit of a commotion from this alleyway. I was thinking about cutting across the top floor of the mill to have a look down from this side, when the fellows causing the disturbance appeared below me. The tide was on the ebb just then. The little mud bank at the bottom of these stairs was uncovered, and this pair had come down the stairs and were standing on it. They were having a regular set-to, Miss French. One big fellow with glasses ... '

'Draper,' Wilson cut in again.

' ... And a smaller chap with a cane.'

'Uncle Hugh,' said Wilson.

'They hadn't yet come to blows,' said Roberts, 'it was just a lot of shouting, mainly from the smaller chap.'

'He couldn't make it out,' said Wilson, 'except for one word.'

Roberts, very tolerant of these interruptions, said, 'The smaller one kept calling the bigger one a "rotter" – "I've known for years you were a rotter", and so on – and that was obviously driving the bigger one mad, not that he was saying much at all; but I could just tell he wasn't going to stand much more of it. I was thinking of calling out for them to leave off before it came to serious violence, when my governor tapped me on the shoulder and called me back in. One of the grindstones was running hot, and there's a danger of fire when that happens, so I had to see to it.'

'And that's all he saw,' said Wilson, with a great frustration in his tone. 'Until the next night.'

Roberts fished in his pocket, producing a tin of cigarettes. 'I assume you don't ...' he said to Kate (who shook her head), before offering the tin to Wilson who rather surprisingly took one. Quite a rigmarole then occurred, because the breeze coming up from the river didn't seem to want cigarettes lit in the alleyway.

'The next night,' said Eugene Roberts, when he'd succeeded in lighting his cigarette, 'I was on an early turn. Well, what *I* call early, which is what most people call late. I was due to knock off at midnight. At about eleven, I was on the balcony out back.'

The river, Kate noticed, was making a new noise: the water was swinging. Either the wind was getting up or the tide was turning, or possibly both. A dark vehicle of some sort rattled along the road at the top of the alley.

'I was looking downriver,' Roberts was saying, 'and I saw something snagged on the little jetty at the back of the pub here. I didn't think much of it, but when I booked off, I stepped into the pub for a nightcap, and I walked out back to look again.' He was indicating the jetty belonging to the pub. 'It was a tangle of rubbish . . . looked like a kind of bird's nest of broken wood, wire and old sacking. There was a swanky-looking cane in there, and I thought again of what I'd seen the night before. I know the fellow who keeps the pub, and he has a little galley that he moors under the jetty.' Roberts pointed to the very boat, which was just then little more than three feet away, rocking gently between the spars of the jetty. 'I climbed down into it and shoved myself over towards the bundle. There was the cane, and a pocket book – but all the paper inside was sodden, and nothing to make an identification.'

'Except the initials,' said Wilson.

'But they meant nothing to me,' said Roberts.

Wilson, turning to Kate, said, 'Mr Roberts might have asked in the pub whether any two men who seemed to be at odds had been in the night before. But he didn't think to do that.'

With perhaps the faintest trace of irritation, Eugene Roberts smiled at Kate, and pointed across the river. 'I was sort of hypnotised by that blue lamp,' he said, 'and I decided to take the stuff over to it. Well, I was already sitting in the boat, with a pair of oars to hand, and a nick's the right place for lost property, isn't it? It's the right place for the "found drowned" as well – because I did wonder whether the fight might have come to something really serious.'

It was very easy for Kate to imagine this kind man rowing quietly across to the blue lamp at midnight.

'And what did they say in the police station?' she asked.

'They weren't so very chatty,' said Eugene Roberts, grinning. 'I spoke to the desk sergeant and he gave me pretty short shrift. An argument – not even a fight – on the riverbank in Sailortown was nothing to him. What would be news would be a *friendly* conflab on the banks of the river. On top of that, he had to get ready for some sort of inspection or big parade or something ... and there'd been no "found drowned" for a couple of weeks. He took the cane and the pocket book, and entered them in a ledger. Then he gave me "Good night" in a pretty sharpish sort of tone, and I rowed back over. Of course, Mr Wilson here's been back there no end of times since.'

'The first time *I* went—' Wilson began, but Eugene Roberts cut him off.

'I'd better be getting back,' he said, tossing his cigarette stub into the river. 'I'll see you again shortly, Mr Wilson, I've no doubt, and it was a pleasure to meet you, Miss French.' And he headed off up the alley.

Wilson was indicating the Spread Eagle. 'I'm not a big one for public houses, Miss French, but it's getting rather cold out here ...'

*

In the tunnel, Art could hear the approach of another train. He ought to have known that the blockage, once cleared, might release another. He now saw a giant moving shadow that managed to emit light from either side, and to send smoke and steam tumbling forwards. The train came on, and he stepped into one of the sideways arches. A moment later, he was right next to something that seemed to have

270

the complexity of a moving factory: all interlocking, sliding and rolling pistons, rods and wheels – and a noise so loud, he found he could not walk and could hardly breathe. After the engine there came a tender full of coal, and then a long *train* of coal that took an eternity to pass. When the end finally came in sight, Art made out what he thought of as a caboose, but which the British called a brake van. As it whirled past, Art noticed that Draper spotted the brakesman of the train standing on the veranda fitted to the front of this vehicle. As Art looked helplessly up at him, he seemed to whirl, with outstretched arms, like a discus thrower. He let out a roar of anger or reproof, and Art felt a thud against the side of his head: his punishment for trespassing on the track. He was dazed for a moment, and choking in the black cloud the train had left behind. He removed his glove and put his hand to his temple. Even in the darkness, he could see that his fingers came away discoloured. He walked on (stumbling against the rail somewhat), arriving at the green light – which turned red as he passed – and finally into the light of the station, where he verified that his fingers were both black and red. He scrambled up onto the platform, pressing his handkerchief to the wound. Two women on the platform stepped back from him in horror as he made towards the exit. His white trousers were now black and white, and his eyes were streaming from the coal dust. In truth, the wound was not much, but the brakesman's shying of the coal had told him that evil was abroad tonight.

*

Kate and Wilson entered the pub, which was warm, wooden, dark, with thick red curtains closed against the river, the sudden disappearance of which was somewhat disorientating. After long negotiation, Wilson obtained for himself what appeared to be a tumbler of hot water. Kate accepted a small port. They sat by a good fire. 'The first time I went to the Marine Police,' Wilson doggedly resumed, 'was on January the third 1894 ... '

He talked slowly. He was a moral man, but without charm, and Kate knew that Art Wakelam must be waiting for her in the Circle Bar of the Hippodrome. The second half would have started by now, and he would be worried; he'd probably enquire at the stage door; he might then be directed to the front, since she believed the doorkeeper had seen her heading towards the river with Wilson, but Art Wakelam must be left to his own devices. It was more important to have the culmination of Wilson's tale, which was the fulfilment of the promise of the visions. As for herself, she must go where the cane and the pocket book led.

Wilson began explaining why he had gone to the police station on that first occasion. He told how, at Christmas 1894, his aunt had not received a card from Brooks. Made curious by this, he had visited the house in Wapping where Brooks had been lodging. The landlady had told him he'd gone to Australia. Wilson had expressed his incredulity with vehemence: 'I was disgusted by the news, Miss French, *disgusted*.' He had then visited the police station, to discover that his uncle did not appear on any of the 'found drowned' lists, but when Brooks happened to mention that he had often carried a cane decorated with a swan's head, he was shown that very cane, and told who had brought it in. And so his friendship – if that's what it was – with Eugene Roberts had commenced.

After hearing Roberts' tale, Wilson had called on Draper in Providence Road, and had been rudely dismissed. The maid, he noticed, had somehow come by a black eye. Some weeks later, Wilson's mother received what purported to be a letter from Brooks in Australia. 'It was an absurdity, Miss French,' Wilson said. 'It made out that he was touring the country. He had spent some time in a place called Wollongong, the name of which derived from the Aboriginal word for clouds. Coal had been discovered there in 1797. It was all out of an encyclopedia, Miss French, and it was type-written. Type-written, on a type-*writer*, Miss French – this by a man who was supposed to be travelling light in Australia, with little more than a knapsack to contain his belongings.'

'But did it not carry an Australian postmark?'

Wilson waved the point away, which of course he was quite right to do.

He had then commenced making enquiries in the Halls, and learnt of Draper's reputation as a difficult and surly man. He had returned repeatedly to the Marine Police. 'They became thoroughly sick of me, Miss French.' But after two years, he had learnt from the Wapping men that they did know a man by the name of Joseph Draper. He was one of the 'regulars' at what Wilson described as 'a riverside establishment'. Two of the girls from this establishment had appeared on the 'found drowned' lists, in 'ninety-six and 'ninety-seven.

'But nothing could be proved,' he said, 'and this has

273

remained their fixed position. Six months ago, they gave me custody of the cane and the pocket book. I had no use for them, except as mementoes of my uncle, but then I read of your act, and so I formed the plan that you saw carried through tonight. I presented the cane and pocket book to Draper and I observed his reaction. I was hoping he would appear disturbed. It's possible he would have retained his composure, but by the extreme quickness of your divination you undermined his defences, and we saw what we saw . . . I was immediately sure that you would know the history of these articles, and that you would wish to speak to the person who had brought them in.'

He was looking about him, as though he had dropped something.

Kate said, 'But where has our talk got us?'

'I am building my case, Miss French, and you have heartened me considerably. I have been at this for five years, and I will continue for another fifty if necessary.'

'But you must have evidence, Mr Wilson.'

'Yes,' he said, and for a moment he looked very sad. Then he glanced under the table.

Kate said, 'You have lost something?'

Wilson eyed her assessingly, as though trying to discover whether this insight came from psychical powers or native wit. 'I appear to have left the cane somewhere. I must have put it down on the steps when I lit the cigarette.'

*

They stepped out of the pub and onto the river steps. Wilson immediately saw the cane, propped against the wall of the

Thames Tunnel Mill. As they approached it, they heard boot steps from the cobbled road at the top of the alley, where stood Draper. He held a gun, which he immediately fired. Kate saw the orange flare from the barrel and heard the deafening sound, which caused many gulls – unseen a moment ago – to start screaming and ascending towards the moon. Mr Wilson was on the ground. He had been shot in the leg, with the result that his leg was at the wrong angle. Then came a distant shout, and the sound of running feet. Kate heard her own name being called. It was Art; he was running along the alley that lay beyond the cobbled road – the one made by the accidental gap between the two warehouses. Only the cobbled road divided that alley from the one she was in, but Draper stood on that road. He was giving an occasional glance behind him. He was aware of Art Wakelam's rapid approach, but he had time to do what he wanted to do, and he was lifting the gun again.

Kate was kneeling by poor Mr Wilson, who had fainted, she believed, from the pain, for he still breathed. She looked towards Draper, and whilst she could see his expression, she could not read it, could not see his mind. So much for mesmerism. 'Oh, do please go away,' she said, 'I have a life to live,' but she might have been speaking to herself. Behind Draper, she saw Art running: she believed she had never seen anybody run so fast, but it was a feat being performed in another world – and then she saw the flare of the gun. She never heard the report.

PART THREE

PART THREE

J ean closed the Word file.

She felt a little guilty at having dispatched Kate in that violent way, but if the book were published, this would only be the start of her life in the imagination of readers. Anyway, Jean had had no choice. As she saved the file onto a memory stick, she regretted the fact that the novel form would not allow her to present the factual underpinning for what she'd written.

She had discovered, first of all, a review of the Friday Fun of 16 December, which she was convinced had been Kate's last performance. The review appeared in the strangely named *Times of the Music Halls*, an obscure weekly printed on green paper, and featuring many advertisements for naughty treats like cigarettes, cigars, alcohol. She had read:

The new darling of Rotherhithe is Miss Kate French, who was again in psychic alliance with Mr Joseph Draper last Friday. What sets Miss French apart is the feminine charm of her bearing on stage and the almost electrical rapidity of some of her divinations. Miss French is heavily blindfolded, but uses – we must suppose – her inner eye to identify the objects offered up to Draper by the auditors. Most impressively of all, she gave the salient details of a cane and a pocket book at the instant they were presented, much to the evident amazement of the auditor concerned, and (it seemed to this observer) of Mr Draper himself. Their performance, at any rate, was the highlight of another grand evening at the Hippodrome.

Jean had found that at the British Theatre Memorial Fund archive on Monday morning. On Tuesday morning, she had disclosed to one of the theatrical ladies that her two principals had lived at King's Cross in the 1890s. The theatrical lady – who was called, not at all surprisingly, Maeve – had tipped Jean off about the *North London Examiner*, a short-lived publication of the late nineteenth century, which had gained an afterlife by virtue of having been digitalised; and it was electronically searchable in the newspaper reading room of the British Library. Jean had gone there directly in hopes of finding mention of the life or death of Kate or The Dad. What she found had caused her to sit, quite motionless, for about five minutes.

SUICIDE OF A RETIRED POLICEMAN

Yesterday at the King's Cross Coroner's Court, Mr Howard Booth held an inquest on the body of Mr Frederick French, aged sixty-seven, a retired police officer, lately of Stanley Buildings, Pancras Road, who was found hanged on January 5th. The circumstances of the discovery were reported in the *North London Examiner* of January 13th. Mr Booth produced a letter which was found in the deceased's pocket and which he read as follows. 'To whom it may concern. I am sorry for the person who discovers this letter. It has not been my intention to cause distress to anybody. But life is intolerable without my beloved Kate, with whom I pray that I may be reunited in a better world. Signed, Frederick French.' Mr Sidney Barley of Hackney, a friend of the deceased, stated that Mr French had been in poor health from a weak chest, and had gone into a serious decline after the disappearance, in the middle of December, of his daughter Kate, a music hall performer. She had failed to return from an engagement at the Hippodrome, Rotherhithe.

The proceedings were interrupted at this point by an outburst from a member of the public. A man identifying himself as Mr Arthur Wakelam, theatrical agent, rose to his feet and made certain allegations, which Mr Booth then summarised as follows: 'Mr Wakelam, you make a number of allegations. Firstly, that the disappearance without trace of Mr French's daughter is to be accounted for by her murder; that this murder was committed by Mr Joseph Draper, who had performed in the music halls with Miss French, and who disposed of her body in the river at a time of fast-moving ebb tide immediately after loosing the fatal bullet; that you observed both the murder and the placing of the body in the river, and might have prevented the crime had you arrived on the scene in time; that a certain Mr Wilson was present at the scene, and that he had also been shot by Wakelam, but not fatally, and was unconscious at the time of the murder. You allege that Mr Draper was also responsible for the murder of Mr Hugh Brooks, with whom he had previously performed in the music halls, and possibly also of two young women found drowned off Rotherhithe in recent years. These allegations are a matter for the police, and I understand that Mr Draper is being sought by them at this present time.' The proceedings were then resumed. The Coroner found no evidence of foul play. A verdict of 'Suicide while temporarily insane' was returned.

Jean had requested a printout of the article, and it had sat on her table that Tuesday evening – alongside a rapidly emptying bottle of chardonnay – as she worked on her denouement, typing with amazing speed. At about two o'clock on Wednesday morning she had located online the telephone number of a body that represented coroners as a professional class. At eleven o'clock, she had broken off from her further researches at the Theatre Fund place to call this number. A very amenable ex-coroner had answered, and he had listened patiently as she read out to him the article from the *North London Examiner*. She then pounced with her question: 'Why did the coroner repeat Art Wakelam's allegations?'

'Oh,' said the ex-coroner, 'he had probably weighed up this Wakelam character and decided he was likely to be speaking the truth. A coroner has privilege against an action for defamation, so he can name names in a situation like that, and he obviously wanted the allegations to get into print.'

'He must have been a very nice man,' Jean had remarked, absurdly.

'We coroners generally are.'

The next thing was that Jean found a letter – dated 20 January 1899 – from Bill Wise of Selwyn & Wise to somebody whose name she did not recognise, and which did not matter. Wise had written:

Yes to Mademoiselle Loyal and her pigeons, but you know my view about animal acts, and I am making it a condition that she keeps the birds off the premises overnight. Yes also to The Vivians. You ask about Art Wakelam. He sailed to the States last week to participate, I suspect, in a shooting act of his own. (He considers New York to have been the likely destination of the fugitive Draper.)

She was thinking of these things as she walked along the Embankment into town, and it was a luxury to have this Saturday for thinking only. But in the absence of any real work, Coates – and his outburst of the previous Sunday – was returning to the fore of her mind. The strangest thing of all, she now decided, had been his statement, 'You've got this detective at King's Cross,' because she didn't really have a 'detective' at King's Cross, but only Tom Anderton, music hall performer, who had impersonated a Holmes-like detective, and had lived at King's Cross. But she must banish Coates. In order to try and do so, she began playing one of her favourite mental games. The set-up was as follows . . .

Jean's future editor, whether male or female, would be a person of great discernment and physical beauty, but they would naturally have a few questions about the manuscript. Nothing to get in the way of the drinks party and formal dinner at a Mayfair hotel that would be held in honour of the book . . . but still a few queries that the editor would mention in a tentative, amused sort of way, anticipating with pleasure the confident riposte they had come to expect from such a (fairly) young and highly talented author. The conversation would be conducted in a sun-dappled, modern office symptomatic of *money*:

EDITOR: How does Draper escape at the end?

JEAN: By boat. The rowing boat moored behind the pub, remember?

EDITOR: And did Wilson survive?

JEAN: Yes. But he was incapacitated at the crucial time, and, indeed, unconscious.

EDITOR: Of course, yes. Do you think we ought to spell that out?

JEAN: No.

EDITOR: And to go back to the moment before: what would Draper have been thinking, when he came across Wilson and Jean at the riverside?

JEAN: He would probably have thought that her psychic powers had enabled her to lead Wilson to the very spot where he had murdered Brooks.

EDITOR: And excuse me for asking such a crass question, but did Kate French *have* psychic powers? That seems to be left rather up in the air?

JEAN: Isn't it always rather up in the air? The question of whether anyone has such powers?

Big Ben was chiming midday as Jean approached a yellow sign. She thought it was something to do with roadworks, until she made out the words WITNESS APPEAL in red; then came the word MURDER, and the capitalisation continued relentlessly: ON OR ABOUT SUNDAY, OCTOBER 22ND A YOUNG MALE WAS FATALLY STABBED AND HIS BODY PUT INTO THE RIVER AT VICTORIA GARDENS. DID YOU SEE OR HEAR ANYTHING? PLEASE CALL US. There was a phone number – two in fact, one relating to this particular inquiry, and the other the more general Crimestoppers number.

Jean stopped walking. She was thinking of those bobbing harlequins, the police boats she'd seen three weeks before when coming out of Embankment Tube station. She consulted the calendar on her phone, wanting to make sure she had no further need to worry. But the calendar did not let her off the hook. It had been Monday, 23 October when she'd seen the boats, so it seemed likely they'd been attending to the body that was being spoken of here. She thought back to the peculiar, bus-oriented phone conversation she'd conducted with Coates from the magic shop. Right on cue, a number 87 bus was coming along the road beside her.

The bus and the sign; the sign and the bus.

Coates had done this murder, and he was worried that she might have seen him do it from the window of an 87 bus. A detective called Anderton was somehow on his trail, and he believed Jean knew this. She rested her right hand feebly on the river wall, like a helpless old lady. She thought she had written a historical story of a paranoid man who believed a young woman could read his mind, thereby discovering past iniquities. But it turned out that, as far as Coates was concerned, she had written a *roman à clef*. To think that she had ascribed Coates's reaction to jealousy of her abilities. The hubris of it! Coates had no interest in her, or anyone's, literary abilities. People in general were *not* jealous of the ramblings of an unpublished – and most likely unpublishable – author.

She walked on again, stopped again. She had asked herself a question: *What is here?* In the mesmerical code, those words denoted the fourth set, smoking paraphernalia, and she was looking down at most of a cigarette. It was flat and dirty, but she picked it up, looking at the small gold emblem of a bird's wings halfway along the paper: the symbol of American Spirit. Jean looked back at the witness appeal sign, which was now fifty yards behind her, but it was double-sided, so there could be no escaping its question: DID YOU SEE OR HEAR ANYTHING?

She could quite legitimately say that she had not seen anything, only this cigarette, which was not the kind of thing the signwriter had had in mind. American Spirit was a slightly exotic, but not completely obscure, brand. Jean got hers from a newsagent's in Fulham that had once been a full-blown tobacconist's. She believed you could also buy them from supermarkets – the bigger ones anyway. But the combination of the brand with the fact of the cigarette being smoked only a centimetre down, in the Coates manner . . . all of that taken together with his keenness to know whether she had been on this road, Millbank, on the Sunday evening of a murder. Jean was walking on, but she wanted to sit down.

What if this was the most important moment of her life?

She ought to throw the cigarette away: she didn't know where it had *been*. But what if she did know where it had been? Did the cigarette carry Coates's DNA? Had she now superimposed her own DNA, and might she herself be accused of the murder if she called the number? And if she called the police, and accused Coates, what did that make her? She would be a grass. Did Coates deserve any sympathy? He had thought that, by the hatefully elliptical means of a supposed literary manuscript, she was conveying to him the simple message, *I know that you killed a man and put him in the river.* Why (he must have been wondering) did she want him to know that he knew? Blackmail? If he thought that, might he not come after *her*? If he had killed a man, why not a woman? She would need police protection. She would probably have to go and live in the New Forest, or Dartmoor, with a hotline to the local police station.

She stopped again. It would be a difficult matter to find out if there were a Metropolitan Police detective called Anderton based in the vicinity of King's Cross ... but a private one? That would be simpler, because private detectives advertised. She forced herself to make the internet search, and her phone — not in the least flustered — politely asked if she had meant 'Anderson'? She looked him up, and it seemed he operated from a street running just north of the station; and there was his number.

As the detective's phone rang in an absurdly melodramatic and portentous way, she was rehearsing her lines. 'So sorry to bother you. You don't know me, but my name's Jean Beckett, and I wondered if I could ask a question in confidence. It's to do with a man called Coates. I just wondered if you knew him. His first name is ...' Of course *he'd* then say, 'What's it regarding?' and she wouldn't know how to deal with that. But voicemail had kicked in, and a surprisingly calm, northern man was asking her to leave a message, and he would call her straight back. Jean hung up. Then she dialled again and left her message.

She walked on, already feeling better. Her voice had been rather shaky, but she had *acted* at least, and she had taken some of the burden off herself and put it onto someone else, which had not perhaps been very nice of her. Was Coates danger-ous? He had not killed her so far, or harmed her in any way, despite the fact that they spent the entirety of their time alone together in a half-empty block of flats. Yes, there was a certain menace about him, but she had put that down to his maleness. Vincent, for example, did not have *enough* menace – was flac-cid – and that was a deficiency in him. It would be very easy to throw this filthy cigarette end into the river, which was loitering a mere ten feet away.

Jean looked up and saw the Houses of Parliament, pictur-esquely offset by a red bus going around Parliament Square. This picture-postcard double act was suddenly very consol-ing. She was in the heart of London, and she'd been very *near* to the heart of London three minutes ago when she'd picked up this bedraggled piece of litter. How many people were in the heart of London with her? Millions. Only a very small percentage of them smoked American Spirits, but even that number must be in the high hundreds if not thousands. Yes, most of those would smoke them all the way down, but there were many reasons for not completing a cigarette, aside from an habitual inclination against doing so. Your bus was coming; your taxi had just pulled up; and it was generally quite difficult to smoke on this road, what with the sideways gale that was always coming off the river.

Coates was moody and arrogant, yes, but who would he

have found to kill on Millbank on a dark Sunday night? And *why*? He was too snobbish to tangle with the kind of drunk who might be spoiling for a fight. It was true that he would mutter to himself, and might that not signify a dangerous mental state? But it might equally be a function of the afore-mentioned arrogance. It was occasionally necessary for him to consult a more intelligent person (i.e. himself) than present company offered, and many people talked to themselves. She, Jean, did it all the time. As for his remark about the detective . . . probably that *had* been his indulgence in literary criticism. It was very likely that, having read in her story of the Sherlock Holmes-like comedy detective Holmfirth (played by Tom Anderton), he was saying in effect, 'I see you've made a half-baked attempt at turning it into a crime novel.'

Also, the Ander*son* she had discovered had not called her back. Yes, it had only been three minutes since she'd called him, but it seemed inconceivable that he was not just then shaking his head as he listened to her message, marvelling at the way private investigators were magnets for loonies. As she continued to walk on, she took her wallet from her handbag, and put the cigarette inside the wallet. She would decide what to do with it by the end of the day.

———

And Jean had a lovely Saturday in the West End, accompanied by autumn sunshine and a phone that remained silent. An hour in Foyle's bookshop, which seemed to have a space reserved for *The Martian Girl* in its window . . . followed by lunch in the Stockpot on Old Compton Street: baked trout and chips and two cups of tea, and moreover she resisted the treacle sponge. She then looked into the record shops on Berwick Street, buying vinyl by Laura Nyro and Al Green. She also got talking to a bloke who said he might be able to put some DJing her way, and gave her his card. She would see the cigarette butt every time she opened her wallet, and it looked grubbier and more negligible every time.

Jean then walked to the Theatre Memorial Archive, and caused a sensation by offering a donation. A cheque was very acceptable indeed, even if only for fifty pounds, and one of the bangled ladies had actually hugged her. Jean had then doubled back quite a long way west and entered the alley of the magic shop, because it was absurd not to enquire after Vincent while she was in the West End.

She pushed open the door braced to encounter the unpleasant Worsley, who would surely be minding the shop if Vincent were indeed absent. Vincent was *not* in the shop, and nor was anyone except a middle-aged, slightly punk-ish woman in a red mohair jumper, who was killing time by manipulating a pack of cards, cleverly shuffling it with one hand. A female magician, then. Jean could not, offhand, remember having seen another one.

'Hello,' she said. 'Can I help?'

'Possibly,' said Jean. 'I was looking for Vincent.'

'Oh, Vincent's off,' said the woman, but she was still shuffling the cards, so it couldn't have been anything very serious. 'He gets a bit stressed, you know,' she said.

'So he's all right?'

'He's absolutely fine,' she said, and she laughed at her disloyalty. 'He'll be in on Monday.'

Jean wanted to ask 'How do you *know* he'll be in on Monday?' but couldn't think of a way of phrasing it. But the difficulty was immediately removed, because the woman said, 'He texted me about an hour ago.'

Jean thanked her. On her way back down the alley she herself began texting Vincent: a cheerful message to the effect that she'd just called into the shop hoping to see him; sorry to hear he was off, but glad he was on the mend. As she headed west again, Jean continued with her text. It became rather prolix and confessional, about how she was extremely grateful for all his help, but she had decided to cancel the show and would be trying it as fiction instead, which was probably futile, but still. She would be going to Tobin's Supper Rooms at six o'clock tomorrow to explain in person to Brett. She was sorry she had not had the chance to explain in person to Vincent, but she looked forward to seeing him soon.

By the time she'd signed off, she was back on Old Compton Street, where Patisserie Valerie emitted its siren call, so Jean went in, and had a raspberry tart and two cups of tea, thereby obviating – or perhaps rectifying – her earlier dismissal of treacle sponge.

Coming out of Patisserie Valerie, she decided to head for Leicester Square in search of a film to see.

———

You wouldn't think there'd be a hotel in a place like Vauxhall, which was really just a dirty roundabout on the south side of Central London, but there was, and Coates had been in it for a week.

He'd grown up in south London, in that overheated, too-carpeted house with the TV always on, so it was full circle really, especially since this room was too hot and carpeted as well, and he'd had the TV playing ever since he'd checked in, because the Head turned up frequently, and it was necessary to keep having a word with him, assuring him that things were all on track for tomorrow, Sunday, and you didn't want people to hear those conversations when you were supposed to be in a room on your own. He had been out in the afternoon, drinking in pubs and making two purchases he was very pleased with. He had decided to give them pride of place in his room, which meant balancing them on top of the television. There was the carving knife, which had been forty pounds in John Lewis on King's Road, and the cut-throat razor. He'd gone to Jermyn Street for that, where all the major ponces – including sometimes himself in the old days – went for their clothes and haircuts. It was carbon steel with a bone handle, and he'd got it stropped in an African barber's shop on the way back to the hotel. He had liked it in there, with the radio playing and all the black guys lounging about and laughing and smiling but waiting for bad things to occur – because they knew the score.

The chief barber had offered to use the razor on Coates, who – thinking he was offering to kill him – had considered the offer, even though it wouldn't go down well with the Head, but when he realised the guy was only offering to shave him, he said no. Coates had not shaved while in the hotel, under orders from the Head, because it was necessary for Coates to be at war with the world of the smooth-shaved men. If all went to plan they'd be reading about him in their papers on Monday, and they'd definitely be intrigued by him, because of the Oxford background and the legal career and the beautiful, dead (as she would be by then) wife. Probably be jealous was well, because their own wives were not beautiful and not dead. First on the agenda was the shamus at King's Cross, then Jean, going into or coming out of that little theatre in Deptford; then Camilla in Chelsea. 'I repeat that I'm not doing Lucy though,' he said. The Head made no reply, so he repeated it again.

'I'll tell you this,' said the Head. 'You're driving down to the mother's if they're not in London. As for the girl ... I don't know.'

'She's called Lucy, and I'm not doing her. We've been over this.'

'Yeah, yeah,' said the Head. 'Do the old fucking mother-in-law instead then. In her fucking manor house in the Cotswolds. She's got it coming, boy one, I tell you.'

'Yes,' said Coates. 'You're right.'

And there was a pause while a man turned up on TV and began to read some news.

'I'm thinking of going out tonight to get a woman,' said Coates, raising his voice slightly to compete with the news.

'Can't you ever settle for a hand shandy, you dirty fucker? Haven't the bloody women got you into enough trouble?'

Coates decided to open a bottle of wine. Stepping into the bathroom where he kept the bottles, he did wonder whether the Head of Chambers was actually gay.

———

Lucy was lying next to Camilla on Camilla's bed. This meant they were in crisis mode – Lucy would usually only be on her

293

mother's bed when properly ill – but neither acknowledged the fact directly, in spite of the unprecedented takeaway pizza in a box on the bed, and the complete absence of Daddy. Lucy acknowledged the situation indirectly by reading her go-to consolation book, *The Little Princess*. Camilla was supposedly reading her own grown-up equivalent of that work, *Pride and Prejudice*, while simultaneously looking at her phone and trying to avoid looking at her phone.

Lucy, propped up Little Princess style on a ridiculous amount of pillows, looked up from the book and said, 'Shall I tell you what's bothering me at the moment?'

Her mother kissed the top of her hair. This was her daughter attempting to soothe her mother's anxiety. Traditionally, Lucy had always put the 'bothers of the moment' to Coates. He used to elicit them, in fact, but then Lucy had started to *volunteer* the 'bothers', which were always of an academic nature.

'A westerly wind,' said Lucy, putting aside her book. 'Is that coming from the west or going to it?'

'Coming from it,' said Camilla, who had heard that one before. Upriver/downriver was another familiar conundrum.

'A jigsaw,' said Lucy, 'is made with a jig-*saw*. Is that right?'

'Yes.'

'So you could write, "He made the jigsaw with the jig-saw."'

'Yes, but then when the person actually completes the jigsaw, you could say she assembles it.'

'*She*, yes,' said Lucy, nodding. 'I always say he.'

Camilla believed that her daughter would be rather more of a feminist if she knew the truth about her father.

'You know a man called Max?' said Lucy, and her mother looked at her in alarm. Given what was going on with her husband, she didn't need the introduction of another strange man.

'No,' said Camilla. 'Who's he?'

'I don't mean a person, I mean the name Max. What's it short for?'

'Maximilian.'

'Oh. And what about Gus?'

'Gus isn't short for anything.'

Lucy nodded. 'Maybe there's something *long* for it?'

Camilla's phone clanged horribly. She answered, walking rapidly from the bedroom. 'Yes?' she said, in the dark hall. She didn't know whether she wanted it to be her husband or not.

'It's Stewart.'

'Who?'

'Stewart. Stewart Anderson.'

'Yes. Hello.'

'Is your husband with you?'

'No. He's gone away for a few days.' She realised she was actually protecting Coates by saying that.

'I've had a call from his girlfriend. Jean Beckett.'

Camilla left a silence, allowing him to deduce her contempt. Then she said, 'I thought, from the pictures you showed me, that my husband had worked out you were following him. Now it seems his mistress has done the same. She told you to leave her alone, I suppose?'

'We didn't speak. She just left a message asking me to call. In those situations, we always consult the client.'

'In those situations when you screw things up completely,

295

you mean?' Jean Beckett was a journalist. This news that Camilla had put a tail on her husband would soon be all over Fleet Street, insofar as Fleet Street still existed.

'Do you want me to return the call?' said Anderson.

'Well, *I'm* certainly not going to do it,' said Camilla. She would be like that pathetic female in the country music song 'Jolene'. Please don't take my man. 'When did she call?'

'On Friday morning.'

'It's now Saturday evening. Why the wait before telling me?'

'We've had a problem up here. Two terriers worrying the sheep. We've had four ewes with their throats ripped out. I'm just setting off back, so I can meet you tomorrow lunchtime at McDonald's if you want to discuss.'

Camilla terminated the call in sheer disgust. It was the curse of Lee Christian. When she walked back into the bedroom, Lucy said, 'Mummy, do you think Gus is the shortest man's name of all?'

She had clearly heard every word of the call.

———

When Jean came out of the cinema, the day was definitely over, and a loud machine was coming along to collect up the remains of it. It approached along the gutter of Charing Cross Road, numerous brushes of varying sizes whirling away. The thing devoured almost every piece of rubbish in its path, and certainly ninety-nine per cent of cigarette stubs. Jean scurried a little way ahead and took the long American Spirit stub from her wallet. She dropped it into the gutter, and waited.

The machine ate up the cigarette stub, and this, Jean thought, was the verdict of fate. Not that it hadn't also been a legitimate scientific experiment. How many times must such a machine have moved along the gutters of Millbank since 22 October, the date given on the police notice? It was inconceivable that the remnant of a cigarette would have survived since then. Therefore the American Spirit she had carried about all day must have been a new one, and the whole idea of Coates as a paranoid killer now seemed ridiculous. *She* was the paranoid one. Had she not, after all, written a whole *story* about paranoia? As she came to the top of Villiers Street, she felt that the hierarchy of her anxieties had been reshuffled. Top of the list now was the possibility that she had somehow offended *Vincent*, who had not replied to her friendly text, but this was as nothing compared to the panic of the morning. Yes, the question remained: why had Coates sulked and stormed out on the previous Sunday? She could not think of an answer. Perhaps a *little* jealousy, though? His own life and career were certainly in disarray, after all. But it didn't matter that there was no definite answer. It was quite normal to have a few mysteries in one's life.

———

At an Indian-run electronics shop late on Sunday morning, Coates pointed to the cheapest mobile phone.

'That one?' said the guy, because it seemed that perhaps Coates hadn't spoken. He *had* hesitated, which was because he had been waiting for the Head of Chambers to come on. 'Yes,' he said, in his own voice, 'that one.' When he took his credit card out of his wallet, the Head of Chambers did come on. 'Pay with cash, you mug,' he said. Or had Coates said it?

Must've done, because the Indian said, 'Cash? No problem.'

Coates paid, and got his phone. Then he stood looking about the shop, at all the flashing electronics, and the young Indians smiling at him from far away. All Indians lived in the past or the future, or both at the same time. None lived now. He walked out of the shop and veered rapidly right, walking fast and heading north. With this new phone in his hand, he could do anything. Pay and go, it said, and he had paid and now would go, which the phone confirmed because all its lights were green. Approaching Euston Road, he took the piece of paper out of his pocket, and the Head of Chambers kindly read the number for him until it was right inside his head; then he dialled it. When he got through to Anderson, he was turning right into the Euston Road.

'This is Anderson,' he said.

'Can we speak?' said Coates.

'About what? It's Sunday. I'm only in the office to collect some papers. I was just on my way home.'

'A surveillance job. Quite urgent.'

'Surveillance is not usually urgent. Who is this?'

'Arnold.' It was something about the roaring sound of a bus going past that had made Coates say that. It had been very weird, but now the bus was gone and the name remained.

'*Mr* Arnold?' said Anderson.

'That's it.'

'Do you know the McDonald's near King's Cross?'

'The McDonald's restaurant?'

'Yes.'

'No. Can we meet at your office?'

'I prefer not . . .'

'I'd rather not be seen talking to you. It's all right, I have the address. Be about five minutes.'

'Well . . .' said Anderson.

As soon as Coates had put away the phone, the Head of Chambers came on again. 'Go by the pubs,' he said. He sounded happy.

'Do you mean drink in them on the way?' Coates enquired (and some people passing by the other way saw him say it).

'Just go by them,' said the Head. 'You'll know what to do when you see the first one.'

The first one was on the left. It was in front of the big flat station. It was called the Euston Arch, and what was needed there was a little jump for celebration as he passed by. The next one was also on the left, and it was called the Euston Flyer, so Coates began to run. Then, on the same side, there was the Rocket, so he really rocketed. But then he was walking slowly as he entered the street of Anderson, which was not called Anderson Street, and was opposite the big pointed station. In this street were lots of staring scruffy people that Coates didn't like. One of them, in a big overcoat, sat drinking cider in a wheelchair.

'Y'all right?' he said, in a grating Scots accent.

'What shall I do?' Coates said, walking very slowly past as the question was repeated. The Head was obviously thinking about what to do, and after a while – during which Coates looked at the pictures of the names of all the little, scruffy hotels that had come into this street – he replied, 'Say yes.'

'Yes,' said Coates to the man in the wheelchair, who had

obviously been very seriously assaulted at some point, and no wonder. The office of Anderson was at the end of the street. It was in a kind of dirty brick box stuck onto the side of one of the taller white houses. Coates knocked, and footstairs came down the steps. *Steps* came down. He knocked again, because they had been slow steps; the knife was all ready in his hand, and he wanted to get on with it. The door opened, and Coates already heard himself speaking: 'Are you Anderson?' He began looking at him, but Anderson was attempting to close the door, so Coates put the knife into what looked like the softest part of him, which was about in the middle. And the knife did nothing but go right into Anderson, because that was where it obviously belonged. And Anderson didn't object very much, so obviously he knew it as well. Blood came slowly at first, then fast, like when you win a lot of money on a fruit machine, and it's embarrassing, and you're looking around, saying 'Sorry about this!' But at the same time you're very glad.

But none of this had taken place, because he was standing outside the door with no idea what Anderson looked like, and there was a kind of eye on him, a tiny camera, looking at him with his knife in his hand from above the door. He looked to the left: just the street. He looked to the right: the Scottish drunk, in his wheelchair and his blanket, practically in his hospital bed. '*Off* him,' said the Head. 'He's half dead anyway.' He was some distance away but he raised up his drink and shouted his shout along the street, 'Y'all right!'

But Coates wouldn't bother about him because he wasn't part of the conspiracy. Coates looked again at the shut door that symbolised the conspiracy. It meant that Jean, who was one of the top two conspirators, might not go to the theatre; but she probably would, because he was sure she would have forgotten she'd told him. He liked to be underestimated in that way, because then the knife would come as an even bigger shock as it was going in.

Now there was a taxi, with the knife beside him in the bag, and the Head shouting all kinds of obscenities at him. The taxi put him off somewhere in east London – 'Sorry pal, you're freaking me out' – because he must have been shouting from time to time. He knew he was on the wrong side of the river and there was no bridge, but he found a way under, which was clever of him: the pedestrian tunnel with a white singing noise as he walked down the steps, then along.

———————

It was not fear that Camilla felt, as she pushed the Prius up to ninety and moved into the fast lane of the M40, but anger: at the ineptitude of Anderson, and the sheer indignity of having to load her daughter, her laptop, her daughter's laptop and most of their clothes, into the car before heading off into the unknown. Anderson had called at 1 p.m. Coates had come to the door of his office with a knife in his hand. It was now necessary for him to bring in the police (that is, the proper, grown-up police) and he would be obliged to give them her details, which struck her as cowardice. He had no choice, she could see that, but he was the sort of person who would always put himself in the position where he had no choice. The police, if and when they called her, would be speaking to her in the country-side. She was going to her mother's, and so heading for a complete capitulation, since her mother had always hated Coates, ever since before she'd met him, when she had asked, 'Where did he go to school?'

But Camilla's mother would be denied the pleasure of pointedly not saying 'I told you so', because Camilla and Lucy would not be staying with her for any length of time. Coates knew where her mother lived, so Camilla would be suggesting that she go away for a few days. Meanwhile, she and Lucy would be going on to stay with Camilla's mother's sister, Elspeth, who lived deeper in the Cotswolds, in what Camilla liked to annoy her mother by calling 'the real countryside'. Camilla thought of the arrangement in science fiction terms: her mother's house was the Mothership, her auntie Elspeth inhabiting some breakaway pod or satellite.

Lucy, on the back seat, was glowering into the rear-view mirror. She had given up reading *The Little Princess* in favour of *being* the Little Princess. 'You do realise,' she had said, sometime around Junction 2, 'that we are about to start rehearsals for the Nativity play?' Thank *Christ* she was not the Virgin Mary. Lucy had nearly been the Virgin Mary. She had got through to the 'final round', but lost out to her familiar nemesis, Verity. Lucy was one of the Three Wise Women, which was at least a speaking part, indicating the star – or concurring when another of the Wise Women had indicated it – and announcing her gift for the baby Jesus, which in Lucy's case was that enigmatic commodity, myrrh. It was better than being in the crowd scene as a shepherd ... which bucolic speciality made Camilla think of Anderson again, and the further consequences of his incompetence. The other woman, Jean. She had better be warned that her lover had gone rogue. Perhaps she already had been – by Anderson or the police – but it would be unsafe to rely on that. The woman had pitched a story to her by email, so she would have the contact on her laptop, and it would no doubt include a mobile phone number. Freelancers, being a rather desperate class of people, always offered their mobile numbers, together with inducements such as, *If I don't pick up, please leave a message and I'll call straight back.* When she saw the turn-off for Junction 5 approaching, Camilla decided to take it.

Off the motorway, she experienced a gradual decompression as the road became increasingly countrified. She stopped and pulled over in some woods, from which a mysterious mist was emanating.

'What's going on now?' her daughter demanded.

Camilla turned around in her seat. 'Will you pass me my laptop, darling? It's somewhere on the back seat.'

Lucy began ferreting about for it, saying quite rightly, 'This is getting more and more ridiculous.'

Camilla opened the laptop. Of course, she would have to get out of the car to make the actual call, since Lucy mustn't hear.

———

Jean had decided to go east on the Thames Clipper, which was a humble river-shuttle of Transport for London, or a fairly luxurious pleasure cruise, depending on which way you looked at it. The Thames Clipper was available to Jean from its calling point at Chelsea Harbour, just the other side of the Monster. Taking the Clipper was part of her strategy for managing Sundays without Coates. She would give herself a little treat every Sunday by way of distraction. She had taken it a couple of times before. It interested her that any journey by public transport could begin with a man throwing, or catching, a wet rope.

The seats were like airline seats and arranged like a cinema auditorium, and the whole experience was cinematic as they pulled away into the middle of the wide water, with afternoon turning to evening, and the sun going down in a silvery part of the sky to the south and east. It was taking its bow in a rather shamefaced manner, not having put on much of a show today, but the twinkling lights on the riverbank offered some compensation. Coming up on the right was the big red circle of the London Eye. Further down, on the left, Whitehall awaited in shades of patrician, muted gold. More immediately to the left was Millbank, and Jean noticed the spot, next to the small strip of municipal garden, where the body had been put into the river, as advertised by the police notice. The whole scene of the crime looked small and negligible. Coates was gone from her life, but not because he had anything to do with that, or any such melodramatic cause. He had simply moved on to some other extra-marital situation. She missed him, probably in the way a person who gives up drinking misses booze: for the jolt of energy, and the excitement of anticipating that jolt. But his charisma had waned disastrously, and if their relationship had been a battle, she had won, because it *had* been jealousy on his part in the end. His almost universal bitterness had finally encompassed Jean herself, and it was contemptible that her slight, fragmentary manuscript had been a sufficient cause. She knew now that she had not really finished the story of the Martian Girl. It had become clear that the real novel must place the historical account of Kate and Draper within the frame of her own relationship with a paranoid man. But before starting this reconstruction, she must dispense with Tobin's, hence her present voyage. The next seven hundred pounds was not quite due. It was *nearly* due, and she suspected there was a term in the contract requiring advance notice of non-payment of it. She had deliberately not re-examined the contract, because it might be necessary to plead ignorance. If she was in breach of any such term, she would not be able to ask for repayment of the *first* seven hundred.

Either way, she would be refunding Coates by means of a cheque in the post, because of course she knew his address in Chelsea even if she had never been there. As for what the accompanying note would say ... She was oscillating between vindictiveness and magnanimity, but she assumed that she would eventually gravitate towards some equilibristic formula. She turned around in her seat and looked towards the bar of the Thames Clipper, because part of its glamour was that it did have a bar, with quarter bottles of chardonnay five pounds a go. If she hit the jackpot with Brett – the first seven hundred returned and the second instalment waived – she would treat herself to one of those on the way back. She realised she was probably the only Londoner on the boat. She was certainly the only Londoner not photographing herself or other people with a mobile phone. She took out her own phone, and saw that it was dead. She thought she'd recharged it that morning, but the connection on the charger was dodgy. So Jean was flying blind on the Thames Clipper.

———————

The white walls continued as he walked up the steps at the other end of the tunnel, on the other side of the river. On resurfacing, what he saw was people, old buildings, river and sky, but no colour. Not even in the little fairground by the old ship that was on display. He knew there must be coloured lights on the merry-go-round but they were not coloured to him. The helter-skelter was black and white, even the little triangular flag on top of it, which fluttered in the grey wind. He turned and tried the river, which was just like black paint – oil-based and with a life of its own. He looked inland again: no redness, not even any green, even though this was Greenwich. He felt he must be wearing dark glasses to bring about all this dullness, and he tried to pull them away from the front of his eyes, but there was nothing there but his face.

It was half past four, so he had an hour and a half to kill before he killed Jean, then it would be a taxi to Chelsea to do his wife, who he could not bear to think of by name. He only thought of Jean by her name because he had no other name for her. (His 'lover'? He hardly thought so.) When he took that taxi, he would have to keep the Head quiet, otherwise they'd be chucked out again.

He paused in the walk he'd been taking into the heart of Greenwich, and he waited. The Head was coming on. 'Fuck you,' he said, in a little sort of burp, and then he was quiet again. Coates walked through the dirty, crowded streets, which lacked the weather to be festive, which was what they wanted to be. Things would be all right in summer, when the light and colour would come back, but Coates somehow suspected he would not be around then. He was standing outside a pub. He thought he might as well go in and drink a lot, because there was nothing left to lose.

The pub was drab, and there was football on a grey pitch on a grey TV. He thought for a while about the phrase 'colour TV'. Nobody ever said that any more. They took the colour for granted, but that hadn't always been the case. As a boy, he'd always thought it would be harder to make the black and white than the colour, but now the black and white was all around him. A barmaid – Spanish-looking, kind of tragic – was frowning at him, which was all the women ever did these days. He appeared to have asked for a glass of wine. 'Large,' he said, but that wasn't the answer. 'Red or white?' she asked. Well, it didn't make any difference. 'I'll have both,' he said. She thought he was mad, but he had the long knife in the little nylon backpack that he used on his bike, so whilst he might be mad, other people were soon going to be dead.

The red and white wine were basically black and white, and he drank the first followed by the second. Then he ordered the same again, and drank them in reverse. He looked towards the door, through which he would soon be going out to start killing. It opened, and a policeman came in. Why? The police were not supposed to drink on duty. The copper began walking through the crowd of the pub, very slowly, saying hello to some people, like a royal fucking visit. He came up to the opposite end of the bar and started speaking to the Spanish barmaid, who was much keener on speaking to the copper than she had been on speaking to Coates. It came to Coates that he was wanted by the police for lots of things. The copper turned and walked out again, because he was obviously very stupid, but Coates's heart was beating as if he'd run a race. He saw a sign above some stairs: GENTS. He descended and entered the brightly lit whiteness, looking forward to seeing himself in the mirror. He had the comb with him, of course, and he would comb his hair with it. He was looking down at the sink; he looked up to the mirror, and there was nothing there to speak of. It was a big mirror, yet still nothing worth mentioning; and then Coates noticed a small crumpled object in the bottom right-hand corner. It was the Head of Chambers. He gave what might have been a smile.

───────

She only knew it was five o'clock when she disembarked because she happened to glimpse the watch on the wrist of the man who threw the wet rope. She walked into Greenwich: maritime heritage, fish and chips, scruffy crowded pubs with MORE ROOM UPSTAIRS, but all under dark grey skies. Jean saw a small bookshop and went in, partly because she thought it must be about to close. It was the more interesting sort of bookshop – second hand – and she began looking to see if it had a Theatre and Performance section or something of the kind. She was in search of music hall books, the story of the Martian Girl being unfinished, and yes, there was a buckled shelf: some dusty film guides, a biography of Clint Eastwood and a bent, slightly damp volume called *On the Halls*. It appeared to be the story of a family troupe of singers and dancers, who were both 'on the Halls' (music hall artistes of the early twentieth century) and *called* Hall, and it was written with jollity by one of their number: a certain Bobby Hall. The index suggested a transatlantic work, with theatres in both Britain and America listed. Under 'D' she saw, *Draper, Joseph.* Turning with rapidity to the page, she read:

Backstage at the lovely Imperial Music Hall on 29th Street, Sue was surprised to be accosted by a big, dirty, drunken fellow who told her that if she came back to his rented room, somewhere nearby, he would teach her mind reading! Whilst this was more original than 'Come and look at my etchings', the purpose was presumably the same. Sue thought so anyhow, responding firmly in the negative. But it seemed the fellow would not take 'no' for an answer. He became abusive, and followed Sue into the female dressing room, whereupon another of the girls summoned Midge from the stage door. Midge, as already noted, is called Midge precisely because he is not a midget, and when he appeared on the scene, the big, dirty, drunken fellow did not look quite so big. He was smartly ejected with a very final warning ringing in his ears, for it appeared he had rather haunted the Imperial in recent months. The next time, Midge assured him, the cops would be called.

Of course, we assumed the man was a total fraud, but Midge said he really had been a mesmerist on the Halls in England; that his name was Joseph Draper, and he had worked with a young lady known as The Martian Girl, who had disappeared in London the year before. The rumour among the Imperial turners was that Draper had killed her. I would hardly think it worth mentioning this somewhat depressing tale were it not for the fact that a week later, we all learned that Draper had been found shot – two slugs in the brain – in some back alley in the Lower East Side, and a police investigation was under way. No culprit was ever brought to book, I believe.

Jean stood with the book in her hand, trying to divine the meaning of the Martian Girl.

————

Coates wandered around the crowded, colourless streets of Greenwich, seeing everybody and nobody. It was nearly six and everything was closing down. The Head came on, and now Coates could see as well as hear him, and he was dancing in a small white place in Coates's head, which must have been a chamber: 'Moment of truth is here, boy,' he sang or said. 'And now let's see what you're made of.' Coates walked towards the river and turned left. On this side of the river there were black jetties, and buildings with rotten, un-coloured wood instead of windows. On the other side of the water was Canary Wharf, with the white light on the top that flashed, never staying lit – like a busted cigarette lighter. In the water were great riveted grey buoys, like chopped-up bits of a sea serpent. And there were pyramids of wood, like bonfires that would never be lit because they were in the water. But a fire might have recently burned on the bank, because everything was blackened and broken. He saw a sign: *In Emergency Ring 999*, and maybe that's what the ringing was, because there were bells going. He looked again to the right: Canary Wharf and its fellow skyscrapers. All those big boys looked set to wade into the water and come and get him. The river would only come up to their knees. The ringing became a church bell, calling all the non-existent people to church, or calling them into the river. He moved rapidly to the water's edge, and suddenly looked down a slimy high wall. Twenty feet below was a black beach of hopeless rubble. If you jumped into the water now you would die because there was no water to jump into. It must be low tide, but at high tide you would be instantly in the water and carried away. The Yob should have been carried away. He ought to have been rolling through the water here, passing the great riveted grey buoys that maybe had bells inside them as they rolled in the water, because other bells were joining in with the Sunday chiming, this being the end of the week and the end of time. He had been brought to a graveyard, and Jean thought it was funny, so she had put him in a story. He had lost everything in his life, and Jean had written a story about it to get money, and let him read the story, so that he would know that she knew.

He had come to the theatre. It looked like a church. TOBIN's, illuminated letters said, except they had not been lit. The building was on the edge of something that might, at best, have been a car park. 'Do her, boy!' the Head screamed, because a woman was walking out of it. He ran towards the woman with the knife in his hand, because the momentum of the run would take the knife right into her, but then he slowed because she had come to the end of a brick wall that was also a corner with barbed wire on top of it; and she turned the corner, going out of sight. So he had to start again.

He was moving more slowly now, down a street that was possibly not a street, just a wall on one side; on the other side grey railings with broken boats beyond. He crossed the road, so that he had the railings and she had the wall. He went ahead of her with the knife held inside his jacket, but there was certainly a problem because the woman was not Jean. He had seen her before though. Where? In the past; he had seen her in the past. She was nearly Jean, and that might be good enough because she was part of the plan against him. Yes, they had sent a woman out of a black and white film to play further games; and they had put him in the black and white film with her. They had got hold of a beautiful woman to do this, and given her a coat with a grey fur collar. 'Does it matter if it's not the right one?' he appeared to ask, but the Head was screaming at him so loudly that he would tear himself to pieces, and the only way to stop it and bring the film to an end was to stop it with the knife. The woman was very well aware of all this, so she was not walking any faster; she was walking more slowly, and she turned and looked at him with a smile of glittering eyes that told him the end was coming, and it was coming at the end of the street, which she was now looking towards.

A battered building approached: a dirty white pub with a big lantern outside. The woman had now gone, because there had been a gap in the wall, but he was looking at the pub. The lantern was not lit but not broken either. This pub *existed*, and there were three people under the lantern. They had been in the pub before and would be in it again soon. They were all smoking cigarettes, that was why. And one of them was doing something else, which was holding quite a small gun, and pointing it at Coates because one of the three people was a woman, and she was pointing something else at

312

Coates, which was the finger she used for pointing. She was pale and thin with high curly hair, and her mouth was open because she was saying something in shock. She was Maxine from Number Four, and the man with the gun was like the dead Yob but older, as was the other man. The gun went off.

EPILOGUE

All the things he would never see. That was one way of
thinking about Coates that could make her cry. He
would never see his fiftieth birthday, or even his forty-ninth.
He would never see the completed conversion into flats of the
Chelsea Monster, or the publication of *The Martian Girl* (if that
were ever to happen). Jean thought that her ability to cry or not
cry almost at will about Coates proved that she was a writer. She
could think herself into any emotion. She did miss him, certainly. Some of her best moments had been experienced when
waiting for him, knowing she would never be disappointed – by
his appearance, at least – when he turned up at her door. On
the other hand, he had tried to kill her. That is, he had surely
intended to kill her by going to the vicinity of Tobin's at the
time she had told him she would be going there. But she had
left the vicinity immediately after reading about Draper in the
book called *On the Halls*. Seldom, she thought, could so trivial
a book have saved a life. Presumably, Draper had been tracked
to New York by Art Wakelam, and shot there – and this would

not have happened had Kate not been killed by Draper. In a somewhat Christ-like manner, she had given her life that others might be saved, because Draper (who, according to Art Wakelam, was responsible for deaths other than those of Brooks and Kate) would probably have killed again. Kate's father had also paid the price, but he was about to die anyway. It had occurred to Jean while reading *On The Halls* that – in spite of being dead – Kate French might save Jean herself.

In reappraising her situation vis-à-vis Coates, she had seen that he was indeed dangerous, and she had performed a swift risk assessment in that secondhand bookshop. He knew where she lived; he also knew she was heading to Tobin's, which was located in a dark wasteland. So she had stepped out of the bookshop and straight into a black taxi. On arrival in Lots Road, she had asked the driver to drive up and down while she verified that the coast was clear. In the flat, she had packed a bag and given her phone some charge, thereby receiving Camilla's warning. 'I know you're seeing my husband ...' Camilla had begun, and that had been one of the worst moments of Jean's life, as Jean had immediately declared on returning the call. She had then set off to her parents' place in Brighton, calling Brett of the Supper Rooms from the train, saying everything she'd meant to say face to face. He'd taken the news of her cancellation calmly (almost, Jean felt, with relief). Not only would she not owe any further payment, he would try to refund much of what she had already paid.

On the Wednesday, there had been the report in the London *Evening Standard*, which liked to keep Brighton informed of all the worst goings-on in the capital: ... *Mr Coates, from Chelsea, was found unresponsive by paramedics at*

5 p.m. last Sunday, November 19th. He was pronounced dead just after 6 p.m. from multiple gunshot wounds. Police have launched a murder investigation into his death.

The first tears had come, and she and her mother and her father had engaged in a three-way hug in the kitchen. Then they'd all got drunk, and she'd showed her mother all her photos of Coates with a certain amount of guilty pride.

The next day, the *Standard* had returned to the story of his murder, this time on its website and with CCTV footage: *This is the moment two men and a woman fled from the scene of a murder in east London last week. Detectives hunting the killers of Mr Coates today released the CCTV footage of the people they wish to speak with.* The two sentences could have occurred in either order, and this was part of the indignity Coates had suffered. She had watched the footage repeatedly: two men in hooded tops and a thin woman in a leather jacket with curly hair piled high – all walking fast down a dark street that was featureless enough to have been part of a light industrial estate. It was just around the corner from Tobin's. She kept thinking of her schooldays, and how three people might gang up on a fourth: that was the usual ratio – three against one.

The police had been very kind in the interview. They would be keeping her abreast of the investigation. They told her Coates had been carrying a knife, and she told them of her suspicions about his involvement in the Millbank killing. Of the two detectives who interviewed her, one listened carefully to this, the other appeared not to. She had been offered counselling, to which she did not feel entitled, having been involved in an illicit affair. All the counselling 'resources' (she imagined that was the word) ought to be for his poor wife and child.

And now she was walking along King's Road on an incongruously sunny Monday afternoon, heading for a meeting with Camilla in the Chelsea Potter, which was – she assumed – a suitably smart pub for a person called Camilla to have chosen. Jean had rehearsed her opening line: 'I am so very sorry about all this. You have a little girl, I think. I do hope she will not be too badly affected. If there is anything – anything at all – I can do to help . . . '

What she was less sure of was how far to go into the tale Vincent had told her three days previously, when he had finally resurfaced. He had called her on the Wednesday of that *Standard* report, but he hadn't seen it – a situation almost inconceivable to Jean, who had immediately read it out to him. After he'd said how sorry he was, he'd asked, 'But who shot him?' It was a good question. Who *were* those three people on the CCTV footage? Jean had wondered whether, having failed to murder her, he had turned on a complete stranger. Or had he been buying drugs? In her mind, Coates was suddenly capable of anything. She had begun speculating into the telephone, and Vincent had uncharacteristically interrupted her: might they meet up? Jean had agreed and suggested Friday evening in London. Vincent said, 'Are you sure you're up to coming back?' and Jean – being in Brighton – thought of a beach and the gentle incoming waves now safe to swim in, the shark having been killed; also the proverbial horse that had to be remounted the moment one fell off.

A mutual failure of imagination had then occurred, and they arranged to meet in the place they had last convened: the Punch Bowl, off Wardour Street.

Vincent had been unencumbered by Little Vince, and seemed more unencumbered generally. He still looked like a head waiter, but a lighter and healthier one, as attested by each of the several antique mirrors around them.

'I'm sorry if I've been a bit elusive recently,' he said. 'I've been feeling a bit harassed. I mean, nothing to what you've been through, obviously . . . '

'The owner of the shop – Mr Worsley?' suggested Jean. 'Is he the problem?'

'He is really, yes. He's married, you see, to a woman quite a bit younger than him. She's a performance artist, and she's a bit strange.'

'Naturally,' said Jean.

'She's called Clare, and she's got this obsession with Kate French, the Martian Girl. She's really the only reason I got to know anything about Kate. She found the footage that I showed you, and Mr Worsley showed it to me.'

'Why?'

'No real reason, just something to do in the shop. I mean, we were getting on quite well back then, and he was telling me about his wife's new project.'

'Oh,' said Jean, and here was something akin to the feeling she'd had when Camilla had called.

'The thing is – Clare's a bit nuts, but she's very pretty and she looks almost exactly like Kate French, so she thinks she sort of owns her, and she was a bit upset when she heard that you were planning a one-woman show about her.'

'Was she planning a show of her own?'

'Well, that's the thing. She was, yes. And she'd wanted to do it at Tobin's, but had been told someone else had booked to do a show on the same subject, which I didn't know at first. I only knew she had an interest in doing *something* eventually. When Mr Worsley found out I was talking to you about Kate French, he got a bit . . . heavy.'

'And is she still planning on doing her show?'

'Well, here's the thing—'

'Could you just say yes or no, Vincent?'

'Well, no. It gets a bit complicated now. When you texted me that you weren't going ahead with your show, I told Mr Worsley, knowing he would tell Clare. I'm not in touch directly with Clare, and I don't think many people are. I hope you don't mind, but I really needed to get Worsley off my back. This was Saturday afternoon. In the evening, Mr Worsley emailed me, saying thanks for letting him know, and Clare would be going in to Tobin's the next afternoon – the Sunday – to ask if she could take over your slot. She wanted to do a kind of audition at the first opportunity.'

'What time?'

'I don't know.'

'Well, Coates was shot just around the corner from Tobin's, so . . . did she see anything?'

'Don't know.'

'She wasn't the one who *shot* him, was she?'

Vincent frowned. 'Why would she do that?'

No; the CCTV image showed the guilty parties: two men and a woman who did not look remotely like Kate French.

'But the upshot of it all,' Vincent said, 'was that she's decided to drop the whole thing.'

'But why?'

'The chap at Tobin's, Brett, talked her out of it. Said you couldn't do a show about mind readers with only one person.'

'That's what *I* told him. I mean, there are ways round it, but—'

'Yes, but they didn't get into that because Brett suggested another idea, and she went for it, which is quite surprising, because she's not usually very open to ideas. I'd better not say too much about it.'

'But it's nothing to do with mind reading?'

'Nothing at all.'

'She'll still be pissed off if my novel comes out, I suppose.'

'Well, maybe it'll be filmed, and you could suggest that she auditions for the part of Kate? She's really very talented.'

It was touching of Vincent to postulate such a happy outcome.

'She's talented . . . but anti-social?'

'She is a bit, yes.'

'She wouldn't welcome a call from me asking about her exact movements on that afternoon?'

'I shouldn't think so, no.'

Jean decided not to burden Vincent with her discoveries about the fate of Kate French. Later, walking back alone to the station, she had called Brett at Tobin's, where he had been busy preparing for an imminent interval. Jean had swiftly, and rather skilfully (she felt), hinted at a personal interest in the shooting that had occurred. She then said she was trying to track down anyone who might have seen anything. She had managed that part less well, and Brett had said, with previously unsuspected sarcasm, 'Sort of helping the police, are you?'

'I think somebody came to see you,' Jean had blurted. 'An actress called Clare. I was just wondering if she might have seen anything as she walked there and back.'

'What makes you think she walked?' said Brett. 'As far as I know, she came here in an Uber, and left in one after we'd spoken. But I have to go now, sorry.'

She had used up all her credit with Brett.

———

She walked into the pub called the Chelsea Potter, where she saw Camilla, rising from her seat to greet her.

'I am so very sorry about all this,' said Jean. 'You have a little girl, I think. I do hope she will not be too badly affected. If there is anything – anything at all – I can do to help . . . '

Camilla was smiling. She said, 'My daughter's pretty resilient, I think. It's five o'clock. Is that too early for a glass of wine?'

The Friday features meeting was under way. Beyond the window, the sky was a very dark blue, offsetting the lights of London, like the velvet on which the goods rest in a jewellery shop. The editor was saying the ABCs were looking good – glossies like theirs were holding their own surprisingly well against online competition – and the magazine would be upping its pagination. Sally Wilkinson already knew this, and she'd been tipped off that she was likely to be given her own books page – made literary editor, in fact – in addition to overseeing 'Real Lives'. The new role might give her the power base she needed to get her novel published. She would be forced to do what Polly Mitchell did so effortlessly: network.

Polly, who'd recently been going on about where you could go to detox after a night out partying (Tufnell Park had taken over from Notting Hill as 'juice bar heaven'), was now texting, which is what she did instead of listening to anyone else speak. If this was some kind of power trip, then Polly ought to know it would be lost on Lee Christian – currently holding forth about adulterated cocaine and ecstasy – who had apparently been born with the conviction that everybody was in love with him. The editor, Camilla, was nodding, which was what *she* did instead of saying, 'Forget it, Lee. This story's old hat.'

Sally liked Camilla, and in a way she regretted that she'd put her through such a hard time as the model for the Camilla of her novel. Of course, if *The Martian Girl* were ever to be submitted to a publisher, she would have to change Camilla's name, which would be a shame, because 'Camilla' was just right for a capable professional woman with a husband going off the rails. As far as Sally knew, the real Camilla's husband was not going off the rails, and it would be a great surprise if he did, because he had an MBE. There would have to be a *lot* of name-changing in the novel's features meeting scene, for which she had more or less downloaded an actual features meeting she had attended six months ago. She would have to begin by changing her own name, since it was bad manners to put yourself into your own fiction without at least pretending that you were not doing so.

It was hard work finding names, but she was pleased with what she'd come up with for her principals. Jean was a better name than whatever had been the name of the bookish, slightly whimsical freelancer who'd come into the magazine to pitch once. Camilla had been too busy to see her, so Sally had fielded her ideas, and the woman had mentioned in passing her interest in music hall, and she'd been sufficiently diverting on the subject to start Sally reading about it on her own account. Sally was also pleased with 'Coates', but any forename had seemed to undermine its somehow narcissistic integrity, so she'd simply avoided giving him one. Where had Coates, as a personality, come from? She didn't know. He was an amalgam of some of the better looking-men she'd known, and, during one of her human misery trawls, she'd looked into the 'client profile' of London's red light trade: the men were from a higher social bracket than you might think, and tended to want to indulge a specialism. Dr Lewin, just then looking at his watch in a doomed attempt to demoralise Lee Christian, had been helpful in the creation of Coates's mind, since he'd been wittering on about psychosis and psychotic phenomena at one of the meetings.

'Very good, Lee,' Camilla was saying, 'How about a punchy twelve hundred words?'

'Honestly, Camilla love,' Lee said, 'I see this as a real biggie. I'd need at least two thousand five hundred to do it justice.'

Sally risked a glance towards Mark, who was going to have to rewrite whatever Lee Christian produced. He was doodling as usual, but now – and just as she had hoped – he glanced upward for an exchange of conspiratorial smiles. Here, on the face of it, was a highly encouraging signal.

But what was he *thinking?*